About the Author

Subhuti Anand Waight is a former UK political correspondent who gave up his journalistic career to live in an Indian ashram. He toured India as part of a troupe of Shakespearian actors and has also written and staged his own musicals and plays. He is the author of four books.

Subhuti Anand Waight

WHEN SHAKESPEARE
LOST THE PLOT

AUSTIN MACAULEY
PUBLISHERS LTD.

A CIP catalogue record for this title is available from the British Library.

ISBN 9781786931696 (Paperback)
ISBN 9781786931702 (Hardback)
ISBN 9781786931719 (E-Book)
www.austinmacauley.com

First Published (2016)
Austin Macauley Publishers Ltd.
25 Canada Square
Canary Wharf
London
E14 5LQ

But this I say, no hesitation,
Will never knew of meditation.
His busy mind was full of chatter
He didn't think the silence mattered.

~ Prologue

INTRODUCTION

It was intended as a tribute. To me, it was an indictment. On April 23, 2016, four hundred years to the day that William Shakespeare departed from this world, the cream of British acting, plus Prince Charles, appeared onstage at Stratford to celebrate the Bard.

They chose, as their theme, the world's most famous quote, taken from the world's most performed play, written by the world's most acclaimed playwright:

To be or not to be.

Tim Minchin, Benedict Cumberbatch, Harriet Walter, David Tennant, Rory Kinnear, Sir Ian McKellen, Dame Judi Dench, and the RSC's current Hamlet, Paapa Essiedu, all offered their own take on how the line should be said and which word should be emphasized:

"To be *or* not to be, that is the question…To be or *not* to be, that is the question…To be or not to *be*, that is the question…To be or not to be, *that* is the question…To be or not to be, that *is* the question…To be or not to be, that is *the* question…To be or not *to* be, that is the question."

Prince Charles also became Hamlet for a moment, walking to the stage from the audience to join the actors and giving the quote its final nuance:

"To be or not to be, that is the…*question.*"

Everyone loved it. Everyone agreed it was a brilliant and witty sketch, a fitting tribute to England's greatest literary genius.

And really, there was only one problem:

Nobody answered the question.

Nobody even tried.

Subhuti Anand Waight

CHAPTER 1
Nearly Not to Be

In seconds, the question shifted from abstract to real. In other words, I thought I was going to die. Shakespeare's most famous line, which had been buzzing around my brain all night, was suddenly laid bare on the road ahead as a huge truck started to roll back down the hill, threatening to decapitate me.

I'd been thinking of Hamlet's dilemma: *To be or not to be?* Now the looming certainty of *not to be* stared at me through the taxi's windscreen.

I'd been writing about Elizabethan executions, in which heads were regularly chopped off. How ironic that I was about to experience it myself.

I'd been scripting a play about life-or-death choices, but now it seemed I had no choice. This real-life drama was about to climax in a fatal and bloody manner.

Just a few minutes earlier, we'd been speeding along a highway leading out of Mumbai in the direction of Pune. My taxi *wallah* was driving very fast, which was a little scary, but basically it was okay because the road was almost empty.

That was how it was supposed to be. After all, it was two o'clock in the morning and I'd timed my flight from Heathrow to arrive in Mumbai after midnight for this very reason: to be able to leave the city and hit the highway with a minimum of fuss.

I knew it would change when we left the coastal plain and began the long climb up the Western Ghats. It always did. Day or night, the hill was busy with slow-moving, heavily-laden trucks. But this time, as I peered ahead into the darkness, I could see it was worse than usual.

Continuous lines of red taillights snaked up the darkened hillside ahead of us, inter-twining like spirals of luminous DNA molecules, glowing in the night, with yellow spirals of headlights coming down in the other direction. It was a beautiful, but daunting sight. The hill was choked with traffic.

Indian drivers don't obey lane discipline. Either they don't know about it, or they don't care, so it was no surprise to find trucks in all three lanes, mixing freely with coaches, vans and cars, all trying to find the quickest way up the hill.

At first, we had a good run, due mainly to the skill of my local driver, who took advantage of every little gap in the traffic to weave his way through the maze of vehicles, including frequent use of the hard shoulder on the left side of the road.

I knew the highway was dangerous. I knew that there'd been more than 2,000 accidents and 400 deaths since it opened over a decade ago. I also knew I could have avoided the road trip by flying from Heathrow to

Dubai, then taking a second flight direct to Pune, but it required too long a wait in the transit lounge.

Convenience won over risk. Somehow, it was easier to fly nonstop to Mumbai, throw my bags in a taxi and use the highway. Besides, to me, this journey was like a rite of passage, announcing my re-entry into the country. Safe arrival in Pune was proof that India still loved me, still embraced me as one of its spiritual sons.

We were about half-way up the hill, on the steepest section, when our luck ran out. With all three lanes occupied ahead of us, my driver again used the hard shoulder to sneak past a truck in the crawler lane. The manoeuvre worked but got us deeper into trouble. As we nosed through on the inside, we found that all lanes ahead – including the shoulder – were blocked by slow vehicles, while those behind us were too close for comfort. We were surrounded, boxed in.

The hood of our little taxi was almost under the tail end of a giant lorry in front of us when that vehicle's steady progress suddenly faltered. It slowed down, stopped, lurched forward, then stopped again. The brake lights blazed in our eyes, flashing a red warning, and a familiar hand-painted sign "Horn Okay Please" seen on the tail gate of every truck in India stared us right in the face.

My driver didn't need the invitation. He hammered his horn in a rapid, urgent staccato, muttering strange words in his local Marathi tongue, while I watched with fascinated horror as the rear wheels of the truck started turning backwards.

Rollbacks on this hill were a real threat. Old, poorly maintained and heavily-laden trucks frequently carried too much weight for their brakes to handle. It was for this reason, in the past, when the highway was a single, badly-paved lane, every truck had at least four men in the cab: the driver, the co-driver and two others who remained unemployed unless and until the engine failed, or the gearbox broke, or a tyre burst, or the truck ahead stalled. Instantly, the two men would leap from the cab holding large rocks and rush to the rear of the vehicle, jamming them under the wheels to prevent a disastrous rollback.

Superstition also assisted drivers on this hill. Back in the seventies, naked sadhus with white, yellow and red streaks on their foreheads would sit under trees at the foot of the ghats and stare with unforgiving eyes at the drivers as they began their climb. The message was unmistakable: "Buddy, if you have any hope at all of making it to the top, you'd better throw us some coins."

Most drivers did. The sadhus have gone, but, even today, the cab of almost every truck contains a little illuminated shrine for some Hindu god or goddess to dwell in; as divine insurance against a dangerous breakdown.

Up to this moment on the ride, my mind had been idly preoccupied with Hamlet's soliloquy, going over the script of a play I'd written around the central theme of the Prince of Denmark's dilemma: *To be or not to be?*

But this was no time for philosophical musing. Faced with real and present danger, Hamlet's problem vanished. Intellect died. Instinct took over. To survive, *to be*, was all that mattered. I flipped open the buckle of my safety belt and slid down in my seat, wondering if I could somehow dive all the way down into the leg space if the truck's tail gate smashed through our windshield and transformed our little taxi into a convertible.

Uttering more curses, my driver turned to look out his back window, pressing down on the clutch and easing his foot off the brake, thinking to let our taxi roll back out of danger, but after no more than half-a-metre, a loud horn from behind warned us not to retreat any further.

The wheels of the truck ahead continued their inexorable backward motion and the tail gate was now clearly over our hood. This was it. One millimetre closer and it would be time to dive down and pray.

But we were fortunate. The truck's roll-back halted, its engine roared, heavy black smoke belched from the exhaust pipe and again the vehicle moved forward, more steadily this time.

A small gap opened on our right and we squeezed through, out of danger and into a zone of faster, freer traffic. We weaved our way up the grade like a cunning fox slipping through a herd of motorized elephants, sped through the tunnel at the top of the ghats, then levelled out as we reached the rim of the plateau.

"Chai stop", announced my driver, taking a slip-road off the highway. It seemed a shame to allow all those people we'd overtaken to pass us once more, but when your taxi driver needs a tea break in the middle of the night, you'd better listen to him. Chai and chewing tobacco are the two stimulants that keep these men awake at the wheel.

We drove into the service station, past the fuel pumps and parked in front of a row of sweet shops and restaurants, all darkened and closed. But a single, stainless steel can of the magic brew stood on a low wall, where a tired-looking man mechanically dispensed small, white plastic cups filled with chai for twenty rupees a shot.

I bought one for the driver and another for myself, enjoying the sweet taste of the thick brown liquid, an intense mixture of strong black tea, boiled milk, spices and sugar. Chai is the Indian working man's espresso. It's normally served mid-morning and again at around 4:30 in the afternoon, but on the highway it's available 24/7.

A few minutes later, we were back on the road. We drove into Pune well before dawn, travelling swiftly through empty streets, and soon I recognized the landmarks – a bridge, a temple, a government building, the back of the railway station – and smiled in the knowledge that my destination, a self-styled 'meditation resort' in a Pune suburb was just a couple of minutes away.

Where to stay? Room charges at the resort's upscale guesthouse were way above my modest budget, as were most of the local hotels, but I remembered one small hostel, just next to the resort, that offered a handful of cheap rooms that couldn't be booked ahead of time, available only for drop-in clientele. First come, first served.

The taxi pulled in and I slowly clambered out, walking stiffly after the three-hour drive. When I got to reception, I had to wake up the concierge, who, quite reasonably at this godforsaken hour, was sleeping at his desk.

"Good morning. You have a cheap room for me?" I inquired hopefully.

He nodded, groping under the desk with one hand for a key and opening the register with the other. Obviously, he'd done this so many times he could do it in his sleep, which was probably just as well – it didn't seem like he was actually awake.

"Number nine... passport please...."

I was in luck. One of the cheapest rooms was vacant. It meant shared showers and toilets, which was not much fun, since the ones downstairs were – I discovered to my dismay – unspeakably dirty, but the upstairs bathroom was shiny and new and the showers had hot water. It was just a little irritating when the hotel staff passed through to say "good morning, sir" while I was cleaning my teeth. How did they expect me to reply?

I took a quick shower, returned to my tiny room, and then lay down on the bed, noticing the rock-hard nature of the mattress beneath me. It didn't surprise me. In India, it's a kind of law: the cheaper the hotel room, the harder the mattress. As for the pillow, it seemed to have been filled entirely with concrete, but it would have to do.

The hotel was right next door to the meditation resort, which was ideal except for the fact that, this year, in a break with my personal routine, I wasn't intending to spend much time there.

Every year, since God knows how long, I'd been coming to India in the winter and spending long, leisurely weeks hanging out and meditating at the resort. Not this time. This year, I was on a mission – mission impossible, perhaps, but a mission nevertheless.

My intention was to take William Shakespeare's most famous line, uttered by Hamlet, and transform it into a denunciation of modern values in favour of timeless Eastern mysticism.

I wanted to stand Shakespeare on his head, give *Hamlet* a happy ending, expose a fatal flaw in Western philosophy and instigate a spiritual revolution.

To be or not to be?

The question had to be answered. Four hundred years had passed since the Bard posed it, and that was long enough.

Lying in bed, looking back on my taxi ride, I remembered how Hamlet's quote had vanished from my mind in the face of death; how the only thing that mattered, in that instant, was *to be*. This, I realized, was the reason no one had ever bothered to answer the Bard's question, because, naturally, none of us wants to die. In real life, *to be* is the only option.

Yet I was aware of another possibility, elusive, mysterious but nevertheless real. I'd been there. I'd tasted it. I'd experienced it: a totally different context in which *not to be* was the only intelligent response, offering an urgently-needed antidote to the stress and superficiality of a society hooked on *to be*.

I'd written a play around this theme and intended to perform it for the public, right here in Pune. But first, I had to find actors and actresses, enthusiastic amateurs who would donate their services for free and commit to six weeks of rehearsals with no guarantee that we could pull it off.

Which, in turn, presented another question. As I tried to relax my weary body on the unyielding mattress, I found myself wondering "Where is Hamlet?"

CHAPTER 2

The Sound of Silence

At sunset, I was standing by the side of a man-made lake, dressed in a long white robe, waiting for permission to cross the water and enter a large, black, pyramid-shaped building on the other side. Tall, ancient trees created a canopy over my head, a crescent moon hung in a pastel-pink sky and more white-robed men and women were arriving every minute, stopping by the lake's edge and waiting silently by my side.

Standing amid this futuristic scenery made me wonder if I'd gotten myself onto a movie set from *Star Wars*, where a group of Junior Jedi were awaiting instructions on how to use the Force.

But no, this was the evening meditation, held daily at the resort. Truth to tell, I hadn't intended to enter the place so soon, but Hamlet, I'd just learned, was still on the beach in Goa and wouldn't arrive in Pune for three to four days, so I had time to kill.

I'd slept little, then spent most of the day unpacking my bags, sorting dirty laundry and applying for a local SIM card for my mobile phone, a simple task made surprisingly difficult by the number of forms and photos required to satisfy Indian bureaucracy. That done, I registered at the resort's welcome centre, bought myself two robes, maroon for daytime, white for the evening, and joined the other meditators in time for the evening programme.

When I first came here, back in the 1970s, the ashram was smaller, funkier and packed to bursting point with young, long-haired Western adventurers in love with the spiritual mysteries of the East. We'd come to experience life with a controversial mystic called Osho.

We wore bright-orange clothes and necklaces of wooden beads with Osho's photo dangling from them in a locket. We called ourselves *sannyasins*. We spent most of our time hugging, meditating, dancing, singing and sleeping with each other.

To outsiders, we must've looked like a bunch of sexualized hippies, searching for the ultimate orgasm, which, if you define meditation as 'orgasm without sex' – as Osho once did – was pretty close to the truth.

The place has changed. *So much water has gone down the Ganges*, as the Hindus say to denote the passing of time. The pressure-cooker intensity of the old ashram has vanished and the number of visitors is down to a fraction of what it was, but the underlying vibe of meditation remains and that's what pulls me back, year after year.

Here, I must confess: I'm not one of the world's greatest meditators. I can't do it by myself. Left alone, I tend to watch the latest offerings by Netflix or HBO rather than close my eyes and observe the inner movie on the screen of my mind. That's why I make a point of spending time in places like this. When meditation is structured into the daily routine, I'm more likely to slip on a robe and join the party.

This evening, especially, I needed help to give my obsession with Shakespeare a rest. I'd been mentally chewing on the script all day and wanted to forget about it for a few hours, so I could look at it again later with fresh, innocent eyes.

We were given the nod to cross the water, filing quietly in a long line of flowing white robes along a narrow walkway, then climbed stone steps to a small doorway on the pyramid's side before disappearing into the interior. Inside, the auditorium was big, square and empty, with a dark-green marble floor, a tall pointed ceiling and sound-proof double-glazing on the windows.

The vibe was rather stark and cold, and you needed to protect your *derriere* with a padded meditation chair or freeze your ass off on the floor. But, for me, it was a fine place to meditate, which, when you consider the fact that it had none of the atmosphere of ancient temples and other holy places, was a remarkable achievement.

I unrolled a long, black mat, placed my chair on it, sat down, put on a pair of white socks, and then wrapped myself in a big, white shawl, feeling warm and cosy, ready for an easy, relaxing, meditative experience.

So much for expectations. Without warning, a sudden tickle in my throat quickly escalated into a massive need to burst out coughing, which was completely forbidden in this silent space.

There was, I knew, a strictly enforced rule: no coughing. If someone even so much as cleared his throat, a robed official would arise from the seated throng, glide noiselessly through the dim light to the offending party and insist that he left immediately. No exceptions. No second chances.

In all these years, I've never had to leave, but this time I was being severely challenged. I was holding my breath, seemingly forever, while tightening my stomach muscles and making strange bodily heaving movements on my seat to contain the hacking sounds that wanted to erupt from my lungs and throat. My mouth was clamped in a grimace and my eyes were squeezed shut. I guess I looked like a very serious meditator.

I've always appreciated the rule of silence in this auditorium. After all, I didn't travel eight thousand kilometres from the UK to listen to a ninety-minute symphony of throat-clearing. I understood that outer silence was needed to support the meditator's quest for inner silence, so when coughers were asked to leave, it was usually okay with me.

But on that particular evening, when it was my turn, I had a different perspective. I really didn't want to have to pick up my things and walk out. It was against my one hundred percent record and my pride.

At the front of the hall, in the left-hand corner, a group of white-robed musicians were picking up their instruments, getting ready to play, and I found myself mentally pleading with them: "Come on, guys, hurry up! Start the music NOW before I rupture my guts holding in this cough!"

Finally, the first notes drifted out across the hall, but to my dismay, they came in the form of a long, meandering, violin solo – way too quiet to hide a cough. Again, I was silently screaming at the musicians: "Where's the beat? Where are the drums? Come ON!" Eternity passed before my eyes and then, at last: "Boom...boom..." in came the drums.

Up went the noise level. I jumped to my feet along with everyone else, and from my throat emerged a carefully muted coughing-release session that continued all the way through the dancing phase of the meditation. Still, it seemed pretty loud to me and I was surprised that nobody was tapping me on the shoulder and pointing to the exit.

Half-way through, I turned around to check who was near me and was alarmed to see a senior resort official standing right behind me. It seemed impossible he hadn't heard, or seen my bodily gymnastics, but he was operating the Wi-Fi pad that controlled the auditorium's sound-mixer, so either he didn't notice, or had other priorities.

The music climaxed, then stopped, and everyone who'd been dancing sat down. I was relieved to notice the tickle in my throat had gone. My coughing fit was over. I could lean back in my chair and relax.

That was when I heard it: the familiar yet elusive sound of my own inner silence, softly flooding into the empty chamber inside my head, gently extinguishing any lingering thoughts. This was how it felt, like some hidden, inner floodgate being raised and a waterfall of calmness pouring noiselessly into my mind. Uninvited and unexpectedly, the blessing of meditation had descended on me.

That's when I realized what an ambitious task I'd set myself with my play: to somehow convey the significance of such a mysterious, subjective experience.

Perhaps I should explain: silence can be shallow, an unremarkable state of every day consciousness that we all know; nothing more than a temporary absence of noise, like a pause in a conversation, or the moment after a television has been turned off, or the hush before a theatre curtain goes up. Nothing special.

But sometimes, when one's energy has been brought to a peak, when, for whatever reason, one's whole mental state has been forced to focus on the present moment, then silence becomes a much more vital experience. It has the potential to overwhelm the chattering mind, dissolve all problems, dissipate all concerns and leave one resting in a deep sense of peace and well-being.

The strain of trying not to cough had done me a favour. Unintentionally, I'd been driven into a highly energized state before sitting in meditation, which had the effect of taking me out of my mental preoccupations and into silence. I knew of several meditation techniques that used such tactics deliberately, but this accidental 'method' had worked well.

It didn't last long. A couple of minutes passed and then my mind, recovering from the surprise of being suddenly struck dumb, clicked into gear. The thinking process started once more and, true to my current preoccupation with the Bard, I found myself wondering:

"And what would Master Shakespeare have thought about not thinking?

CHAPTER 3

Frying Eggs for Hamlet

Hamlet answered the door in his underwear, in a pair of boxer shorts, to be precise. Besides which, he wore a sheepish grin and nothing else.

"Sorry, guess I overslept," he mumbled, then turned and led me to the kitchen.

Ophelia, I assumed, was still in bed and yawning, stretching her sweet young body under the covers, stealing a few more minutes, not yet ready to face the bright morning sunlight.

Hamlet and his girlfriend had gotten off the bus from Goa early yesterday morning, but were obviously still recovering from the trip.

"Coffee?" he inquired.

I nodded. He put on the kettle and took three dirty cups out of a pile of dishes in the sink, washed them, and then reached for the large Nescafe jar on the counter.

"If you wanna make fried eggs, I'd appreciate it."

That sounded reasonable. I'd eaten a small bowl of porridge two hours earlier and was peckish. I lit the gas ring, took a box of eggs from the fridge, cracked them and started frying. Hamlet made coffee for three, pushed one cup towards me, and took the other two out onto the patio. It was already warm out there. Nights can be cold in India, in the beginning of December, but as soon as the sun comes up, the temperature soars to a comfortable twenty-five degrees Celsius.

Hamlet sank heavily into a plain, white, plastic chair, reached for a pack of tobacco on the little table in front of him, and began rolling a cigarette. A short while later, Ophelia appeared, a friendly but ghostly apparition from the bedroom, wearing only an elegantly ripped t-shirt. Her blonde hair was a delightful mess and her bare, slim legs were bronzed from the Goan beaches.

Peering in my direction through half-closed eyes, she nodded a silent 'good morning' and wandered sleepily across the living room, out onto the patio, sat down beside Hamlet, took a sip of coffee, and rolled her own cigarette.

When the toast and eggs were ready, I gave them both a plate, then sat down next to them. Nobody spoke. It was clear that both Hamlet and Ophelia needed their morning shots of nicotine, caffeine and protein before joining the world of the awakened.

Hamlet knew what I was thinking. I could tell from the way he didn't look at me; just kept studying his plate with an amused, unfocused stare. He knew what I'd come to hear. Still, he had to finish his eggs, take another sip of coffee, and stub out the burning butt of his cigarette before making eye contact. When he did, his face lit up with a mischievous smile.

"We've decided we're not going to work in the resort this year," he informed me.

I laughed in surprise, delighted at the news, and pretty soon Hamlet and Ophelia were laughing with me. They knew how much these words meant to me.

These were the words that opened the door. They completed my casting and made the play possible. They gave me the green light to go ahead and rent the most expensive theatre in the City of Pune and put on a play that would lose several thousand dollars of my personal money. But I didn't care. It was worth it.

Like me, Hamlet and Ophelia were in the habit of coming to India every year to meditate, work, or hang out at the resort. Like me, they were willing to give it up in order to tread the boards of dramatic romance.

Hamlet was Korean-American, born in Seoul and raised in Los Angeles. He was forty years old with a flat, moon-like face and long, black hair that made him look like a cross between Jackie Chan, Bruce Lee and an Apache warrior.

If you're thinking "Hmm, not your typical Prince of Denmark," I can only agree. But he was good-looking, brimming over with youthful energy and had great stage presence even though he was only a beginner at acting. Wait, let me qualify that: he used to be a City of London banker, which, according to my cynical view of global finance, definitely requires acting skills – after all, you have to convince the public you're trustworthy.

But Hamlet gained my trust in a different way. He flipped the bird to mainstream values, left the City and took off for the Mystic East, seeking deeper answers to life than brokering hedge funds and selling snake oil.

In India, he met Ophelia, a twenty-five-year-old German art student with tattoos on her body, a ring through her lower lip and a sense of adventure that made her impulsively jump on the back of Hamlet's motorbike and drive off into the sunset with him.

One year previously, before they came on board my project, they'd spent several months living and working inside the resort. Hamlet was the driving force behind the Events Team, which had the task of staging nightly diversions for visitors, ranging from black-and-white disco parties to *Meditators Got Talent* variety shows.

He loved nothing better than to pick up a microphone in front of a crowd and say "Good evening, everyone…" And, of course, as an American, he was genetically disposed towards showbiz. The resort managers loved him and wanted him back for another season, but the appeal of my theatre project won out. He was hooked on Ham.

Ophelia, his girlfriend, adored the idea of playing the famous role and I adored her, because she already looked the part. Admittedly, in daily life, she seemed far too happy, but otherwise her pale skin, blood-red lips and long blonde tresses would all look terrific under moody stage lighting. Add a long white diaphanous gown and a mournful expression, and there you have your classic, doomed, despairing, youthful tragedienne.

It was, in short, a package deal, an extension of a real-life love affair, a theatrical marriage not exactly made in heaven – neither of these two was going win an Academy Award – but good enough for me to declare "Yes, this show is going to happen!"

At that particular moment, before rehearsals with the full cast began, it was just Hamlet, Ophelia and me in the apartment. It was a moment to relax, enjoy my casting success and catch my breath before the long pilgrimage to showtime. Watching the two of them, sitting in casual intimacy on the patio, I was struck by the fact that normal life rarely, if ever, gets onstage. Entertainment, by definition, is created by drama, and drama by the unusual, the unfortunate…and the tragic.

Look at it this way: let's suppose, for a moment, that Hamlet's uncle didn't kill his father. I'd like to refer to his father by name, but it seems that ghosts don't have names, so we never get to know what Hamlet's father was actually called…Frederik, perhaps? Or Christian, Rasmus, Cnut….? I'm partial to Cnut. That was the name of the only Dane I ever learned about in my high school history lessons, although we Anglicized it into 'Canute'.

Back in the early eleventh century, after invading England and slaughtering an impressive number of Anglo-Saxons, Cnut the Dane became a most pious and humble monarch. So much so that, on one famous occasion – and this is the reason why he elbowed his way into our history books – Cnut placed his throne before the waves at the English seaside and ordered the incoming tide not to wet his shoes and garments.

No, apparently, he wasn't 'cnuts'. Rather, the king was exposing and ridiculing the empty flattery of his own courtiers. As the waves soaked his socks, Cnut declared: "Let all men know how empty and worthless is the power of kings, for there is none worthy of the name, but He whom heaven, earth, and sea obey by eternal laws."

Cnut then hung his gold crown over a statue of Jesus nailed to the cross and vowed never to wear it again, which makes we wonder why he bothered to invade England and slaughter all those Anglo-Saxons in the first place. School history books never answer the interesting questions, do they?

Anyway, returning to Hamlet: let's imagine his father is alive, well and still married to Queen Gertrude. Meanwhile, Uncle Claudius, instead of pouring poison into his brother's ear, is off hunting, riding with his hounds, chasing and killing deer instead of family members.

Now picture this peaceful scene: Hamlet is sitting on a patio, somewhere in Elsinore Castle, enjoying breakfast with his beloved Ophelia. They could not have enjoyed this cosy togetherness for long. Even if Uncle Claudius had suppressed his sibling rivalry, something out of the ordinary would *have* to happen:

- Fortinbras, Prince of Norway, arrives unexpectedly at Elsinore Castle to claim half of the land of Denmark and also the hand of Ophelia in marriage, pushing Hamlet aside and starting a deadly feud between the two young men....
- Ophelia's younger sister is jealous and seduces Hamlet by slipping into his bed on a dark night during a thunderstorm, when he can't tell the difference, until suddenly Ophelia appears and he realizes his error, too late....

33

- Hamlet's mother murders Ophelia because she is not of royal blood and therefore not good enough for her wonderful son....

I'm sure you get the point. Entertainment demands extraordinary occurrences and this, in turn, means that sooner or later the characters are going to find themselves struggling through scenes of conflict, intrigue, violence and death.

The basic dynamic of almost every tale, whether told in a play, book, movie, or TV series, is conflict resolution: set up conflict early in the story, then keep your audience on the edge of their seats, preoccupied with the question 'will it all turn out okay in the end?' Will we find out who shot JR in the TV series *Dallas*? Will Marshal Gary Cooper outgun the bad guys in *High Noon*? Will Frodo make it to Mount Doom and destroy Sauron the Necromancer? Will amateur magician Harry Potter kill Voldemort, or vice versa?

Psychologists in America and Europe routinely publish social research studies showing that when children are exposed to violent entertainment as teenagers, they are likely to be more aggressive and less sensitive to the pain and suffering of others. In other words, the line between who shot JR, who shot JFK and who shot the next-door neighbour's cat tends to get a little blurry.

These findings don't make a scrap of difference. Nothing is going to change. As long as human beings need entertainment, they are going to want something with higher adrenalin voltage than the sight of a boyfriend and girlfriend sitting cosily together, sipping coffee, eating fried eggs, gently awakening to the day.

Hamlet and Ophelia will need to struggle, risking defeat, despair and, indeed, death itself, so that my play can entertain people.

Will it turn out okay? See next gripping episode.

CHAPTER 4

The Bard and the Queen

The Englishman's romance with India stretches back, of course, much further than when my own humble feet touched the subcontinent's soil for the first time. It predates the British Empire and the glory days of the Raj.

It began well before the Battle of Plassey, when, in 1757, that notorious soldier of fortune, Robert Clive, defeated the Nawab of Bengal thanks to the treachery of one of the Nawab's own generals and opened the way for the East India Company to sink its vampire-like fangs into India, sucking thirstily at the country's wealth. No, to find the first, faint heartbeat of the Anglo-Indian love affair we must go back much further to Shakespeare's time. In 1583, shortly after the Bard had married Anne Hathaway and before he'd written his first play, a small group of English adventurers set off from London, financed by the Levant Company, which was trading mainly with Turkey. Their mission? To probe the mysteries of the East and find a way to break Portugal's vice-like monopoly on trade in the Indian Ocean.

They nearly didn't make it. Sailing down the Persian Gulf, they were arrested as spies at the Portuguese trading station of Ormuz and sent to Goa as prisoners. An English Jesuit priest procured their freedom, and eventually they arrived at the court of the great Mughal Emperor, Akbar, located in Agra.

Little happened in the way of trading agreements, but here the party split. Ralph Fitch, leader of the expedition, was hungry for more sight-seeing. He went on to explore the River Jumna, the Ganges, Bengal and even pushed into Burma, Siam and the border lands of China. He wanted to cross the China Sea, but the ever-vigilant Portuguese stopped him at their massive fortress at Malacca.

Another member of the party, William Leedes, a jeweller by profession, got a well-paid job with Akbar and remained at the Mughal's court in Agra. It's just a guess, but one might speculate that Leedes' decision was swayed by the presence of Akbar's *nautch girls*, beautiful young women who wandered half-naked through the palace, available for sexual pleasure with anyone who felt like it.

Another man, John Newberry, either set himself up as a shopkeeper in Goa, or was murdered in the Punjab, depending on which historical source you care to believe. Personally, I prefer the Goa version, since this bestows on Newberry the dubious honour of being the first British tourist, opening a pathway to Goa's sunny beaches which, four hundred years later, would be crammed with holiday makers desperate to burn their white skins to a bright lobster-pink.

It is worth noting that none of these early English adventurers seems to have been interested in meditation. Perhaps they never saw beyond the colourful pantheon of Hindu gods and goddesses: Shiva, Parvati, Ganesh, Indra, Laxmi, Krishna, Kali....

Perhaps, in all their wanderings, they never met a self-realized soul.

By the time Ralph Fitch returned to London in 1591, eight years after setting out, Shakespeare was also there, having just arrived from Stratford and having written his first play, *Henry VI Part II*. Fitch rejoined his old guild, the Worshipful Company of Leathersellers, while Shakespeare rose to fame as a playwright. It is unlikely the two men ever met.

Four centuries later, I made my own pilgrimage to India and I rather fancy that if the Bard had accompanied me, he would have understood much of what he saw. The trains and cars, of course, would have been new, but many of the sights would be familiar: cows in the streets, beggars on the sidewalks, bullock carts creaking and clattering over badly-paved roads, shoemakers and tailors plying their trades in narrow alleyways, and a noticeable absence of public toilets.

He might have walked with me, in 1976, along a certain unpaved dirt track leading out of the Pune suburbs, past banyan trees, coconut palms and fields of sugar cane. The vegetation would have been unfamiliar to him, naturally, but as far as the epoch was concerned, Shakespeare would have seen little that might indicate he wasn't living in the sixteenth century.

What a difference forty years can make! If we tried to walk along that same path today, the Bard and I would be knocked flat in seconds. That narrow dirt track, now known as 'North Main Road', has mutated into one of the busiest dual carriageways in Pune, choked with cars, trucks, buses and motorbikes from dawn 'til dusk…and way into the night.

What happened? Well, when India abandoned its protectionist economic policies in the mid-nineties, foreign investment poured into the country and Pune became an economic boom town, doubling its population every ten years. Yesterday's suburbs have become today's inner city; agricultural fields have disappeared beneath apartment blocks; bullock carts are out and Mercedes and Saabs and are in.

Nowadays, the Bard would be simply overwhelmed as, indeed, I tend to be, sitting in the back of a motorized rickshaw, speeding along North Main Road, with a scarf held over my nose in a futile attempt to filter out the worst of the traffic fumes, heading for Hamlet and Ophelia's apartment.

On this auspicious day, we begin rehearsals of a play that will make the Bard's ancient bones turn in his Stratford grave. On this day, the full cast meets for the very first time, and I need to have the eggs-and-coffee ritual completed before 9:30 am, the appointed meeting hour.

As I mentioned earlier, the other acting roles in addition to Hamlet and Ophelia had already been filled, so maybe this is a good moment to introduce two more of them:

The Bard himself. Well, that was me. I decided to play the part of William Shakespeare. At sixty-seven years of age, bald and bearded, English and intellectual, I could just get away with it, although I have to admit that my grey beard made me look older than the only known portrait of the Bard – the rakish-looking fellow, sporting a gold ring in his left ear, who gazes out of the Chandos painting. Not surprising, really, because Will died at the age of fifty-two.

This may seem premature to us, but when you consider how many times the London theatres were forced to close because of bubonic plague sweeping through the city, it's a miracle he lived that long.

Plague was rampant at the end of the sixteenth century, and the Globe and other theatres were ideal places for catching it. The whole country suffered, but London, fittingly enough, was deemed to be the plague capital, so much so that on one occasion Queen Elizabeth I fled to Windsor, erected a gallows and declared anyone coming from London should be hanged.

The Bard survived long enough to write thirty-eight plays and 154 sonnets. He retired at the age of forty-nine to Stratford-upon-Avon and soon thereafter expired. He may have died of the plague – nobody really knows.

It's strange that I wrote a play about Shakespeare because I hated him with a passion when I was at school. I guess all the kids of my generation did; well, anyway, the middle-class kids who went to 'academic' schools and were force-fed Shakespeare's plays in dusty classrooms on sunny days, when we all should have been chilling at the beach.

But then, I have to grudgingly concede that Shakespeare saved my life. I'll come to it later.

So, I was holding down the Bard's role. The role of Good Queen Bess was taken by a long-time friend of mine. She was born to play it. In her mid-sixties and raised in Hampstead, London, she uttered the Queen's English with an impeccable upper-middle-class accent, exuding an effortlessly superior demeanour and was therefore a shoo-in for the role.

Don't get me wrong. In real life, Her Majesty was a gentle soul, a caring and generous friend to me and something of an emotional anchor in times of instability, chaos and stress – which tended to happen to me fairly frequently, due to my insecure lifestyle as a spiritual gypsy.

But like I said, she was a class act. I don't think she ever thought of herself as superior to anyone, but that's how she came across. I remember one time: Over lunch one day in the resort's canteen, a group of us were discussing how difficult it was to arrange to shift some furniture from one house to another in Koregaon Park – the Pune suburb where we all lived.

Her Royal Highness looked at us in a puzzled way and enquired, with the genuine innocence of the aristocracy, "Can't the ayahs do it?"

Of course, we all cracked up laughing.

In fairness, though, I have to say that we all had *ayahs* – our favourite term, borrowed from the days of the British Raj, for female Indian servants. They were cheap, readily available, spoke Pidgin English and were eager to work for Westerners, whom they could manipulate and cheat far more easily than their local, mean-and-wealthy Indian employers.

No, it was the way Elizabeth said it that tickled me – that, plus the comical image of our fat, lazy *ayahs*, struggling in their saris to carry a chest of drawers across Koregaon Park.

During the past six months, my poor Queen had been suffering severely from rheumatoid arthritis, something I wouldn't wish on anyone, but it's an ill wind that blows nobody good and her gaunt face and pained expression, combined with a limping gait, were perfect for the part of an aging, bitter, old monarch determined to impose her bad mood on her luckless subjects.

Like me, Queen Bess had spent many years in Pune. We both arrived here in the seventies. We both lived in the ashram. We both explored Osho's vision of sex, love and meditation, although not necessarily in the same bed. We both stayed on after the guru died in 1990.

I became a global commuter, choosing to spend my summers in Europe and my winters in India. But Elizabeth settled in Pune. She found herself a cosy apartment and a cat, then spent her days collecting and publishing personal stories from people like me about life with Osho. She no longer worked in the ashram – which by this time had completed its mutation into a resort – and was therefore free to indulge my desire to make her Queen.

Every morning, during our rehearsals, Elizabeth would arrive on her bicycle at Hamlet and Ophelia's apartment, having braved the chaotic rush hour on North

Main Road, which, in my estimation, earned her a gold star for courage.

I'd started bicycling in Koregaon Park, years ago, for health reasons – to keep fit. I gave it up for a similar reason – to stay in one piece. The traffic got so crazy I knew, sooner or later, I'd get squashed on the tarmac. Indeed, I even heard a rumour that trainee surgeons from around India came to Pune hospitals to practice their skills, because there were more traffic accidents here than anywhere else. It didn't surprise me.

But the Queen…the Queen rode on, defying some of the worst drivers ever to be found on four wheels. I should know, I took my driving test in Pune. One quick circuit of an empty parking lot with the examiner, a modest amount of *baksheesh* and it was all over. Pass.

Perhaps the very sight of my Queen intimidated other road users, for her lower face was hidden behind a large air filtration mask, her eyes behind a pair of dark glasses and her hair under a huge floppy cap. With this tall, alien-looking creature bearing down on you, it's understandable you might suddenly swerve to let her pass unharmed.

And so, from various parts of Koregaon Park, the cast gathered at Hamlet and Ophelia's apartment. This would be our routine for the weeks ahead: rehearsals in the morning, chill-out time in the afternoon, meditation in the evening.

A play to rehearse. A show to put on. A gamble to see if a bunch of amateurs really could produce a piece of theatre worth watching.

"Let's do it," said Hamlet. And so we began.

CHAPTER 5

The Mark of Greatness

Normally, I don't like Prologues. I find them boring and irrelevant. They insinuate themselves between the audience and the plot, delaying the action while stating the obvious.

But when it came to directing my own play, I really had no choice. Somehow, I was having visions of an Englishman with a great baritone voice walking out onto the stage in a pair of puffy, Tudor-style breeches and leg-hugging tights, unrolling his scroll and introducing my play.

Sure enough, that's what happened. I needed two 'extras' in my play to be the Queen's attendants, to perform various practical functions onstage such as shifting props around, and also to occasionally join in the action, such as supporting Ophelia with an up-tempo dance routine – no, really, I mean it.

As soon as they volunteered, I realized one of them would make a superb Prologue. He had the stature, the voice, the presence, the BBC newscaster accent. He radiated the sheer Englishness the task required. When he opened his mouth, I had no choice but to bow to destiny. Indeed, I had only to look at him and rhyming couplets started proliferating in my head.

He was in his fifties… tall, bald, clean shaven and in appearance not totally dissimilar to Patrick Stewart playing Captain Jean-Luc Picard in *Star Trek: The Next Generation*.

I didn't know him well, but enough to remember he'd been around the resort for a good number of years and was something of a loner. He tended to be hidden away in air-conditioned offices, editing translations of Osho's discourses, and I don't recall ever seeing him at a disco party. For this reason, I was surprised at his willingness to join the action; surprised and pleased.

And lo, it came to pass: at the appointed hour of the appointed day, the Prologue walked out onto my recently-rented and ruinously expensive stage, unrolled his scroll, and addressed the audience thus:

The mark of greatness as we know
Is left for history to bestow.
And who of us, now sitting here,
Will be remembered through the years?
Whose name to others will be shown
In golden letters carved in stone?

One thing I learned from the Bard: use the Prologue to engage the audience by addressing them directly. Get them involved. So here is the first hook for Joe Public: everyone wants to be famous, recognized in one way or another, leaving a mark on history.

What did Steve Jobs say?

"We're here to make a dent in the universe."

Personally, I disagree with Jobs. As far as I can tell, we're not here to dent the universe. We're here to dance with it. But Jobs' statement reflects a common human ambition: to make a difference and to be recognized for it.

Who of us will achieve it? You…me…the guy next door? Brain food for my audience to chew on. Which brings us, speedily enough, to the man who, in literary terms, made the biggest dent of all:

> *William Shakespeare: there's a name,*
> *Four hundred years of global fame,*
> *His plays show man in good, in badness,*
> *Our vanity, our pride, our madness,*
> *The rise and fall of kings and queens,*
> *Blind ambition, broken dreams.*
> *Shakespeare's mighty pen described it,*
> *What unkind critic will deny it?*

The point I make in the first half of the prologue is hardly original: Shakespeare was a genius, poetically portraying the heights and depths of human nature. That done, I offer a slightly different take on the Bard:

> *But this I say, no hesitation,*
> *Will never knew of meditation.*
> *His busy mind was full of chatter*
> *He didn't think the silence mattered.*
> *His characters did everything*

But close their eyes and look within...

For all the millions of lectures delivered in British schools and universities on the subject of William Shakespeare, I may be the first person to point out the lack of meditative awareness in the Bard's plays. Hardly surprising, really, because meditation has never been part of Western culture, which is why some people in India take the view that the West has never known culture at all. After all, they argue, how can you know culture if you don't even know yourself?

Anyway, this is the main thrust of my story: to show what might happen if a little touch of meditative awareness is added to the Bard's literary equation.

At this point, my Prologue stopped speaking, but it was not the end, merely a lengthy dramatic pause. He ceased to look at his scroll, gave the audience a friendly smile and engaged them more informally:

So... come with me, let me invite you
With this small drama to excite you,
And meet Will Shakespeare and his wife
And give them both a different life.
And what we poor players lack in skill
Let your imagination now fulfil.

One of the things I like about *A Midsummer Night's Dream* is the humble apology Puck offers at the end of the play, when he asks the audience to forgive the fact that a fantastic fairy tale has been offered on stage by ordinary actors:

If we shadows have offended
Think but this and all is mended,
That you did but slumber here
While these shadows did appear,
And this weak and idle theme
No more fleeting than a dream...

The same kind of thing happens in *Henry V* when the opening Chorus asks for 'a Muse of fire' to tell the story of the Battle of Agincourt, adding:

But pardon, gentles all,
The flat unraised spirits that have dared
On this unworthy scaffold to bring forth
So great an object....

It's a nice dramatic device that makes the audience feel good and that's why I included a similar apology at the beginning of my play. It reduces expectations, invites sympathy from the audience and asks them to become involved, supporting the story with their imagination.

One minor difference, though, between me and the Bard: he really didn't need to do it. I did.

CHAPTER 6

Amleth to the Rescue

Will is in trouble. He has incurred Royal displeasure. This calamity occurs right at the beginning of my play. The aging Queen Elizabeth stomps on to the stage, waving Shakespeare's recently-completed script of *Romeo and Juliet* in the air, barely able to contain herself.

"I will not have this play performed in my court, not while there is a single breath left in my body," she declares angrily. "No, no, no, Master Shakespeare!"

Will is in shock. He thought he'd hit the jackpot with this romantic tale. Instead, it looks like he's heading for the Tower. Pleadingly, in his best servile manner, the Bard tries to persuade his royal patron to change her mind.

"But Your Majesty, it is a worthy play...."

"I commanded a tragedy, Master Shakespeare."

"But *Romeo and Juliet is* a tragedy, Your Majesty."

Elizabeth gives a snort of Royal contempt: "Ha! Do you take me for a fool?"

Since no sane person, wishing to keeping his torso and head joined together, would ever dream of saying 'Yes' to such a question, Will's response is unsurprising:

"No indeed, Your Majesty."

"It is a love story, Master Shakespeare, and what is more, it is an *indecent* love story! Will you have me sit on my throne, in front of the entire court, and watch while a young girl, *barely thirteen-years-old*, shares her *bed* with her *lover*?"

The Queen savours her words, like feasting on forbidden fruit, the saliva of self-righteousness almost dripping from her mouth. It's not often that a frustrated old maid has the chance to use such pornographic language – well, porn to an Elizabethan prude, anyway.

It's a bit like the Clinton-Lewinsky scandal of the nineties, when Public Prosecutor Kenneth Starr's team of inquisitors relished extracting every salacious detail from poor Monica Lewinsky, urging her to confess exactly how Bill Clinton played with her breasts and in what manner she gave oral pleasure to the president's private parts. The prosecutors' insistence on laying bare the naked truth, lick by lick, mouthful by mouthful, was, of course, purely for the noble purpose of defending public morality.

"But they were married, Your Majesty," whimpers Will.

"A hasty, secret wedding, performed against all wise counsel. It cannot excuse the scandal you will have us watch."

Will has one last try. He pulls out his ace: the tragic ending.

"But they both die in the end, Your Majesty."

It doesn't work. He knew it. The Virgin Queen is having a full-on tantrum and nothing is going to mollify her.

"Too late, Master Shakespeare, much too late! The romance has already happened. I will have none of it!" To Will's horror, she rips up the manuscript and throws it on the floor. As he instinctively bends to pick up the pieces, the Queen forbids it.

"Leave it there, I command you! And write me another play, to be performed within a week...or risk my deep displeasure. Do I make myself clear, Master Shakespeare?"

It's another no-brainer for the Bard. It's an historical fact that one of his relatives on his mother's side, a gentleman by the name of William Arden, was arrested for plotting against the Queen, sent to the Tower and executed. Shakespeare's chief patron, the youthful and impetuous Earl of Southampton, was condemned to death for similar reasons, but had his sentence commuted to life imprisonment. Therefore, mindful of the ease with which his own cranium might suddenly find itself detached from the rest of his mortal form, Master Shakespeare bows in slavish acquiescence.

"Very clear, Your Majesty."

The Queen storms out and Will, somewhat belatedly, has had enough of kissing royal ass. Thinking his patron is out of earshot, he declares loudly, "My God, what a bitch!"

But the Queen is blessed with acute hearing. She stops, turns slowly and inquires with deliberate menace:

"What did you say, Master Shakespeare?"

Will has slightly less than a nanosecond to avoid decapitation. His rhyming skills are urgently required to cast a smokescreen of confusion around the word 'bitch'. Smiling obsequiously, he stammers:

"Er…I said…that I am *rich*!

Your patronage prevents me…

From falling in a *ditch*!"

The Queen gives another contemptuous snort of displeasure and exits. Will is left alone on stage, but not for long. As he glumly begins to pick up the pieces of his torn script, two members of his theatre troupe come bounding in, full of good spirits, delighted to have the opportunity to tease the playwright – nothing like kicking a Bard when he's down.

These two players, by the way, are my real-life loving couple, who will shortly be slipping into the roles of Hamlet and Ophelia. Right now, they are just a couple of actors in *The Lord Chamberlain's Men* – the name given to Shakespeare's drama troupe during the reign of Elizabeth.

One might speculate that such youthful players suffered under the Bard during long, tedious rehearsals of his works at The Globe, and therefore seized any opportunity to poke fun at him. They speak in rhyming couplets, which, for some reason, I find easy to compose. Ophelia is First Player, Hamlet, Second Player:

First Player (gloating): "How now, what grave misfortune have we here?"

Second Player (ironically): "Her Majesty was not too pleased, I fear!"

First Player (with mock pity): "Why Will, what ails you man? Why this distress?"

Second Player (with feigned innocence): "Have you been fighting with our Royal Mistress?"

The luckless Bard is in no mood to jest:

"Leave me alone, good fellows, I entreat you.

I lack the time and humour now to meet you."

The two young players have no intention of leaving him alone. This is too good an opportunity to poke fun. Snatching up fragments of the torn script, they take huge delight in over-acting the parts of Romeo and Juliet.

First Player (*playing Juliet*): "Oh Romeo, Romeo! Wherefore art thou Romeo?"

Second Player (*playing Romeo*): "But soft, what light through yonder window breaks? It is the East and Juliet is the sun!"

First Player throws away her script and opens her arms wide in a passionate invitation: "Take me, Romeo, for I am yours!"

Second Player runs towards her crying: "My love! My angel!"

They collapse on the floor together in a passionate but comic embrace, engulfed by fits of laughter.

Will has had enough:

"Stop it, both of you! Leave me in peace.

For I must write a tragedy, within a week."

First Player (getting up): "What story will you tell? Hast thou begun?"

Shakespeare: "Alas, I know not. Inspiration have I none."

The two players look at each other and nod in unspoken agreement.

Second Player: "Will, we can help you..."

First Player: "...if you so desire."

Shakespeare is suspicious. "How now? What mischief do you two conspire?"

First Player: "Last month, in Denmark, we played before the king..."

Second Player: "In his great castle did we dance and sing..."

First Player: "A mighty feast was held, with many plays..."

Second Player: "Heroic tales and legends from the grave..."

First Player: "One story was admired above them all..."

Second Player: "The greatest tragedy, wherein a king did fall..."

First Player: "The king's own brother did most treacherously take his life..."

Second Player: "And then he forced the Queen to be his wife!"

Shakespeare's curiosity is roused. They have his attention. Might this obscure Danish folk tale offer, perhaps, the possibility of personal salvation?

"So far so good... and then?" he ventures.

First Player: "Then her poor son, Amleth, tortured by this stealth..."

Second Player: "Knows not whether to kill the new king, or himself..."

First Player: "And so he struggles on, quite desperately,"

Second Player: "Not knowing whether to be, or not to be."

By now, I'm sure, you are beginning to grasp the story-line dynamics: I create the dramatic tension by putting Will under pressure from Queen Elizabeth, then introduce the concept of *Hamlet* as a solution. But I don't want Shakespeare to pull the idea out of thin air, because in real life things don't happen that way. All creators need inspiration and even the greatest minds need a trigger from which to fire off a new fantasy.

Historically, it may well have happened the way I'm describing it.

In the summer of 2012, I paid a visit to Kronborg Castle, near the Danish town of Helsingør. This was Shakespeare's *Elsinore Castle* where Hamlet was supposed to have lived. To tell the truth, I wasn't much interested in the place and would normally never have gone there. I'd come to Copenhagen to visit a beautiful Danish woman with whom I'd enjoyed a delightful love affair a few months earlier. I was eager to renew our sexual connection, but to my dismay, upon my arrival, she announced that from now on she wanted us to be 'just good friends' – a phrase which, as we all know, conveys the kiss of death to any lover.

However, her desire to be with me was genuine. She really wanted us to be friends and begged me to stay, but I was in such a foul mood it didn't seem possible. In desperation, she suggested a trip to Kronborg as a distraction and I agreed, sulking all the way in the train. It was only when we got to the castle that I started to cheer up and take an interest in my surroundings.

Kronborg overlooks the Oresund Strait, a narrow strip of water that separates Denmark from Sweden. In the sixteenth century, from this vantage point, the kings of Denmark, backed by fleets of warships, imposed taxes on goods carried by every merchant vessel passing between the North Sea and the Baltic. The revenue was huge and placed them among the richest monarchs in Europe.

Even when the merchants tried to cheat by understating the value of their cargo, hoping to pay less duty, the kings foiled them by imposing the right to purchase goods carried in any ship at the price set by the merchants themselves.

The traders were royally squeezed. If they declared the real value of their goods, they had to pay heavy taxes. If they tried to make the goods cheaper, the king would buy everything at the declared rate and make a handsome profit.

All this revenue was lavished on Kronborg Castle. In Shakespeare's day, King Frederick II transformed his simple medieval fortress into a magnificent Renaissance castle and held great feasts there, accompanied by much dancing, singing and theatrical events. So did his successor, Christian IV.

While walking through the Great Hall where all this happened, I was told by our guide that Elizabethan players from London were occasionally hired by these

Danish kings to perform at their feasts. Most probably, this is how a version of the famous Norse legend of *Amleth*, whose story-line closely follows that of Hamlet, reached London. Shakespeare picked up the idea from returning English thespians.

Good hypothesis? Well, if you ask me, it's a lot more plausible than some of the off-the-wall theories surrounding the Bard. Take, for example, the 2011 movie *Anonymous*, which claims to show how Edward de Vere, 17th Earl of Oxford, wrote Shakespeare's plays. I don't buy that for several reasons:

1)   The noble earl inconveniently expired in 1604, before many of the plays were written.

2)   Oxford happily published his own plays under his own name – humility and anonymity were not his strong suits.

3)   He was the patron of his own troupe of players, the Earl of Oxford's Men, who were in direct competition with Shakespeare's company.

Moreover, as John Cleese and the creators of Monty Python would no doubt have observed, Edward de Vere showed every indication of being an 'upper-class twit' with plenty of talent for sexual debauchery, losing money and sudden outbursts of violence, but little in the way of genius.

Advocates of the Oxford candidacy argue that Shakespeare wasn't cultured enough to be familiar with the legends, history, folk tales and international gossip that make up the stories of his plays. What nonsense! Even an ordinary journalist like me, who once worked as a political reporter in the Houses of Parliament, could easily weave stories together out of rumour and gossip – in fact, that's what I was paid for. And I rather fancy, had I lived 400 years earlier, I could have done the same at Elizabeth's court, picking up tales from travellers coming from abroad and fashioning them into my own creations.

If a Fleet Street hack can do it, what to say of a poet like Shakespeare? Two London players return from a gig at Kronborg Castle, pass on the basics of a good tale to Will, and without difficulty, Amleth becomes Hamlet. After all, it's the poetry and depth of human character that counts with Shakespeare, not the historical detail, with which the Bard improvised freely. How else would a bunch of English fairies – Oberon, Titania and Puck – find themselves in a Greek wood outside Athens in *A Midsummer Night's Dream*? It's bizarre, nothing to do with Greek culture, but it works wonderfully.

A brief theatrical aside: In this context, I feel a pang of regret that Shakespeare never met with Ralph Fitch, the first Englishman to explore India. Picking up stories from Fitch, the Bard might well have created an Anglicized version of Ramlila, the hugely popular Indian drama, enacted every year in towns and villages across the country. Ramlila depicts the life of Lord Rama, the abduction of his wife Sita by his enemy Ravana, and the ten-day battle that gave Rama final victory.

It would have made a nice addition to Shakespeare's foreign-based plays: Antony and Cleopatra in Egypt, Romeo and Juliet in Italy, Othello and Desdemona in Cyprus, Rama and Sita in India.... It would have fitted snugly among the Bard's epic tales of passion and extended the geographical range of his plays by several thousand miles.

Although the theory has slid out of fashion, I suppose I ought to say something here about the other chief candidate proposed by the "anybody-but-Shakespeare" school of historical conspiracy theorists. I refer, of course, to Francis Bacon, the philosopher, statesman and scientist, whose life and career paralleled Shakespeare's, passing somewhat bumpily through the reigns of Queen Elizabeth and King James.

Frankly, I can't buy this one, either. As far as I can see, Bacon was far too busy generating his own prolific writings, managing his turbulent political career and struggling with his lifelong inability to stay out of debt, to have time to pen a weighty folio of plays and poems on the side.

In any case, Bacon left his own mysteries for historical detectives to probe: he might have been a Rosicrucian, he might have been a Freemason, he might have been gay, and he may possibly have been a paedophile.

He is called the father of modern scientific method but in real life, Bacon couldn't add two plus two correctly because he died £23,000 in debt equivalent to £3 million at today's value. Shakespeare, on the other hand, was a shrewd businessman, forming a joint-stock company with the actors he employed in his plays, taking a share of company profits, earning a fee for each play he wrote and dying a wealthy man.

Oh yes, and one more thing: Bacon couldn't write poetry to save his life. On this ground alone: case dismissed.

By the way, it's quite remarkable how certain myths find their way around the world. The legend of Amleth doesn't originate in Denmark. Earlier versions have been found in Byzantine, Greek and Roman myths, so you see how ideas move and mutate.

A couple more historical titbits:

1) Christian IV of Denmark was a cousin of King James I of England – who succeeded when Elizabeth died in 1603 – and the two enjoyed watching theatre together, including Shakespeare's plays. However, by the time the Danish king visited London in 1606, *Hamlet* had already been written, so Christian wasn't the one who passed on the plot.

2) It's claimed that a play with Hamlet's theme existed in London prior to the Bard's epic, but, if so, it could have been similarly inspired – by players returning from the Danish court.

Basically, it's a great story. In the Danish version, Amleth is the son of Horwendil, King of Jutland. Horwendil is murdered by Feng, his brother – I love these Viking names – and then Feng becomes the new king and marries Horwendil's wife, Gerutha. Meanwhile, Amleth feigns madness to avoid being killed by Feng, then leaves the country, teams up with the King of England by marrying his daughter, and invades Denmark. He burns the Great Hall, incinerating a large number of drunken nobles in the process, then slaughters his uncle, thereby avenging his father.

Stirring stuff! Clearly, Amleth was more a man of action than Hamlet, who, poor boy, was prone to long periods of intellectual agonising and little in the way of swashbuckling heroics.

And here, if you will, another small theatrical aside: I have to apologise for the way my two players explain the legend to Will, because, as you may have noticed, they say that Amleth was in mental torment, wondering whether to be or not to be. Not a chance. Amleth was a Viking, born and bred, and these gung-ho warriors were renowned for head-chopping, not mind-fucking. But I need to bring in the famous 'to be' line somewhere, so it will have to do. If Shakespeare can take liberties then, by God, so can I.

Listening to the tale told by these two players, Shakespeare's mood changes from despair to hope. Out of the blue, they have thrown him a lifeline. Now he wants to hear the whole story, which he intends to shamelessly plagiarise in order to meet the Queen's deadline.

"It is a worthy tale, what happens next?" he asks.

But it's not going to be that easy. The two players scratch their heads, look at each other and affect mischievous ignorance.

"Er... we forget," says one.

"Oh no!" Shakespeare throws his hands up in frustration, until they reassure him thus:

First Player: "It matters not, Will, draw upon thy skill..."

Second Player: "And let your clever mind write what you will."

First Player: "Just make it up, you shall invent the rest. "

Second Player (*smirking with irony*): "After all, it is what you do best!"

First Player: "As long as they all die when the play ends..."

Second Player: "The Queen will love you..."

First Player (*rubbing her fingers to indicate money*): "...and make sweet amends!"

The Bard is convinced. After all, he really doesn't have much choice if he is to write, produce and perform a finished drama in seven days. The die is cast.

Shakespeare: "It shall be done. I'll write this 'Hamlet' now.

For I must save my precious neck somehow!

Henceforth, Will Shakespeare's plays shall ever be,

Remembered for their gloom and tragedy!"

CHAPTER 7

Heroes, Zeroes, Kings and Villains

It is time to introduce my dear wife, Mrs Shakespeare, a key figure in my play, a wise woman who is not afraid to speak her mind. As such, she puts her playwright husband to shame.

According to my highly personalized view of Elizabethan court politics, Will is basically an ass-kisser, weaselling his way into favour with Queen Elizabeth and trying hard to convince her that it is a good idea *not* to chop off his head. He retains his precious image as a genius wordsmith, but doesn't have much backbone.

His wife, however, is outspoken, fearless, with a finely-tuned, ironic sense of humour and thus a very different creature from the obscure and silent Anne Hathaway, the Bard's historical wife.

About Anne we know little, except that she was eight years older than Will and three months pregnant when she married her eighteen-year-old husband. She bore him three children and was famously bequeathed the 'second best bed' in her husband's will. But who she really was...what she thought...what she said to Will over breakfast…whether she was the inspiration for his love sonnets or the long-suffering wife who had to read about Will's romantic feelings for other women in his poems…alas, we have no clue.

I discovered my own Mrs Shakespeare at a seaside café in Greece, on the island of Lesbos, in the summer of 2012. We met over coffee, then sprawled on a pair of blue, leather bean bags on a wooden deck that jutted out over the beach, talking for hours about theatre while those around us tucked into Greek salads, tzatziki and lemon curd cake.

She was thirty-seven years old, Swedish and had immersed herself in Stockholm's home-grown world of Scandinavian showbiz, exploring a variety of *personae* such as theatre actress, TV drama queen, comedienne and singer.

"I can do pretty much anything onstage," she explained matter-of-factly, without a trace of hubris. "It's just a matter of focus. But, when times are hard and other work is scarce, I earn my living as part of a pop group that imitates ABBA. I'm Frida, the dark-haired one."

I liked her hypnotic blue eyes, pale skin, brown hair and the deepening sense of intimacy that grew between us as the morning progressed. We became so intimate, in fact, that I wanted to invite her home, but, with superbly inconvenient timing, I'd just vacated my holiday apartment and was waiting for the taxi to take me to the airport.

Many months later, I learned she was coming to India and, without holding out much hope, sent her a copy of my script and an invitation to join the acting team. To my delight, she accepted. I sighed with relief, because I knew her professional talent would anchor my play. I knew, now, that it would work.

It wasn't just her acting skills I needed. It was her golden tones as a singer, because although I thought of my play as...well...a play, it was, in fact, a musical. Or maybe it was a bit of both. Strictly speaking, it didn't conform to the musical format, because although it had enough songs to qualify, there was way too much dialogue.

Let's take a moment to examine the genre. The first musical I saw was the counter-culture rock musical *Hair* which I caught up with in London in the late sixties. As you can imagine, its anti-establishment offering of sexual freedom and illegal drugs was immensely appealing to me as a young man, fresh out of university and now working as a straight journalist during the week, while mutating into a dope-smoking hippie at the weekends.

Hair, like most musicals, had minimal dialogue and plot development. It had sensationalism, for sure – guaranteed by the nude scene – but its main strength was its songs, many of which were embraced by the anti-Vietnam-war movement in the States.

Leap-frogging over approximately forty years, the most recent musical I saw was *Mamma Mia*, which I must confess I enjoyed in spite of its mildly nauseating 'feel good' nature. Somehow, for me, any song written by Björn Ulvaeus and Benny Andersson has that 'nice and wholesome' feeling, all clean and tidy, like a

Swedish village on a Sunday morning. Even when Björn and Benny are trying to be deep, they end up on the surface.

I didn't see the stage show, but felt pulled to the movie by an irresistible force: for the life of me, I couldn't visualize a talented actress like Meryl Streep agreeing to take part in a sugar-coated reprise of ABBA's most successful chart-busters. I had to check it out.

Sure enough, there was Streep, living in a villa on the mythical Greek island of Kalokairi, convincing me that, yes, any of three men could be the father of her daughter and, yes, this confusion offered a perfectly good reason for her to sing *The Winner Takes It All*. It was a thin, implausible plot, but, thanks to the catchy ABBA hits, it boomed at the box office, earning an impressive $600 million on a $50 million budget.

What I'm saying is that, generally speaking, musicals are short on dialogue and sketchy in plot, using just enough of both to string the songs together. My offering, on the other hand, contained lots of dialogue and a detailed story line, so the addition of seven songs made it a strange beast, neither one thing nor the other.

The opening number occurs immediately after the Bard's decision to write the tragedy of *Hamlet*. The whole cast comes onstage and forms a chorus line, except for the Queen, who stands apart and listens while the rest of us sing:

> *Another drama for you to see,*
> *Another ending in misery,*

It's oh-so tragic, it has to be
It's for her Royal Majesty.
Another drama to make you sad,
Another story that's going bad
If you enjoy it
You must be mad!
It's for her Royal Majesty.
Heroes, zeroes, kings and villains
Kill each other with precision.
Cleopatra's destiny
Dying with Mark Antony,
Juliet as we all know
Killed herself for Romeo,
Star-crossed lovers, heartbreak endings
Tragedy and gloom descending
Is there more that we can't see?
Is this all that's meant to be?
Another drama for you to see,
Another ending in misery,
It's oh-so tragic, it has to be
It's for her Royal Majesty.
Another drama to make you sad,
Another story that's going bad
If you enjoy it
You must be mad!
It's for her Royal Majesty... we're going
crazeeeeeeee!
It's for her Royal Majesty.

The tone is ironic. Really, it's a kind of complaint,
sung by a troupe of players who are being forced to be

gloomy against their will; hence the hook line: 'It's for her Royal Majesty....' Each time we sang it, the whole chorus line bowed humbly in her direction, emphasizing our lack of choice.

But I don't allow gloom without humour, so we created a pantomime to illustrate the absurdity of it all:

Heroes, zeroes, kings and villains, kill each other with precision...

The two attendants walked forward and, with clockwork military precision, turned to face each other, drew their swords and ran each other through the guts, sinking down together in a crumpled heap.

Cleopatra's destiny, dying with Mark Antony...

Mrs Shakespeare and I walked forward and she performed a classic faint, a dying swan, passing away elegantly in my arms, while I clasped my forehead in mock despair.

Juliet as we all know, killed herself for Romeo...

Hamlet and Ophelia walked forward and she died in his arms, stabbing herself with an imaginary dagger. With piles of neatly paired corpses, we made our point:

Star-crossed lovers, heartbreak endings...

And here, we added what to me was a delightful touch, using only male voices, going deeper and deeper, slower and slower, with:

Tragedy and gloom descending....

So with 'descending' we ended up in the deepest basement of gloom and doom.

By the way, we didn't actually sing. A week earlier, we'd all hopped in a taxi, bringing with us two or three extra singers, and were driven to a Christian theological college in a nearby suburb of Pune to meet Father Edwin, the quietly efficient manager-producer of the college's recording studio.

I don't know why the college had a studio. Maybe it was for nuns to record devotional chorales in their high, pure, soprano voices, or for monks to growl *Te Deum* in basso profundo tones. Anyway, a couple of musicians at the resort turned me onto it as the only reasonably-priced studio within striking distance of the ashram.

They assured me that Father Edwin was not averse to helping Osho sannyasins, even though our approach to spirituality might not be – how shall I say? – in perfect synchronicity with his own theological views.

His studio looked retro, like something out of the sixties, but was impressive, with soundproof rooms, an endless supply of microphones and bundles of cords, and a mixing board offering God-knows how many tracks, illuminated by rows of pinhead-sized green and red lights. The whole thing had an 'Abbey Road' feel to it, as if George Martin might walk in any moment and start working on a track from *Sergeant Pepper's Lonely Hearts Club Band*.

And so, while Jesus gazed down upon us from his cross on the wall, we recorded *It's For Her Royal Majesty* and other would-be show-stoppers. This meant, of course, that we would be lip-synching the songs during our live action onstage, which was fine with me.

Only one of us was good enough to sing live and that was Mrs Shakespeare, who, in one of her many showbiz incarnations, had been part of a fairly successful, all-female, electro-punk band. Queen Elizabeth had a decent enough voice, too, but the rest of us were useless.

As for me, I could hold a tune only with constant practice, which I gained by picking up the mic at the resort's weekly karaoke event and – ignoring groans from my long-suffering friends – singing ballads requiring little vocal range, like Eurythmics's *Sweet Dreams Are Made of This* or Simon and Garfunkel's *The Sound of Silence*. It was only after months of cautious progress that I dared to sing my all-time favourite karaoke number, the fast, rock 'n' roll, tongue-twister *Johnny B. Goode*, penned by the immortal Chuck Berry.

On that fateful night, after I'd put down the microphone, a well-wishing musician friend came up to me and whispered, "You sang the whole song out of key. I thought you'd want to know that."

Thanks.

With only one professional in the cast, we had no option but to pre-record all the numbers. And, besides, we couldn't trust our rented radio mics to produce anything like the sound quality required for live singing.

Two decades earlier, pop-rock pioneer Madonna had paved the way for using live, chic, headset mics – not to mention pink, cone-shaped brassieres – with her iconic *Blond Ambition* tour, but we, alas, lacked the vocal talent to dare to follow in her footsteps.

Over to you, Father Edwin.

CHAPTER 8

Firewood, or No Firewood?

Time is a great forgiver. We love the Bard and revere him as a national treasure. If, however, he was alive and writing his plays today, he would be reviled and condemned as anti-Semitic, anti-Black, anti-French and generally xenophobic enough to be branded as dangerously nationalistic. Even the UK Independence Party might have hesitated before welcoming him into their ranks.

It was no accident that, in 1944, when the British government gave Sir Laurence Olivier the funds to make a film of *Henry V,* the country was at war. The government recognized, quite rightly, that in offering his audiences the chance to relive the English victory at the Battle of Agincourt, Shakespeare had created a superb piece of patriotic propaganda.

The image of a small English army with its back against the wall, triumphing against fearsome odds, nicely mirrored how the British people saw themselves in the struggle with Nazi Germany. The fact that the Bard was putting down the French, rather than the Germans, didn't really matter. It was the anti-European solidarity of an island race refusing to be conquered that struck a nationalistic chord in his audience.

However, leaving aside patriotic fervour, it is in the domestic relationship between man and wife that we find Master Shakespeare most lacking in liberal attitudes. In other words, the Bard was a male chauvinist, respectably so, for an Englishman in the late sixteenth century, but a chauvinist nevertheless.

For example, in one of his best-known comedies, *The Taming of the Shrew*, Shakespeare created a plot in which an Italian nobleman had two daughters, both of marriageable age. The younger one, Bianca, was beautiful and had several suitors, but her father had sworn not to give Bianca away until her elder sister, the shrewish Katherina, was married off.

In desperation, Bianca's suitors recruited Petruchio, the play's heroic woman-tamer. By employing reverse psychology, pretending every harsh thing she said to him was kindness and a number of other tactics, he eventually succeeded in subduing Katherina. In the final scene, where three newly-married men argued about whose wife was the most obedient, a thoroughly tamed Katherina won the contest by declaring:

> *Thy husband is thy lord, thy life, thy keeper,*
> *Thy head, thy sovereign, one that cares for thee....*

If she had stopped there, we could have pardoned the Bard for his misogynistic leanings, but, alas, this was not all. Kate continued:

Then vail your stomachs, for it is no boot,
And place your hands below your husband's foot:
In token of which duty, if he please,
My hand is ready, may it do him ease.

In modern terminology, Kate was saying: "Walk all over me, Petruchio, I don't mind, as long as it makes you happy."

The play was written and performed around 1591-94 and one wonders what Queen Elizabeth might have been thinking if she saw it. Certainly, no man was ever allowed to walk over her and several lost their heads both figuratively and literally for trying.

As I wrote my own play, I wasn't seeking to redress the historical imbalance caused by British male chauvinism down the ages, but, to a certain extent, that's what happened.

When Mrs Shakespeare first appears, wearing her demure, long-sleeved, floor-length, Elizabethan dress, she is apparently confined to the role of dutiful wife, although even at this early stage there are signs of rebelliousness.

The scene opens with the Bard seated in an old-fashioned wooden chair, stage left, feverishly engaged in writing the script for *Hamlet*, his quill pen racing across the parchment on his lap, his mind gripped by the implications of this saga, borrowed from Danish mythology.

Will pauses, gazing into the distance and musing to himself, while tapping his quill on his cheek: "To be or not to be, that is the question.... Yes! That is *the* question...."

He writes the immortal line while already mentally groping for the next, knowing time is short.

Mrs Shakespeare enters with a crochet circle in her hand, a fitting enough occupation for an Elizabethan wife. She looks at her husband, recognizing that he is preoccupied, yet hopeful he might be persuaded to help with some practical necessities of household life.

Will: "Whether 'tis nobler in the mind..."

Mrs Shakespeare (softly): "Will dear...."

There is no response. Will is totally absorbed by his poetic creativity.

Mrs Shakespeare (a little more firmly and loudly): "Will...."

Again, no response. His wife has no alternative but to turn up the volume.

"WILL!"

Startled by her shout of frustration, the Bard looks up at last.

"Yes dear? What is it?"

Mrs Shakespeare picks up a large basket from beside the fireplace and offers it to her husband.

"Fetch another basket of firewood, there's a good fellow."

Will seems to have difficulty leaving his imaginary world and focusing on so mundane a task in the real one.

"Er... what?"

Patiently, Mrs Shakespeare repeats: "Wood, dear, the fire's going out and there's a winter chill in the air today."

However, the Bard is in a full creative flow and another brilliant line has just occurred to him: "To suffer...the slings and arrows of outrageous fortune.... Yes, I like that!" He bends his head and his quill is scratching rapidly once more.

Mrs Shakespeare sighs in resignation. "Writing again, I see."

The Bard does not look up.

"Not another tragedy I hope," she adds, a sarcastic edge to her voice.

This gets his attention. Looking at his wife, he frostily reminds her of something they both already know.

"Her Majesty Queen Elizabeth, happens to be very fond of tragedies."

"That's because she's old and sick and dying," retorts his wife.

Will is shocked...and scared. His wife's bluntness could bring disaster on them both. Now she has his full attention, as he seeks to silence her.

"Hush, woman, hold your tongue! Such things may not be said without threat of immediate arrest and punishment!"

But Mrs Shakespeare is undaunted. "Everyone's saying it except you," she replies. "The gossip is all over London that the Queen will die before the year is out."

Historically, we are in the right ballpark here. It is believed that Shakespeare wrote *Hamlet* in 1601, only two years before Elizabeth's death. She was sixty-eight years old at the time and soon to fall into a prolonged period of melancholy and depression, triggered, perhaps, by the need to execute Robert Devereux, Earl of Essex, her one-time court favourite, plus the untimely but natural deaths of several of her closest female friends.

Will, however, is more concerned about the fate of his theatrical troupe, *The Lord Chamberlain's Men*.

"Alas, I fear it," he confides in his wife. "And what will happen to our poor company of players then?"

He needn't have worried. King James I, it turned out, was even fonder of theatre than Elizabeth, and honoured Shakespeare's troupe by renaming them *The King's Men*. But this, of course, had yet to be determined. Nobody was even sure that James VI of Scotland would be offered the Crown, since Elizabeth refused to discuss the issue of succession almost until her last breath.

Shakespeare's mood has softened to one of vulnerability and doubt, which in turn allows his wife to show her affection. She puts down the basket, comes over to stand behind Will's chair, leans gently forwards and rests her head lovingly against his own.

"Will, sweetheart, write me a nice comedy. Something to make me smile and laugh, like you used to in the old days...to please me?"

Here, we begin to see Mrs Shakespeare's not-so-hidden agenda: to steer her husband, his plays and his characters away from tragedy, towards light-heartedness and happiness. It's going to be an uphill task.

However, I must confess I am diverging from historical accuracy. Shakespeare didn't write comedies first, then follow up with tragedies. During the final decade of the sixteenth century, he produced a fair mix of history plays, comedies and tragedies.

It was only in 1601, with the death of his father, John Shakespeare, that his mood shifted and he began a seven-year stretch in which almost all of his plays had a dark, heavy, brooding quality. This was a creative outpouring that included *Othello*, *Macbeth*, *King Lear* and *Antony and Cleopatra*. This 'dark' period commenced with *Hamlet*.

At first, Will seems to respond positively to his wife's request for cheerful drama. Patting Mrs Shakespeare's hand, he assures her, "Dearest, I will..."

She beams with pleasure, but too soon.

"Er...but not now!" he adds.

The Bard jumps to his feet, excited to share his latest creation with her. "This new play, *Hamlet*, is going to be my greatest triumph. The tragedy of the young Prince of Denmark, torn between action and inaction, decision and indecision, life and death..." He ends with a dramatic flourish: "To be, or not to be, that is the question!"

Mrs Shakespeare is unimpressed. Picking up the basket once more, she thrusts it towards her husband.

"Firewood, or no firewood? *That* is the question. Now get along with you or we'll both die of cold tonight."

Will acquiesces and takes the basket. "Oh very well..." Then inspiration strikes once more: "But wait! I see how it must continue..."

Immediately he drops the basket and sits down, picking up his quill and writing furiously:

"To sleep, perchance to dream – aye, there's the rub: For in that sleep of death what dreams may come...?"

His pragmatic wife shrugs and accepts defeat. "I give up. Give me the basket." She picks it up herself, then turns and address the audience directly:

"Equal rights for women is going to come a little late for me. But I have my ways…."

She smiles, looks deviously at her husband, then sidles over to his chair and rests a hand on his shoulder.

"Buy me a new dress, Will," she says seductively, "And I'll forgive you everything."

Will does not look up. His brain is overloaded with Hamlet's soliloquy, but a small part of it somehow registers that his wife wants something and, if he is not to be disturbed any further, it will be better to simply agree to it.

"Yes dear."

"Ha!" Mrs Shakespeare skips across the stage in delight and again addresses the audience. "You see? It's better to *be*. How can you wear a new dress if you choose *not to be*?"

She laughs and disappears with the basket, while the Bard writes on. It is a small victory, to be sure, but one that reveals Mrs Shakespeare's ingenuity in getting what she wants. And this is just the beginning.

CHAPTER 9

The World Is an Illusion

Hamlet walks on stage carrying a skull. He spies Will Shakespeare, still sitting in his chair, hunched over his manuscript. As the Bard, I'm on stage the whole time, throughout the play. I wrote it that way, which could make me a megalomaniac writer-director-actor, but, as a theatrical device, it works pretty well.

Shakespeare's presence lends continuity to the storyline, which, as I mentioned earlier, draws its pace and dramatic tension from his urgent need to please Queen Elizabeth before she cuts off his head. Anyway, that's my excuse.

Hamlet strolls across the stage, coming close to Will, inadvertently thrusting the skull into the Bard's face. In the original play, of course, this skull is the last remains of Yorick, whose transformation from 'a fellow of infinite jest' into a decaying set of dentures provides Hamlet with yet another opportunity for lengthy melancholic musings on the futility of life, commencing with the famous line:

"Alas poor Yorick! I knew him, Horatio…"

Somehow, this grave aside – if you'll excuse the pun – has remained fixed in people's minds, generation after generation. Even today, when you google the word 'alas', Yorick pops up as one of your first options.

In my play, however, the arrival of a skull onstage has yet to be explained. Hamlet waits to be noticed by the busy playwright and then, when he is not, coughs impatiently to make his presence known.

"Ahem…excuse me, Will."

Will looks up from his writing and is confronted by two hollow eye sockets staring blankly at him. He freaks.

"Aaaargh! For God's sake, man, what do you think you're doing?"

"Sorry, Will. I've come for the audition."

"What?"

"The part. I've come to play Hamlet."

"But why the skull?"

"Well, you said it's a tragedy, so I brought along my grandfather to add a little atmosphere."

Will recovers his composure, takes the skull from Hamlet and inspects it curiously. "Oh, very well. After all, if I fail to please the Queen, this is what I will look like in a week!"

He puts down the skull by the side of his chair, fumbles through his manuscript, pondering over what he's written, then hands a piece of parchment to Hamlet. Getting up, Will takes Hamlet by the hand and brings him to centre stage.

"Stand here, face the audience and read this."

Hamlet holds the script before him, striking a dramatic, overly-theatrical pose that reminds me of Laurence Olivier, who, in 1948 brought *Hamlet* to the silver screen and in so doing won the only Academy Award ever given to an actor playing a Shakespearian role.

However, as anyone who has met an American tourist in Stratford-upon-Avon will know, our friends across the Atlantic tend to go gaga over Shakespeare and lose their critical faculties, over-awed by anyone who can recite the Bard's Elizabethan poetry and prose with a crisp English accent.

If you ask me, this is what happened to Hollywood's Oscar-givers in 1948, because Olivier never impressed me as an actor, even when, as a teenager, I saw him play Othello at the Chichester Festival Theatre.

For me, he was an orator, not an actor. He had a wonderful voice and could stride around a stage, delivering epic lines in ringing tones, but with little genuine emotion. Even when murdering his beautiful wife, Desdemona, brushing off his jealousy with 'It is the cause, it is the cause, my soul', I couldn't feel his passion in it.

A black man killing a white woman? That scene should have set the world on fire. But, no, we had to wait another thirty years before O.J. Simpson fulfilled this scenario's headline-gripping potential.

Sir Larry was old school, pre-Method. He could *act* his characters, but he couldn't *be* them. That's what made it so humiliating for him to play alongside Marilyn Monroe in *The Prince and the Showgirl* in 1957. Up close to the camera, he lacked the ability to convey his feelings, whereas Monroe oozed emotional authenticity in every scene.

It's one of those oddities of destiny that Olivier's name has become synonymous with good acting. The annual awards for excellence in London plays and shows are now called the Olivier Awards.

The bust on the award does, however, depict Olivier as King Henry V, a straightforward action role in which he was much more comfortable. And, let's face it, a play about the English beating the crap out of the French can't fail in the United Kingdom, neither in Shakespeare's time nor our own. The fact that Agincourt was an isolated victory in a ruinous, century-long war in which England lost almost all its French possessions is conveniently ignored by the Bard and everyone else.

Another peeve about Olivier: it's hard to forgive his introductory comment, at the start of his *Hamlet* movie, where he announces: "This is the tragedy of a man who cannot make up his mind."

That is way too banal for my taste, Sir Larry. It's like saying *Macbeth* is the story of a henpecked husband, or *Romeo and Juliet* is about a young couple with family problems. Which makes me wonder: did Olivier have any depth at all, or was he just a voice?

Meanwhile, onstage in Pune, Hamlet begins his audition, clearing his throat and loudly proclaiming the most famous line in the history of theatre:

"To be, or not to be, that is…"

He pauses, shrugs and laughs… "*such* a stupid question!"

82

Will is gobsmacked. He can't believe his ears.

"What do you mean, man?" he asks angrily. Shakespeare has just posed the deepest philosophical question that his brilliant mind could have imagined, and this young creep blows it off like a cheap slogan for a TV commercial.

"Explain yourself!" he demands.

"Nobody asks questions like this, Will."

Offended and indignant, Will shakes his head. "I don't believe this! You and your colleague gave me that line yourselves, from the play in Denmark!"

Hamlet shrugs, conveying his indifference to the alleged brilliance of the line. "I guess it sounds better in Danish."

Highly miffed, Will stabs an authoritarian finger at the parchment in Hamlet's hand. "Just read the script," he orders, testily. His ego as London's literary-genius-in-residence has been deeply dented.

Dutifully, Hamlet completes the audition, declaring:

"Whether 'tis nobler in the mind to suffer

The slings and arrows of outrageous fortune,

Or to take arms against a sea of troubles,

And by opposing end them."

He gets the part. Of course he does. In real life, as I already mentioned, he and Ophelia are deeply in love, so they come as a package. Moreover, we are obliged to do all our rehearsing in the living room of their apartment as we don't have any other space in this over-crowded city. So, one way or another, he's hired.

Now, let's fast forward from Elizabethan England, or rewind from the present-day, and pay a visit – if you will

– to a stuffy classroom at a high school in the south of England, where a seventeen-year-old boy is reading the part of Hamlet.

I remember the date exactly: it is October 24, 1962, and happens to be my birthday. The Cuban Missile Crisis is at its peak and somewhere, far away in Washington and Moscow, John F. Kennedy and Nikita Khrushchev are contemplating blowing the world to pieces.

It happened more than half a century ago and nobody bothers about it now. But allow me to remind you: never, in the long chronicle of madness we call history, have we ever come so close to destroying the human race as we did in 1962. The two World Wars that preceded it were just parlour games compared to the shit that was about to come down on *Homo sapiens*. Hundreds of megaton nukes were poised, aimed and ready to fly in a push-button apocalypse.

"To be or not to be..."

I remember reciting that line aloud while secretly thinking, "Who the fuck cares?"

To be accurate, I probably didn't use the f-word. The social usefulness and linguistic flexibility of 'fuck' had yet to be introduced to me. But, still, I remember that moment. I couldn't articulate what I was feeling, but it was as if a curtain was being lifted, revealing my own rebellious intelligence, which until then had been hidden – even from me – behind an unquestioning acceptance of whatever was being taught to me under the guise of education.

I saw the difference between the intellectual and the existential. Hamlet's oh-so-profound question was a mind-fuck. It appeared to be deep, but it wasn't. In fact, in that moment, the whole laborious process of British education seemed utterly phony to me.

At such a moment, what should we have been doing? Running naked through the streets shouting "The end is nigh"? Throwing a cake and cookie party for the whole school to celebrate humanity's moment of supreme insanity? Breaking into the girls' school next door for a few final hugs before the Big Kiss-Off?

Well, looking back, I'd say any of those options would have been more appropriate than sitting at our desks, reading from text books, doing the British 'carry on as usual' routine while the fate of the entire world hung in the balance. It seemed so unreal.

Many years later, when I came across Adi Shankara's philosophy of Advaita Vedanta, I noted with interest his assertion *"Samsara maya hai"*, the world is an illusion. Well, maybe it is, and maybe it isn't. But, for sure, at that precise moment in history, in October 1962, the study of English literature by a group of teenagers seemed utterly illusory to me.

What was real, what was pulsating as an invisible presence in our little classroom, filled with nicely-uniformed schoolboys and a fusty old teacher with chalk dust on his gown, was the very real possibility that suddenly, without warning, we would all be vaporised by a nuclear blast. My birthday might be my deathday.

Maybe for Nikita Khrushchev the question was real. *To be or not to be?* If that pig-faced little Russian had opted for *not to be*, we'd have all been toast, or perished slowly in the ensuing nuclear winter. One minor consequence of the fall-out from such an epic event, by the way, would be that you wouldn't be sitting where you are now, reading this book.

So, that's when I started to figure out the difference between thinking and living.

To be or not to be? Eventually, I came to the conclusion that *not to be* is the only way to be. But this paradoxical insight comes later in my tale.

CHAPTER 10
Free to Be Me

Mrs Shakespeare is looking at me with a bright, sardonic smile, as if seeking answers while knowing that whatever I tell her is going to be ridiculous. Perhaps she is right. As we have already seen, she is free from the influence of politics and not afraid to speak her mind – especially to her husband.

Mrs Shakespeare has just returned with a basket filled with wood and has stumbled upon the ongoing Hamlet audition. Here, I insert a freeze-frame in the audition itself, so that the Bard's wife can have her say.

"So, let me get this straight," she muses, inspecting the solitary young man standing motionless in the middle of the stage. "This handsome-looking young man is called Hamlet...."

"Right," says Will.

"Hamlet's father was the King of Denmark, but the king was killed by his brother. The brother becomes the new King of Denmark and marries Hamlet's...mother?"

"Right," says Will. When his wife is speaking, Will keeps his answers short. I wrote the script that way – you can't say I didn't learn anything from my love relationships with the opposite sex.

"Hamlet wants to kill the new king, to revenge his father, but instead spends a long time wondering whether to be or not to be, which makes everything very complicated. And how does it all end...?"

"In tragedy," says Will.

As if she doesn't know. Mrs Shakespeare is well aware that Queen Elizabeth has become a bitter, angry old woman who is forcing her husband and his troupe of players to perform dramas that end only in suffering and death.

Historically, it's not true. The Virgin Queen seems to have enjoyed comedy as much as tragedy. But I'm using her to make a point: Shakespeare became England's greatest playwright, revered down the centuries, because people were impressed with his tragedies.

Humour doesn't count. Even today you can see it, in Hollywood's annual glam-fest known as the Oscars. It's the actors playing 'serious' roles who usually bag the gongs. Dustin Hoffman won his pair for *Rain Man* and *Kramer vs. Kramer*, not for his brilliant, gender-bending, comic performance as the title character in *Tootsie*. Renee Zellweger won hers for *Cold Mountain*, a tear-jerking war drama, not for her hilarious portrayal of Bridget Jones. Sometimes the things we respect most do us the most harm.

Meanwhile, back on stage, my wife is about to drive home this point, with needle-like precision:

"Hamlet dies...?" she asks.

"Yes," says Will.

"Hamlet's mother dies?"

"Yes."

"The new king dies?"

"Yes."

"The king's prime minister dies?"

"Yes."

"The king's prime minister's son dies?"

"Yes."

Our one-sided dialogue is interrupted by a vision of loveliness, a hauntingly beautiful figure who glides slowly across the stage. I was right: this young woman is stunningly charismatic as the heartbroken, doomed Ophelia.

Mrs Shakespeare pauses and takes her in, appreciating, along with the audience, this gorgeous sacrificial pawn, ghost-like with her pale face and scarlet lips, soft and vulnerable in her white, flowing gown.

"And who might this young lady be?"

"This is Ophelia, the Prime Minister's daughter. She's madly in love with Hamlet."

"Ah, something to be happy about, at last!"

Will is forced to disillusion his wife, who, one suspects, already knows that happiness is not a major theme in this politically-driven saga. "Not exactly," says the Bard, cautiously. "You see, the murder of his father has driven Hamlet almost mad, so he rejects Ophelia. Watch and see!"

Hamlet, who has been standing motionless all this time, suddenly comes to life and, true to form, cruelly abuses his former beloved. Here, for a few lines, we stick to the Bard's original script:

Hamlet (*sneering disdainfully at his former love*): "I did love thee once."

Ophelia (*nursing her wounded heart*): "Indeed, my lord, you made me believe so."

Hamlet (*callously*): "You should not have believed me, I loved thee not!

Ophelia (*stricken with grief*): "Alas, I was the more deceived!"

And this, as we all know, is where Hamlet loses it, screaming:

"Get thee to a nunnery! Why wouldst thou be a breeder of sinners? Or, if thou wouldst marry, marry a fool, for wise men know well enough what monsters you make of them. To a nunnery go, and quickly, too! Farewell!"

Ophelia sobs and sinks to the floor in despair. Mrs Shakespeare waits for Hamlet's tirade to end and then returns to her task of husband-hunting.

By the way, maybe I should remind you, Mrs Shakespeare is not your stereotypical Swedish blonde. As I mentioned earlier, she has dark-brown hair, penetrating blue eyes and the kind of neutral face which, while attractive in its own right, can be made up as a clown, a femme fatale, an innocent child, or an Elizabethan housewife.

She's got that chameleon quality of an experienced actress and for this reason, her presence always makes me feel slightly unsettled. I'm never sure who I'm with. I can't grab hold of her personality and fix it. In a way, our relationship nicely mirrors that of Mr and Mrs Shakespeare – Will can never be sure whose side his wife is on. Right now, she's on a roll, so we need to get back to the action.

"So Hamlet told Ophelia he loved her, and now he doesn't...and now what will she do?" she asks her husband.

Will would love to escape at this point, but all the exits are blocked. He is cornered. He has no choice but to be struck by the twin arrows of irony and sarcasm now speeding towards his chest, shot from his wife's verbal bow.

"Er... she will throw herself in a lake."

"And drown herself and die?"

"Yes, in her grief and her despair."

Long dramatic pause. "Will..." she says slowly.

"Hmmm...?"

"Don't you think you're overdoing it, just a teeny bit? All this doom and gloom...?"

Just a teeny bit. Mrs Shakespeare's use of understatement is superb, especially when one considers that this was the longest of all the Bard's plays, a four-hour marathon of nonstop misery. In fact, she hates the whole idea of *Hamlet* and is determined to rescue all the characters and transform them into happy human beings. Her campaign begins with Ophelia.

But first, Will has to fight a short, hopeless rear-guard action.

"The Queen will love it," he protests.

"Yes, well, the Queen is sixty-seven years old and still a virgin," retorts his wife. "But what about all the young women who will watch your play? *Get thee to a nunnery...? Breeder of sinners...?* What kind of example are you giving them?"

Will waves a dismissive hand while uttering the classic cliché used by all men who are forced to surrender to feminine wisdom while pretending to remain intellectually superior.

"Oh, you don't understand, woman!"

Mrs Shakespeare is not impressed. "Oh, but I rather think I do. Come here, sweetheart," she murmurs, taking the poor girl by the hand and raising her up. "Now listen, you're much too young to go drowning yourself in a lake."

Ophelia turns her beautiful head to cast a soulful look in the direction of Hamlet.

"But...but I love him!"

"Yes, well, there are plenty more idiots where that one came from, I assure you," retorts Mrs Shakespeare in a brisk, no-nonsense manner. "Now what you need is a role model..."

Ophelia is puzzled. "What's a role model?" she asks.

By way of reply, Mrs Shakespeare turns and speaks directly to the audience, in one of several theatrical asides she will deliver during this performance.

"Oh, I forgot, that phrase doesn't come into fashion for another 400 years..." She again faces Ophelia. "Well, someone to look up to... someone to give you hope... someone to show you a new vision of life."

Ophelia is bewildered. "Like who?" she wonders.

Mrs Shakespeare thinks for a moment. Then it dawns on her. "How about Lady Raga?"

I have to confess, when I wrote the first draft of this play, I had Mrs Shakespeare say "How about Lady Gaga?" Gaga was an obvious choice, a symbol of young, rebellious, *'do anything I fucking well want onstage'* female liberation. Of course, this was a few years back, before Miley Cyrus eclipsed Gaga by swinging naked on a wrecking ball, then twerking onstage with American singer Robin Thicke. Now Gaga's envelope-pushing dramatics seem positively conservative.

Anyway, I was going to have Ophelia sing Gaga's *Bad Romance* to Hamlet, then turn away from him and proclaim her independence by singing *Born This Way*.

However, it's better to be original whenever possible, especially when it comes to avoiding royalty fees, so I composed two new songs for the occasion and also changed the name of the role model from Gaga to 'Raga' for my India-savvy audience. As many of you know, a *raga* is a piece of classical Indian music, so it was a perfect *double entendre*.

Two courtly attendants, dressed Elizabethan style, bring on a purple curtain which they hold up in front of Ophelia while, with Mrs Shakespeare's help, the young woman does a quick onstage change.

Funky, bluesy music begins to play and then Ophelia rips away the curtain and struts out towards the audience, dressed in a glitzy, white tank top and matching mini-shorts, with white stockings. It's an all-blonde outfit and looks sensational. This is where the plot comes unglued and Will starts having a coronary arrest.

"Hey, what's going on? This isn't in my script!" he exclaims, but no one is listening, least of all Ophelia, who belts out the blues:

Raga and her Baba, we don't get along,
Raga and her Baba, this man he done me wrong.
Broke my heart in pieces and threw it on the floor,
Still I come back crying, begging him for more....
It's a crying shame.... oooh yes it is... it's a crying shame...

I wrote the lyrics and a Russian musician in St. Petersburg, a friend of mine called Ravi, did a great job adding the tune. One of the advantages of my lifestyle is that I'm connected with a worldwide network of talented and artistic people – Ravi is one of them. He's in his mid-forties and does his best to look sad and mournful, like a soulful musician should, burdened by his own penetrating insights into the injustices to be found Russian society – we won't even mention the name 'Putin' in this context.

By nature, however, Ravi is a bliss-addicted, happy-go-lucky kind of guy. Rather like Leonard Cohen, the melancholic Canadian songwriter and musician, he found that, in spite of discovering many excellent reasons to be depressed about the state of humanity, "cheerfulness kept breaking through". That's Ravi.

As I indicated earlier, Ophelia is lip-synching. It's actually Mrs Shakespeare's fine voice with which she moans onstage about her obsession with her *Baba*.

Ophelia has a highly individual way of dancing. It's odd. It's...well...a kind of sensual wriggle, arms and legs going everywhere at once, and no amount of choreography will change it. But somehow it works. She's all over Hamlet, slinking up to him, grabbing him then pushing him away, blaming him for her unrequited love. He's the *Baba* she's singing about:

Raga and her Baba, the man I love to hate,
Raga and her Baba, a passion that can't wait.
Broke my heart in pieces and threw it on the fire,
Still I come back crying, burning with desire...
It's a crying shame... oooh yes it is... it's a crying shame....

Mrs Shakespeare, observing from the side-lines, watches her protégé drape herself on Hamlet and slide erotically down his body in a masochistic gesture of addiction, but then the older woman intervenes, stopping the music.

"You've got the right idea, sweetheart," she encourages Ophelia, "but you're still focusing on Hamlet. Take all the energy back and give it to yourself." She pauses for a moment, takes Ophelia's hands, looks lovingly into her eyes and delivers the key line: "You are free to be you."

Ophelia gasps in astonishment at this unexpected revelation, liberating her from the Bard's cruel pen. "Free to be me?" she echoes.

Cue for a song, if ever there was one. Mrs Shakespeare drags Hamlet to the side of the stage and

Ophelia stands alone, facing the audience. After a moment of silence, a solo Spanish guitar comes in, flamenco-style, strumming dramatically in the background as Ophelia slowly and powerfully sings:

It's not the first time that you've made me cry,
It's not the first time that you've said goodbye,
But this time I have found a golden key,
Without you, I have freedom…to be me!

There's a sudden surge of music with a driving beat, and Ophelia breaks into a fast rock tune, titled *Free to Be Me*, again composed by the Subhuti-Ravi team:

I'm free to be me, yeah, free to be me,
Free to be me, yeah, free to be me….
Free to say "No!" and free to say "Yes!"
Free say "Hi!" and "Goodbye!" to the rest
Free to cut loose and dance all night long
Grab any guy and this is my song.

While Hamlet watches in astonishment, Ophelia takes advantage of her new-found freedom to flirt with the two attendants who, along with Mrs Shakespeare, are doing a pretty-damn-cool backing routine, wearing shades and strutting their stuff in time to the music. One of them, of course, is my oh-so-English Prologue, whose transformation into an MTV disco-dancer adds comedy to the chorus line.

Ophelia homes in on the guys and flirts shamelessly with them:

Free to say "Hi, I'm single and free,"
Free to say "You! You're coming with me!"
Free to say "Guy, are you looking at me?"
Free to say "Yeah, now, you're coming with me!"
I'm free to be me, yeah, free to be me,
Free to be me, yeah, free to be me...

As the song fades, the two attendants lift her up and carry her off, while she waves glamorously to the audience, obviously ecstatic about her new-found freedom.

I admit, theatrically speaking, it's a bit of a stretch, switching so fast from helpless victim to liberated superwoman. But personal transformation is like that. One moment you're trapped inside a belief about yourself that grips your heart and mind so totally you can't imagine escaping from its clutches. Next moment, you're free to fly like an eagle across the sun, leaving no footprints in the blue sky – two metaphors used by mystics to describe the state of spiritual liberation.

So, early in my play, Ophelia has a euphoric moment of liberation. But it's not going to be that easy. This young woman has greater challenges to face if she is to succeed in avoiding her dreadful fate. Queen Elizabeth, the all-powerful, all-miserable, all-English sovereign, has commanded a tragedy and, by God, that's what Will is determined to give her – if only to save his own neck. The Bard, you will note, is a pragmatist, not an idealist.

But he's up against his own wife, a highly resourceful and clever woman, so he's squeezed between a rock and a hard place.

This is how I set up the dramatic tension to carry the play towards it climax: Who is going to win? Mrs Shakespeare or the Queen? How does Will get out of this dilemma? Can Hamlet and Ophelia find true love? And what, you may be wondering, does all this have to do with meditation and starting a revolution of the soul?

Well, as the working men of Athens said to Duke Theseus in *A Midsummer Night's Dream*, when presenting their 'merry and tragical' play about Pyramus and Thisbe:

"Wonder on, till truth make all things plain."

CHAPTER 11

Meanwhile, Behind the Curtain

Now that we are well into the plot, I can tell you how this play came to be written. It began with a vision, or a fantasy or maybe it was just a scam. Sometimes it's hard to tell the difference. Sometimes all three can be true together.

One year previously, out of the blue, I'd received an invitation to participate in an arts festival in Delhi, including several nights of cultural entertainment, featuring a musical concert, a classical Indian dance performance and a theatre play. The general idea was to feature sannyasin artists and thereby demonstrate that meditation and creative expression can go hand-in-hand.

The festival was to take place in a modern auditorium with a seating capacity for 5,000 people. We would be flown to Delhi from Pune, and we would stay in three-or-four-star hotels. All expenses would be paid. I was invited to provide a play for the evening of drama. It sounded great.

At first, I had no doubts about the festival, although the presence of a slight knot of tension in my stomach informed me that I had considerable doubts about my ability to produce a play to match the occasion. Searching for a quick solution, I thought back to the musical shows I'd written and staged in the nineties, wondering if perhaps one of them might do the job:

The Professor Who Lost His Mind. The tale of an American psychology professor who, accompanied by his wife and two children, goes inside his own mind to rescue his beautiful 'inner woman' from his male chauvinistic 'inner man'.

The Beautiful Princess. The story of a medieval prince and princess whose families hate each other and who find true love by making a *Tardis*-style time trip to the Pune ashram and doing past-life regression therapy.

Amrapali & the Wheel of Dharma. A beautiful courtesan from the days of Gautama Buddha emerges from a 2,500-year-old sleep to do battle with a power-mad Tibetan lama over who should control the next turn of the Wheel of Dharma.

Meet Me in Maroon. Four meditators at the Pune ashram try to save the world from a space vampire who threatens to suck the life out of the human race if they won't give him the secret of 'the key of life'.

All four musicals were comedies and all had been well received, when performed at the ashram. But there was a problem. It was indigenous theatre, written by a sannyasin, performed by sannyasins, for sannyasin audiences. Not necessarily the kind of thing that would be appreciated by a sophisticated audience in the Indian capital.

I'd also written a play called *Journey to Mount Kailash*, based on a true incident in Kathmandu, Nepal, in which a friend of mine, wrongfully jailed for smuggling heroin, tried to prove his innocence from within the prison by setting a trap for the woman who set him up. But, again, not the kind of thing to stage in a Delhi arts festival.

To be relevant, our theatre show had to convey some quality of meditation while keeping people entertained and also – most crucially – avoiding the awful trap of proselytizing. Nobody needed, or wanted, to have meditation rammed down their throats, and I certainly didn't want to be guilty of it.

It was my memory of Osho's discourses that gave me the key. Over the years, I'd listened to a lot of them and recalled a couple of occasions on which the mystic had toyed with Shakespeare's most famous quote: *To be or not to be.*

For example, in 1987, responding to a question from a friend of mine about the significance of the Bard's utterance, Osho said:

Shakespeare is a great poet, but not a mystic. He has an intuition into the reality of things, but that is only a glimpse, very vague as if seen in a dream, not clear. His question in Hamlet *shows that unclarity. 'To be or not to be?' can never be asked by a man who knows, because there is no question of choice. You cannot choose between 'to be' or 'not to be'.*

In existential terms, not to be is the only way to be. Unless you disappear you are not really there. It looks a little difficult to understand, because basically it is irrational. But reason is not the way of existence;

existence is as irrational as you can conceive.

Here, those who think they are, are not. And those who think and realize they are not – they are.

This understanding is as old as India itself. It not only predates Osho, it goes back further than Gautama the Buddha, who was teaching the art of *anatta*, or no-self 2,500 years ago.

In this spiritual paradigm, ego is the barrier ego, not in the Western sense of someone who has an inflated notion of self-importance and who needs to be more humble, but, more fundamentally, ego as the idea of 'self' itself. Osho explained it thus:

The idea that 'I am' is just an idea, a projection of the mind. But the realization that 'I am not' comes only as a flowering of meditation. When you realize, 'I am not', only the 'I' disappears and there remains behind a pure existence, undefined, unbounded, unfettered, just a pure space.

'I' is a great prison.

It is your slavery and bondage to the mind.

The moment you enter beyond the mind, you are – but you don't have any notion of being an ego, of being an 'I'. In other words: the more you think you are, the less you are; the more you experience that you are not... the more you are.

The moment the soap bubble of your ego pops, you have become the whole existence.

Osho's comments gave me the clue. I would use Hamlet's dilemma to contrast Western intellectual attitudes with Eastern spirituality. I would challenge the West's faith in the rational mind, opening the way for the East's insight into 'no mind'.

In a way, I was challenging my own past. I had studied philosophy at university, steadily chewing my way through the works of Locke, Berkeley, Hume, Descartes, Rousseau, Kant, Hegel…only to realize, after discovering meditation, that the effort by all of these philosophers to find truth via the workings of the human mind was a waste of time. Not only was the mind the wrong tool for the job. Mind itself was the barrier.

Also, I was determined to write a comedy, off-setting Shakespeare's morbid play with a more positive, humorous and upbeat vision of life.

Most people think that if you're going to use art to present weighty issues, like East versus West, then you need to create something serious. But I disagree. I want people to laugh, chuckle and enjoy themselves, *and* take home something to think about.

So that's how I came up with my tale. On one level, it was about Will Shakespeare's dilemma of being forced by Queen Bess to kill off his characters, while his wife did her best to prevent him. On a deeper level, it showed how his characters could escape their fate by using meditation to change their beliefs. At the deepest level it was a dismissal of the whole Western way of thinking.

But still, even if such a play could work as a piece of theatre, there were things about the Delhi festival that didn't seem plausible. For one thing, you cannot put on a play in front of an audience of 5,000 people. It won't work. Most of them will be seated too far away from the stage and, even with radio mics clipped to each character, you will lose them.

Even Sir Larry, playing at Chichester, didn't have to face more than 1200 people. Rock superstars like Mick Jagger and Bruce Springsteen can handle audiences that size with massive video screens and towers of audio speakers, but not actors, and certainly not a bunch of amateurs with an obscure play. After a while, people are bound to feel restless, start chatting among themselves, coughing, scratching, checking their mobiles, walking out....

For us, it would be challenging enough to perform in a small, intimate theatre with a maximum of 500 people – 250 would be better.

Besides, I'd already burned my fingers in Delhi. Back in the seventies, when I was part of a group of travelling players called *The Rajneesh Shakespeare Company*, we toured India offering two of the Bard's plays, *A Midsummer Night's Dream* and *As You Like It*.

Basically, it was a PR exercise – conceived by me and approved by Osho – aimed at offsetting the ashram's notorious reputation as a place of nonstop 'free love' where we ran around stark-naked all day, having sex with multiple partners. Nothing like an evening with the Bard, I reasoned, to cool the Indian public's over-heated fantasies about our mass orgies.

Our theatre company had a few excellent English actors, but the rest of us were rank amateurs and, of course, there were challenges to face. The guy who played Duke Theseus in *A Midsummer Night's Dream* looked noble enough, but had great difficulty memorizing Shakespearian lines. Oberon, King of the Fairies, and Demetrius, one of the young lovers, were rivals, competing for the same girlfriend, who happened to be our stage manager.

Several of the Mechanicals of Athens were regularly stoned during rehearsals. Bottom the Weaver was on harder stuff, but it never seemed to affect his acting. He wore his donkey's head with aplomb and was at ease issuing commands to the little fairies like "Scratch my head, Peasblossom."

As for me, I was busy with publicity but found time to play Aegeus, the angry father who sets up the comedy-conflict in the *Dream* by refusing to let his daughter marry the man she loves.

We made costumes in traditional *sannyas* colours – from yellow through orange to red – and injected truckloads of enthusiasm into the project. We had a great time, travelling around India by bus and train, strutting and fretting our hour upon the stage.

We did well in Pune, Mumbai and other cities, but, alas, we bombed in Delhi. The main reason was that I'd been given the last-minute task of choosing between a large auditorium and a small, intimate theatre for the play's venue. So many people seemed interested in coming that I chose the auditorium, but failed to hire a sound system to amplify our voices – there were no radio mics in those days.

As a result, only about a quarter of the audience could hear our lines and the capital's newspapers, eager to prove their cultural superiority over a bunch of upstart foreigners, gleefully shredded us.

So, having learned a bruising lesson, the projected size of this festival audience didn't make sense. It wasn't a deal breaker, this early in the game, but it bothered me.

As a first step towards Delhi, I agreed to meet Ragni, a young Indian woman with showbusiness links in Bollywood who – so I was told – would make a video of the play, while it was being performed. We met over coffee at Dario's, a chic Italian restaurant next door to the resort.

Ragni walked in half-an-hour late, wearing a casually-elegant black silk blouse and matching pants, with her designer sunglasses pushed back on top of her head and her long, black hair cascading down over her shoulders. She weaved her way elegantly through the tables towards me, waving a friendly 'hello' while talking with cool efficiency into her shiny, white Samsung Galaxy. Jackie Kennedy herself couldn't have made a better entrance.

We shook hands, ordered cappuccino, and pretty soon she was offering me good news and bad news.

"I like your script, and I want to be involved," she told me, having read the copy I'd emailed to her. This, of course, was the good news.

"But to be honest with you, I don't think this festival is going to happen," Ragni confided bluntly. "The organiser keeps shifting venues and dates. I don't think he's got his act together."

Reluctantly, I had to agree with her. I'd gotten a similar message from a friend of mine, an English-born musician called Chinmaya who'd also been invited to perform at the festival. Chinmaya wasn't an internationally-known musician, but he'd had the distinction of playing at Paul McCartney's marriage to Heather Mills at a castle in Ireland in 2002.

McCartney had been impressed with Chinmaya's album *Celtic Ragas*, released one year earlier, in which my friend, playing his sarod – a stringed instrument half-way between a guitar and a sitar – had transformed Celtic ballads into classical Indian music. Since the ageing Beatle was willing to spend £3 million on the wedding, he happily paid for Chinmaya and his band to perform.

It was difficult to reassemble the musicians who'd accompanied Chinmaya on the recording of *Celtic Ragas*, because, as sannyasins tend to do, they'd scattered across the planet. But back they came and yes, on that fateful day in June 2002, in the grounds of a remote castle in Glaslough, Ireland, Paul and Heather stood before Chinmaya's band while they played their Anglo-Indian mix.

That, of course, was the high point of Paul and Heather's ill-fated marriage. All too soon, she realized she could never replace McCartney's first wife, Linda, in the Beatle's wounded heart. All too soon, he understood that this woman was no submissive, fawning geisha, awed by his name and fame, but an untameable lioness with a full set of fangs. Their love affair died almost as quickly as the band dispersed after the gig.

Eleven years later, Chinmaya told me he'd agreed to participate in the proposed Delhi arts festival, but was forced to withdraw when no money was available for him to book and retain other band members. McCartney could pay up front. Our festival *impresario* in Delhi could not.

"I'm afraid the organiser's a dreamer; he's all hot air," Chinmaya added.

The festival was disappearing, but a new friendship was forming. Ragni and I liked each other. To me, she was attractive, intelligent and capable, with just a touch of steel beneath her soft exterior. She was twenty-eight-years-old, about to produce her first movie in Mumbai and had her own production company.

We got along well for three reasons: we both loved show business, we both liked new creative projects and we were both sannyasins. Oh yes, and we both wanted to put on the play as quickly as possible, if not in Delhi, then in Mumbai; if not in Mumbai, then in Pune.

Mumbai seemed too expensive, so we opted for a two-night-run in an old, dilapidated Pune theatre that was so funky it was hilarious. The stage had no wings, there were no lighting bars and no sound system. Everything had to be rented and imported from outside.

One poor man, who'd waited all afternoon to buy a ticket, came to Ragni just before curtain-up to complain that the back of his seat was missing. He had nothing on which to lean while watching the show! The place was like that, falling apart, as if nothing had been done to it since the departure of the Raj.

Also, I have to admit, the actors weren't really up to par. They did their best, but we had no time to recruit talent. So Hamlet turned out to be a young Indian guy with a broad Australian accent. He lived in Melbourne and by nature was far too cheerful to hold down the role, while Ophelia was a last-minute discovery: an English backpacker who happened to be staying in the same guest house as myself and who, as a starry-eyed teenager, had once dreamed of playing Ophelia.

"I'll play the part if you let me keep the wig and costume afterwards," she bargained.

It was an offer I couldn't refuse.

"Deal."

The show went ahead. We got away with it, but I knew we could do better.

Twelve months later, we'd shifted from the worst theatre in town to one of the best: an open-air amphitheatre with seating for 650 people, surrounded by a shopping mall that shielded it from traffic noise. When the sun went down and the lights were turned on, the place looked magical.

It was outrageously expensive by local standards, costing US $2000 per night, which few production companies could afford, so most of the time it was unused, looking forlorn and abandoned. Moreover, the wooden floor, exposed to an annual cycle of ferocious summer heat and continuous monsoon rains, was so little used that it became too rough for actors to walk on without hurting their feet.

Over the years, efforts had been made to persuade the owner of the shopping mall to lower the rental price, but she wouldn't budge. She didn't need to. Her husband was the owner of some huge Indian petrochemical conglomerate and I suspect he gave her the mall as a plaything to keep her occupied.

She did, however, give us a cheaper deal for the second night, so we could just about afford to put on our play for two consecutive evenings.

It was a great venue, but intimidating. When I first walked out onto that stage, one sunny afternoon, a couple of weeks before showtime, my stomach knotted in fear once more. It was a massive, circular, empty podium. To give you an idea: the London Palladium, arguably Britain's most famous theatre, has a stage that's twelve metres across. This one, constructed in some obscure shopping mall and virtually unknown – even in Pune – was over sixteen metres wide.

How could we, a small, disparate group of amateur actors and actresses, create a convincing dramatic atmosphere on this oversized pill?

The venue came stark-naked, with no frills attached, so again we had to hire everything: a generator to supply power, a lighting system, radio mics, amplifiers and speakers, a vast expanse of hessian matting to cover the rough floorboards, plus a huge set to span the width of the stage.

Racing around Pune in motorized rickshaws, Ragni and I discovered a central depot which supplied theatre sets to nearly all of the city's playhouses. Together, we sorted through masses of scenery, constructed according to English theatre format: scenes painted on big canvas sheets stretched over light, rectangular wooden frames.

At Glyndebourne Opera House, where I was once a stagehand, we used to call them 'flats'.

But, of course, there was no European scene among them. We looked at so many Moghul palaces, complete with ornate turrets and Arabian-style windows, that we almost despaired of finding anything suitable, especially when peacocks, tigers and elephants were painted in pastoral splendour outside the palace windows. As far as I know, Hamlet never owned a pet tiger.

Finally, we found a nondescript-looking set made of castle walls built with huge square stones that might pass for Elsinore, and no exotic beasts in the background. The rental was a real bargain: for about £100, a crew from the depot came to our stage with the set, erected it, waited until we'd finished our performances, and then came once more to take it down and cart it away.

Nevertheless, the overall costs kept mounting. I had some great sponsors, including wealthy sannyasin friends who handed over generous amounts of cash, but the bills kept coming, and in the end, I had to dig into my own pockets.

However, there is a delightful bonus that India offers to theatrical entrepreneurs like myself: cheap clothing fabrics and cheap tailoring. We were able to design and create beautiful costumes for the play. All the guys wore doublets, a kind of cross between a shirt and a jacket, and below the waist they wore breeches, puffy, inflated shorts, much in demand by Elizabethan gentlemen to show off their stocking-sheathed legs.

But we drew the line at showing off the crotch. This, may I remind you, was done with codpieces, those strange pouches attached to the front of men's trousers in medieval times to either accentuate their potency, or to conceal the fact that their genitals were swollen and rotting from syphilis, which, so some historians claim, was rampant in Europe at the time.

Since genitals were not highlighted in the script and since codpieces were fading from fashion by the time Queen Elizabethan came to the throne, we deemed them to be an unnecessary distraction. In any case, I didn't want to risk the kind of 'wardrobe malfunction' – to borrow phrase immortalized by Janet Jackson – that would occur if one fell off.

The women, of course, wore long dresses, with long sleeves, befitting the modesty of the era. Mrs Shakespeare had a lovely green gown. Ophelia had her dreamy, creamy, diaphanous dress. But the real eye-catcher was Queen Elizabeth's dazzling, all-gold, shoulder-to-ankle outfit, made of a silky, shiny fabric that we found while shopping in downtown Pune.

Really, India has so many fabrics at affordable prices it's a designer's paradise. And we had a lucky break: we found a tailor, close to the ashram, who was probably the only one in Pune who'd studied Elizabethan costumes as part of her education. When we showed her the design photos of our characters, culled from internet images, she nodded and said, "Yes, I can do it."

Her name was Ritu, she was in her late thirties and she earned her bread and butter by making robes for the Osho Resort – as I mentioned earlier, everyone visiting the ashram had to wear these plain, anonymous robes as part of the experience.

But Ritu had a serious problem creating Elizabeth's ruff – that stiff, white fan of delicate, white lace that is shown in almost all portraits of the Virgin Queen. Our version of the ruff just wouldn't stay up. I guess, in the old days, they used some kind of whalebone frame, sitting on the Queen's shoulders, but 400 years later, in deepest India, we found ourselves short of whales.

In despair, after many failed attempts, Ritu told me the only way to keep the ruff erect would be to tie it to the Queen's hair, at the back of her neck. I had no problem with this last-resort strategy, but we hit a roadblock: my English lady friend refused to contemplate it. In the end, we decided to let it flop.

The secret of Elizabethan ruffs had eluded us.

One more important detail about the Queen's attire: in the early scenes of the play, she wore a gold mask around her eyes, as if attending a Venetian-style masked ball. It made her look more menacing, but that wasn't the point. The mask symbolized her personality and, more universally, the phony social masks that we all wear, all the time.

And yes, that does include you and me.

CHAPTER 12
Our Royal Jailers

Hamlet's dead father irritates me. What did he think he was doing? Coming back as a ghost, walking the castle at night, scaring everybody and then driving his son crazy by revealing he'd been murdered by his own brother, the new king, who'd also married his ex.

Everything was going just fine until he showed up. His former wife, Gertrude, seemed happy enough with her new husband, King Claudius. True, Hamlet was in a bit of a dark mood, following his father's unexpected demise, but he was sincerely in love with the beautiful Ophelia – and she with him – so one got the feeling he would soon snap out of it.

Moreover, Hamlet was going to rule the country, sooner or later. Providing Claudius and Gertrude produced no children to complicate the issue of succession, Hamlet would eventually wear the Danish crown. No problem. Situation sorted.

But, oh no, this miserable ghost had to come and spoil the party. I grant you, it's not very nice to have poison poured into your ear by your brother – or, indeed, by anybody – while you're asleep, thereby being deprived of your mortal coil, but once it's done, you may as well get used to it.

If I'd been a Danish political reporter in Elsinore Castle after all the main characters in Shakespeare's play had been killed, I would have interviewed the ghost and asked him: "Are you happy now? Now that your son is dead? Now that the woman you once loved is dead? Now that your brother is dead? Now that *everybody* is dead? Do you have any comment for the obituary column of *The Disembodied Times*?"

I'd like to have heard his answer. But Shakespeare doesn't deal with that, which is odd because, when all the bodies are lying on the ground at the end of the play, one might, at the very least, expect the ghost to make one last appearance and say to his slain son, "Job done, Hamlet. Good boy!" The two ghosts could've walked off, arm in arm.

This is one of the reasons why, in the mid-1970s, Osho caused a sensation in India, making a scandalous departure from traditional Indian spirituality by introducing therapy groups in his ashram. Don't see the connection? Look at it this way: Hamlet needed therapy. Why? Because he wasn't free of his father's grip. He was ordered to take revenge and he obeyed like any frightened, dutiful little child.

The only alternative he could imagine was to kill himself, hence his epic speech "To be or not to be…" It was good poetry but poor philosophy. It did not occur to Hamlet, at any time, to rebel against his father. There was no room to manoeuvre outside his narrow psychological box, unless you include the possibility of going mad.

I can't easily forgive the Bard for giving Hamlet such a narrow view of life. After all, Will himself was familiar with the fallibility of fathers, having witnessed the phenomenon at first hand in the form of his own dad, John Shakespeare.

John was an upwardly mobile glover and leather worker in Stratford-upon-Avon, whose fortunes prospered so much that he rose to become the town mayor. Then he fell on hard times. My school books told me it was for 'unknown reasons'.

Ha! What rubbish! Were these teachers trying to protect their precious Shakespeare by concealing facts about his unscrupulous father? The truth is, John got busted for smuggling wool to avoid government taxes, a hugely lucrative but highly illegal business in Elizabethan times. That's why his fortunes crashed and his poor wife, Mary Arden, had to sell off her property just to keep the family afloat.

The ageing couple, John and Mary, lived for years in poverty until their genius son exploded into stardom on the London stage and basically took care of them for the rest of their lives. He even bought a coat of arms, thereby restoring respectability to the Shakespeare name.

You'd think Will's willingness to rescue his own father would have allowed him to paint Hamlet with a broader brush. Surely, our luckless hero didn't need to be so cowed, so obedient, so acquiescent, instantly agreeing to take on his dead father's lust for revenge?

I have to concede, however, that the theme of obedience to one's elders continues to be a powerful force in our society, even today, especially in royal families. I remember a remark made by Prince William, a couple of decades back, when he was about eleven years old. At the time, he must have been feeling uneasy about the pressure on him, as a future British monarch, attending weekly meetings with his grandmother to discuss royal duties, plus having to deal with his younger brother Harry's envy and resentment at being left out.

In a moment of unscheduled honesty, Wills remarked to Charles, his father, "Actually, I'd just as soon *not* be King."

We don't hear anything about that from Wills these days. Any hint of personal preference on such matters has been thoroughly suppressed, and with a grandmother like that sitting on his head, I'm really not surprised.

One more royal anecdote: back in the 1980s, soon after Charles and Diana were married, they were sitting with the Queen at a public event when the band struck up the national anthem. As the music played, Charles, in a rare moment of spontaneity and playfulness, leaned over to his young bride and whispered, "Darling, they're playing our tune."

Diana giggled a little too loudly, whereupon the Queen slowly turned her head and administered what the newspapers afterwards described as 'a killing stare' to her son and his wife. It shut them up in a second.

I've been on the receiving end of that stare myself, when I was a political correspondent. MPs from the Commons had been invited to Westminster Hall, close to the House of Lords, to congratulate the Queen on one of her anniversaries – she's had so many I've forgotten which one. Most probably, it was her twenty-fifth year as Queen. Anyway, we Lobby Correspondents came along to watch the show and report the event, standing high above in the gallery.

A fanfare of trumpets announced the Queen's arrival, whereupon one of the MPs shouted, "Three cheers for her Majesty!" The sequence of 'hip-hip-hoorays' that followed was, without doubt, one of the phoniest demonstrations of good cheer I have ever witnessed.

Then the Queen, Prince Philip, Charles and the rest of the Royals walked slowly through the hall towards the exit beneath us. The Queen raised her head and allowed her hostile, unforgiving eyes to rest upon the media whom, of course, she both hated and needed, just like all the politicians behind her. I felt a strong impulse to wave a hand, or at least give her a smile, but I knew it would cost me my job, so I just stared back and declined to bow my head in loyal subjugation.

I don't want to give the Queen a hard time, but the truth is she acts as society's chief jailer, the ultimate role model, keeping us all safely locked inside the prison of correct social behaviour. And what, you may ask, is wrong with *correct social behaviour*? Well, nothing. Except it kills you. It shrivels your life energy to the point where you may as well be dead.

Osho introduced therapy groups to help us break loose from those psychological and emotional prisons – prisons built with lots of good intentions by our mothers and fathers, not to mention schoolteachers, university professors, members of the clergy... and my own favourite role models: stiff, formal, well-spoken BBC television newscasters.

To me, watching TV back in the sixties, these news announcers looked so incredibly cool, talking about the chaos of world events without a flicker of emotion:

"Good evening, here is the news. Famine in Ethiopia has killed at least half a million people according to a report published today by the World Health Organization..." etc., etc.

As a young man, I wanted to be like them: professional observers of life, totally in control, untouched by anything faintly resembling human feelings. Maybe that was my motivation for becoming a journalist and also why, a few years later, I fell in love with the meditative image of Gautama Buddha.

Siddhartha's blissfully enlightened state, sitting cross-legged with a permanent smile on his face and a golden halo around his head, seemed like the ultimate escape from the ordinary ups and downs of human emotions. He was out of it. Safe. Beyond reach.

So you can imagine my alarm when I discovered that Osho was encouraging us to go *into* our emotions. He wanted us to feel *more*, not less. He wanted us to take the lid off the pressure cooker of self-control that had been steadily building steam ever since mom and dad first said to us "Be quiet! Don't pick your nose! Don't laugh, it's not funny! Big boys don't cry! Sit up straight..." and all the rest.

119

Osho invited us *not* to keep it bottled up inside any longer. He wanted us to lose it – big time. Therapy with Osho was exciting and scary, because we had lots of emotional baggage to unload. We needed to scream, we needed to cry, we needed to shout and laugh and go nuts; we needed to dance around naked, hug each other, roll on the floor... feeling for the first time what it was like to be free of all restraint.

I remember one amazingly liberating moment when we were all naked, lying on our backs on the floor of the group room in one big circle of bodies, playing with our sexual organs – okay, call it 'masturbating' if you like – laughing and waving to our imagined parents, saying "Hi Mom! Hi Dad!"

Somehow I can't imagine Prince William doing that, can you? Maybe Prince Harry on a trip to Las Vegas...

Returning to the irritating spectre of Hamlet's father's ghost, it seems to me this apparition is symbolic. He is the voice of our internalized morality, of all our 'shoulds' and 'should nots', of all the things we ought to be doing – or not doing – if we wish to be recognized as good, obedient members of society.

In the UK, of course, the ultimate reward for this dutiful attitude is to receive a knighthood or some other decoration from the reigning monarch. And it's never too late to repent and rejoin the mainstream, because even a lost sheep can return to the cosy safety of the establishment fold.

Thus it was, on December 12, 2003, Michael Philip Jagger, after more than forty years of sneering, hip-gyrating, rebellious rock 'n' roll, after decades of terrifying parents with sexualized songs that invited young people everywhere to cut loose from moral restraint, arrived at Buckingham Palace and bowed down before the royal presence to receive his knighthood. The Queen couldn't bring herself to present the award to Jagger personally, so it was left to Charles, Prince of Wales, to do the deed.

Arise, Sir Mick.

"Have you seen your mother, baby, standing in the shadows...?"

Actually, it wasn't your mother, Mick. It was the ghost of Hamlet's father.

CHAPTER 13

The Prince Must Die

Hamlet is smiling. That's odd. I don't recall any point in the Bard's tale when Hamlet is cheerful. But maybe it's because my version of the play is a little different and this young man has just watched his girlfriend, Ophelia, strip off her courtly gown and dance around the stage as Lady Raga, wearing little more than a pair of sunglasses.

As a playwright in urgent need of gloom and doom, Will must put a stop to this.

"Hey, what are you smiling at?" he enquires icily, getting up from his seat and crossing the stage towards him.

Hamlet, still distracted, beams at Will with a stupid grin on his face, and says, "She's kinda cute, isn't she?"

Ruled, as all young men are, by their surging hormones, Hamlet has forgotten all about sending Ophelia to a nunnery. Testosterone seems to have triumphed.

"Young man, I am a genius in the use of English language and the word 'cute' does not appear in any of my plays," Will curtly informs him. "Ophelia is a tragic figure, doomed to drown in a lake."

He takes Hamlet by the arm and brings him downstage towards the audience.

"Now then, the big question is: how should you die?"

The smile disappears from Hamlet's visage – that's better. Let's have little respect for the impending disaster that is about to descend on the luckless pair.

"Do I have to, Will?" he asks, pleadingly.

It is Will's turn to be cheerful, slapping Hamlet on the back as if it's the most natural thing in the world. "Of course, man. How can *Hamlet* be a tragedy if you don't die?"

Turning towards the wings on the right side of the stage, he calls out loudly, "Where are the instruments of death?" Immediately, an attendant comes walking towards him, bearing a tray that carries a wine cup, a bottle of poison, an old flintlock pistol and two swords.

Which is it to be? Let's go for poison, since it's already a dominant theme in this tragedy. Warming to his task, Will picks up the bottle, then shakes a few drops of poison into the wine cup, telling Hamlet, "Now, suppose the new king pours a glass of wine, sprinkles poison in it, and then offers it to you to drink?"

Hamlet reluctantly accepts the cup, looks at the audience, winks, slowly brings it to his lips and then, at the very last moment, drops it on the floor. With a look of mock astonishment on his face that fools no one, he turns to Will and exclaims innocently, "Ooops! Sorry, I dropped it."

Slightly irritated but undeterred, Shakespeare picks up the old flintlock pistol and hands it to him: "Or, perhaps, in your despair, you put a pistol to your head and pull the trigger..."

Historically speaking, I'm not sure whether this type of pistol was available in Elizabethan England. I fancy it was invented much later, but some dramatic licence is needed – I can't think of other convenient ways to kill off this guy.

Again, with extreme reluctance, Hamlet slowly brings the muzzle of this weapon to the side of his head. Closing his eyes tightly and grimacing with anticipated pain, he squeezes the trigger and there is a sharp "click," but no report, no sound of a gunshot.

Looking surprised and relieved, Hamlet inspects the weapon then says to Shakespeare smugly, "Will, you forgot to load it!"

At this point, Will has reason to become extremely upset, but another idea has already entered his fertile head and he immediately jumps on it.

"I have it! Hamlet must die in a sword fight..." He grabs the two swords from the tray and offers one, handle first, to the doomed young man in front of him.

"Come on man, take one of these and defend yourself."

Gingerly, Hamlet takes the sword while Will poses like one of the *Three Musketeers*, his blade outstretched at arm's length, ready for some scintillating swordplay. But his young opponent is in no hurry to cross swords, engaging the audience in a series of theatrical asides while trying to figure a way out of the situation.

"My God, do I really have to fight?" he ponders nervously. Then inspiration dawns in the form of a time warp that allows him to mimic one of Hollywood's hardest, meanest showdown specialists.

"Maybe I can scare him with my Clint Eastwood impersonation," Hamlet conjectures, then squinting through half-closed eyelids in classic spaghetti western style, he looks at the Bard and drawls slowly, "Go ahead, make my day."

Theatrical aside: Yes, I do know that this line was uttered by Harry Callahan in 'Sudden Impact' and is therefore, technically, not of the spaghetti western species. But Eastwood was tutored as a director by Sergio Leone, master of the genre, and, anyway, as far as I'm concerned, Dirty Harry is just an updated version of Eastwood's character Blondie in the Italian director's classic 'The Good, the Bad & the Ugly'.

Shakespeare, however, is unimpressed by Hamlet's cross-cultural performance.

"You can't threaten me, I'm a master swordsman!" Will scoffs, making a couple of passes in front of him with a swish and flourish.

Hamlet persists with his teeth-grinding, menacing tone, "Will, you've got to ask yourself one question, 'Do I feel lucky? Well, do ya, punk?'" He's really doing a mean impression of Callahan, but now Will has had enough.

"Where are you getting these corny lines from? Fight man, fight!"

Hamlet shrugs in a gesture of resignation and confides to the audience, "When all else fails: Arnold Schwarzenegger..."

Turning towards the Bard, he suddenly charges at him with alarming ferocity crying, "Hasta la vista baby!"

Will is taken by surprise and is beaten back by Hamlet's oncoming fury. He doesn't have a chance to use his skill, he's too busy defending himself. Staggering backwards, he can't see where he's going, trips and falls. Hamlet stands over him, the tip of his sword pointing directly at Shakespeare's heart.

Now it's Will's turn to seek inspiration and, remembering that he is, after all, the one writing the play, he raises a hand and exclaims, "Wait! Wait! I forgot. There must be treachery involved."

He calls to the attendant who is still holding the tray: "Give me that bottle of poison!" Pulling out the cork, he carefully allows a few drips to stain the edge of his blade.

"Your enemy has put poison on the tip of his sword," he informs Hamlet. "One small cut and all is lost..."

In act of ungentlemanly subterfuge, he then points across the stage, behind Hamlet, with his free hand saying, "Look over there!"

Poor Hamlet. The innocent young man turns to look where Will is pointing and the cowardly Bard stabs him in the thigh. Immediately, the poison takes effect and Hamlet groans and staggers across the stage in a classic death scene reminiscent of many a 1950s B-Western movie in which the bad guy has been shot. After many moans and groans, he finally collapses in a heap.

Will is unrepentant and immensely satisfied.

"That's much better," he announces, standing up and dusting himself off.

A fanfare of trumpets announces the impending arrival of royalty and, sure enough, Queen Elizabeth sweeps onto the stage.

"Where is our playwright, Master Shakespeare?" she enquires, looking above the heads of the audience as if she cannot see the Bard humbly bowing before her. This is an effective strategy used by people in power since time immemorial. They act as if they can't see you, or as if you aren't there, reminding you of your insignificant status.

Will must therefore attract her attention.

"Here, Your Majesty. Your humble servant awaits your bidding."

"We are interested in the progress of your new play," declares Good Queen Bess, allowing a faint touch of menace to be heard in her voice. She likes to keep Will on a short leash. She knows she can't trust artists, actors, entertainers, or, come to think of it, anyone else in her court, or, indeed, in the entire country. Surrounded by conspiracies and enemies, her forty-five-year reign was a miracle of survival.

"Yes, Your Majesty, it's coming along nicely," says Will, fawningly. He's so obsequious, it's really quite disgusting.

"What is this drama to be called?" she enquires.

"*Hamlet, Prince of Denmark*, Your Majesty."

"Indeed? We are curious as to how you intend this play to end..." The supreme power pauses for a moment and then, ratcheting up the menace factor a notch or two, she asks, "In *tragedy*, we trust?"

Now here's a stroke of luck for Will, who, let's face it, could use a break. He's had a rough time trying to keep control of his play, but just at this particular moment there happens to be a dead body lying on the stage.

Pointing to the crumpled heap of flesh, Will nods and smiles, saying, "Oh yes, indeed, ma'am. All the main characters die."

For a moment, her Royal Majesty allows her eyes to rest upon the heap, whose impressive lack of any sign of life indicates her wishes are being obeyed.

"Excellent," she pronounces. "Our people must be continuously reminded that life is filled with melancholy, suffering and death."

To Will's relief, the Royal presence turns away and exits whence she has come. Making sure the Queen has gone, the Bard gets off his knees and strolls over to Hamlet's prone form, nudging it with his foot.

"Arise, oh corpse!" he commands.

Surprised and puzzled, Hamlet raises his head to look at Shakespeare. "But I'm dead," he reminds the playwright.

Will shakes his head impatiently. "No, no. That was just a temporary death to keep Her Majesty the Queen off my back." He grabs Hamlet's hand and pulls him to his feet, then adds encouragingly, "Don't worry, you will die permanently, later in the play."

Hamlet rolls his eyes in disbelief.

"Gee, thanks Will!" he mutters and leaves the stage.

Pulling back from the action for a moment, one might enquire, at this point in the play, where the audience's affection lies. Obviously, with the lovers, Hamlet and Ophelia. Who will not wish for this youthful couple to avoid a dreadful fate? Also, with Mrs Shakespeare, because if anyone can navigate through these treacherous political waters and bring all the characters to safe harbour, it is she. And I'm pretty sure the audience has some sympathy with Will, caught as he is between the conflicting willpower – no pun intended – of two strong women.

If there is any kind of archetypal 'bad guy' it must be Queen Elizabeth, because she is the one driving the plot development towards tragedy. She has her excuses, being so old and friendless, but still, there's no need for her to take it out on others.

In any drama, you've got to have a bad guy to create tension and there's a peculiar thing about being bad: it's subject to the law of relativity. I don't know if Albert Einstein ever noticed, or applied his discovery to cinema dynamics, but good guys can also be bad, providing the bad guys are *really, really* bad.

In other words, the more evil the bad guy, the more nasty the good guy is allowed to be. That's how Clint Eastwood was able to triumph at the box office with mean, tough, Harry Callahan, and other roles like him. The villains in these movies were so revoltingly psychotic that the hero could do pretty much what he liked in the way of being vicious.

Our own villain, Queen Bess, is more straightforward in her approach – she simply wants everyone to die – so there is no need for so crude a hero as Mr Eastwood might provide.

If there is to be a happy ending, it is likely to come through ingenuity and inspiration, not through pointing a gun at someone and saying, "Ask yourself, 'Do I feel lucky?'"

Well, do ya, Will? 'Cos it sure looks like you're gonna need it.

CHAPTER 14

So Great a Thing

I need to tell you how Shakespeare saved my life. It shows the power of the Bard to impress the English psyche, even in modern times, and in so doing change the destiny of mere mortals such as myself.

It happened when I was working on a daily newspaper called *The Birmingham Post*, tucked away in obscurity on the business desk, filing stories about local companies making ball-bearings and gear boxes for the Midlands motor industry.

I hated Birmingham, which is really unfair because it was an important step on my road to journalistic success. Well, to give you the full picture, I'd better start from the beginning...

You see, after graduating from Bristol University with a degree in Politics and Philosophy, I was somewhat dismayed to realize I needed to earn a living. My free ride had lasted three years – student grants didn't need to be repaid in those golden days – but in the end I had to step out into the big, wide, intimidating world, forge a career for myself and earn a buck.

My degree seemed useless. I was too intelligent to go into politics and bored stiff by philosophy. But journalism looked attractive because writing came easily to me and it didn't feel like 'real work'. So I got a job as a cub reporter on a newspaper called the *Evening Advertiser*, published daily in an unremarkable little town called Swindon.

Mostly, it was boring stuff, like council meetings, but once in a while it was fun, such as the time I exposed a local factory for covering people's allotments and vegetable gardens with a dusting of deadly cyanide powder that was pouring out from its chimneys.

However, eighteen months into my new career, there was a problem. My girlfriend, graduating two years behind me at Bristol, had just completed her final exams and wanted to spend the whole summer exploring the Greek islands.

I, on the other hand, was allowed only two weeks' holiday. I asked the editor for an extra four weeks unpaid leave and was promptly refused. This left two options: lose my girlfriend or walk out the door, knowing I would not be allowed back.

I was scared. If I quit, it might destroy my career. But something in me rebelled against the idea of having to wait until I retired at the age of sixty-five in order to enjoy life. Why should I be subjected to such economic slavery? Why should I sacrifice 'now' for the promise of a good time 'then'?

I quit. I collected my two weeks' holiday pay, received a bottle of whiskey as a parting gift from my disbelieving colleagues in the newsroom – they didn't think I would go through with it – and in a display of bravado told them, "By the time I've finished this bottle, I will have forgotten all about you, and you will have forgotten all about me."

I flew to Athens with my girlfriend. We took ferry boats around the islands...Paros, Naxos, Ios, Crete... We made love by moonlight on deserted beaches.... We took horseback rides over mountains... We fought once in a while, got sunburned occasionally, but mostly had a good time.

Six weeks later, back in the UK, I put in a call to a friend who'd also worked on the *Advertiser* in Swindon but was now a business reporter on *The Birmingham Post*, which in those days was a prestigious morning newspaper - now it's just a low-circulation weekly.

"Any jobs up your way, Des?" I asked him.

His reply astonished me. "Yes, mine. I'm off to study Russian at university for four years."

I wrote to his editor, was interviewed for the vacancy on the newspaper's business desk, and was promptly hired. I didn't say anything about breaking my contract with the *Evening Advertiser* and apparently my new editor saw no need to obtain references – thank God, because he wouldn't have got them.

Through this remarkable turn of events, I gained new understanding about the way life works, not just for me but for everyone. Life, I realised, is a different creature from the beast we're warned against by our parents, teachers and other well-wishers. Life, according to them, is dangerous, full hazards, not totally dissimilar to Hamlet's view, expressed in his famous soliloquy, that in life we are helpless victims, at the mercy of 'outrageous fortune'.

We're advised to be cautious, hard-working, obedient, looking for job security, pension rights, health insurance…trying to create as many safety nets as we can.

The spectre of living recklessly and then finding oneself huddled inside a cardboard box under Charing Cross Railway Bridge – rather like George Orwell in *Down and Out in Paris and London* – shivering with cold with only other poor bums for company, is a powerful image to instil caution in us all.

What I discovered, however, was just the opposite. Life appreciates gamblers, people with guts, people willing to take risks. I'm not talking about stupid risks like putting your life-savings on a horse in the Grand National, or trying to swim the Atlantic Ocean without a lifejacket (or even with one). I'm talking about taking risks that help you lead a more fulfilling life.

One of the first things I heard Osho say was: "Existence always supports those in search of truth." In other words, life isn't something alien, hostile and antagonistic to you. It's on your side. It wants you to be courageous, independent and free.

I didn't understand this all at once, just by landing a job on *The Birmingham Post*. It came in instalments, over the years. But it's always been true for me and I have the feeling it's true for everybody.

For a few weeks, I was happy to be employed as a journalist once more. But, all too soon, I realised that business reporting in Birmingham was a terribly dull affair. The motor industry dominated the West Midlands and this might have been an interesting gig, especially test-driving the latest cars, but the *Post* already had a special correspondent for everything moving on four wheels. I was confined to the windshield wiper and ashtray department.

To give you an example, I was asked to write about a newly-invented emergency fan belt for cars. It was a handy device and I actually used it myself, after breaking down on the M1 motorway, but well...it wasn't exactly an epic story, was it? It didn't send shock waves of astonishment through our readers.

I had a vague feeling I was destined for greater things.

To save myself from increasing despair, I viewed the job as a temporary stepping stone. I had my eyes set on London and figured that, with a little luck, I could eventually make my way onto a national newspaper like *The Guardian* or *The Times*. With even more luck, I might eventually land a really interesting job like political reporting.

But then my girlfriend moved to London, rented a flat in trendy Muswell Hill, got herself a fun job at Thomson Holidays and promptly dumped me. Suddenly, I saw myself through her eyes: a third-rate journalist going nowhere, trapped in the Midlands, far from the action of Swinging London.

From then on, Birmingham became unbearable. Recalling my bold decision to leave the *Advertiser* and travel to Greece, I was ready to take new risks, but I couldn't figure out which way to jump. I felt increasingly suffocated, but with no clue how to change things.

Now comes the Bard to the rescue. One day, sitting in the office, I received word that a pub was going to open in South Birmingham, near the Bourneville chocolate factory, owned by the Cadbury family. This sounds, on the face of it, a less than earth-shattering announcement. But it was much, much bigger than one might think.

The Cadbury family was deeply religious and, back in the nineteenth century, had looked after its workers far better than anyone else in England's industrial heartland. At a time when there were no unions, no minimum wage, no safeguards of any kind, the Cadburys were model employers, building whole neighbourhoods near their factories to provide housing for their workers, setting up schools to educate their kids…taking care of just about everything.

There was only one golden rule: No booze. No pubs. No alcohol. This rule had held for over one hundred years, but now, as the family loosened its grip on the area, the first pub had finally appeared.

How to present the story? What came to me was a line from *Antony and Cleopatra,* which I'd studied at school. The play, as we all know, is a power struggle between Octavius Caesar and two passionate lovers, Antony and Cleopatra. Caesar wins a crucial battle and, rather than face surrender and humiliation, Antony impales himself on his own sword.

Not to be upstaged, Cleopatra then picks up an asp, a poisonous snake, and allows it to bite her, ending her mortal existence. When I picture this scene, inevitably I think of Elizabeth Taylor, dressed all in gold, her cleavage well displayed even in death, lying on a white bier, at the end of the most expensive movie ever made (this was 1963). I was an eighteen-year-old teenager at the time and quite impressed, both by Taylor's cleavage and the movie's price tag.

Anyway, when Caesar hears of the deaths of Antony and Cleopatra, he is astonished and declares:

"The breaking of so great a thing should make a bigger crack!"

Caesar imagines that, in keeping with such momentous news, there should be earthquakes, thunderstorms, lions walking in city streets...there should be great dramatic events as nature responded to these deaths.

So that was my headline, my intro to the Cadbury story:

The breaking of so great a thing should make a bigger crack! One hundred years of teetotal puritanism gone down the drain, shattered by a single pub.

The editor loved it. He thought it was marvellous. From then on, he appreciated me as a writer. So when, a few weeks later, his political reporter in London asked for an assistant to help with the workload at the Houses of Parliament, he fingered me for the job.

It was deliverance. A gift from the divine. Suddenly, out of nowhere, I was freed. Not only that, I was promoted. Not only that, I was being asked to do political reporting – the very thing for which I'd been aiming, with many steps in between, further down the road.

There and then, I was ready to buy my train ticket to London. But the business editor, a dour Scotsman called Mac, had other ideas. Squinting at me from under his bushy eyebrows, he grunted, "Weeell, ye canna goo 'til we've orl hud oor soomer holidees."

His roadblock stopped me in my tracks. Of course, he was right. The business desk had to be manned while its reporters took their well-earned vacations. In any case, Parliament was going into summer recess, so there was no need for two reporters until the annual party conferences in the autumn. But I couldn't wait. Another two months in Birmingham? Impossible. I had to get out...now.

I went to the editor. "It's going to take me a while to find an apartment in London and also to find my way around Westminster, learning the ropes," I explained. "Is it okay if I leave now?"

The editor had no problem with it. I returned to the business desk, saying nothing, and an hour later two white envelopes were delivered by the editor's secretary to Mac and myself. We opened them simultaneously. It was a directive from the editor that I would be leaving for London within the week.

I had a split second to find my way around Mac's wounded ego before he stormed into the editor's office to protest. Looking at him with as much gratitude as I could generate, I smiled thankfully and said, "Gosh, thanks Mac!" making it seem like he'd been the one to send me off.

It was an Academy Award-winning performance, spontaneously scripted in a moment of urgent need. But would it work?

Mac hesitated, scrutinising my face for any sign of duplicity, then grunted, "That's okay laddie", and let it pass. My love for the acting profession was born. Three days later, I was at New Street Station, boarding the train for King's Cross. So long Birmingham.

During my time at Westminster, I used Shakespeare quotes a couple more times as intros for news stories, but none of them worked as well as the first one.

However, there was something strange about the job itself, which I need to mention before ending this part of my tale. As far as I could see, there was absolutely no need for *The Birmingham Post* to have two men in Westminster. For a regional daily, this luxury didn't make sense. One man was more than enough.

If I'd been the editor, I'd have told the guy in London "You feel overworked? No problem. Just do what you can and we'll pick up the rest from the wire services."

But I wasn't about to argue. Offering silent prayers to some unknown deity, I stepped off the train at King's Cross, joined a couple of friends in an apartment near Marble Arch, bought myself some snappy Village Gate suits and headed for the House of Commons.

Thank you, Will Shakespeare. Thank you, God. Thank you, Colin Silk, the eccentric old English teacher at Lewes County Grammar School for Boys who introduced us to *Antony and Cleopatra*. Thank you, John

Lewis, political correspondent for *The Birmingham Post*, who pleaded with the editor for an unnecessary assistant.

Why am I so grateful? Because, even though I was thrilled with my new job as a Lobby Correspondent, the excitement didn't last. Within two years, I was bored with British politics and wanted out. Not just out of Westminster, but out of the country, out of my made-in-the-UK personality and out of my mind.

I made it. But that's another story.

CHAPTER 15

The Force Awakens

I do beseech you, gentles all,
Haste ye to your local movie hall
And there watch Star Wars in 3D
Sci-fi as it's meant to be,
Normal life is all forsaken
When you see The Force awaken!

I will return shortly to the theme of my play, but first, let me invite you to pay a visit, if you have not already done so, to the latest Star Wars movie, *Episode VII – The Force Awakens*.

Walking into the cinema, putting on your 3D glasses, you are transported into a wonder-world of special effects, breath-taking action, gallant deeds and loveable characters that totally distracts you from your personal, everyday life.

The movie cost $200 million to make and has already earned $2 billion in revenue, breaking several box office records and indicating how popular this film has proved to be with the public.

I saw the movie in Pune and happened to go to a morning show. Afterwards, walking slowly out into the bright, warm Indian sunshine, carefully crossing a busy road and then relaxing in an outdoor café, drinking a cup of coffee, I could feel how dazed I was from the impact of the movie I'd just seen.

I was struck by the contrast between fantasy and reality, between India and outer space, impressed by the intensity of an experience that allowed me to leave 'normal life' for a couple of hours and escape into a spectacular drama.

If you can relate to what I'm saying, if you, too, have tasted the skill with which movie producers and directors can spirit us away into unknown worlds, it will give you some idea of how the Elizabethan public felt about theatre plays.

Plays were the *Star Wars* epics of their time. Theatres were at the leading edge of social entertainment. Public drama on this scale was something new, risky and very exciting. It wasn't respectable, but it was very, very attractive.

Until Shakespeare's time, theatrical players had a poor reputation and were often regarded as little more than vagabonds and thieves. Wandering minstrels and actors would come into town, erect a temporary stage in the yard of an inn, perform to a crowd of no more than a couple of hundred people, pass the hat round and move on.

But when, in the 1560s, licenses were granted to the nobles of England for the maintenance of their own troupes of players, the first drama companies were formed. Responding to demand, it wasn't long before an enterprising businessman called James Burbage erected London's first successful, purpose-built theatre in Shoreditch.

Shakespeare's troupe, *The Lord Chamberlain's Men*, were frequent users of The Theatre, but then in 1597, the lease expired and a quarrel broke out with the owner of the ground on which the theatre had been built.

The man wanted so much money to renew the lease, Shakespeare's players decided it would be cheaper to dismantle The Theatre, piece by piece, and carry the building materials to the South Bank of the Thames, where they were used in the construction of The Globe. The new project was financed mainly by James Burbage's son, Richard, one of the most celebrated actors of his day.

The Globe was simply the most magnificent theatre London had ever seen. It was designed along the lines of the Roman Coliseum, enclosed and roughly circular in shape, with three tiers of seats, plus a standing-room-only 'pit' area at ground level in front of the stage.

Other theatres also sprang up and some of them, like The Globe, could accommodate an audience of 3,000 people, which was a huge number compared to previous theatrical locations.

This became a new and revolutionary form of entertainment, equivalent perhaps to the serial breakthroughs of movie-making in the twentieth century as it evolved from silent films to the 'talkies', from black-and-white to colour, from conventional celluloid film to digitalized effects created by computers.

It is said that young people, especially, were attracted to the Elizabethan theatres and there were many complaints from guilds, tradesmen and merchants that these plays were distracting apprentices from their duties as hundreds of young men slipped away from work to catch the latest show.

A disreputable sub-culture grew around the playhouses. Next door to The Globe there was a bear-baiting arena; there were also brothels and gambling houses nearby, some say even within The Globe itself, and all kinds of stalls were erected outside the entrance, selling food, ale and merchandise.

The festive and unruly atmosphere was driven by the promise of large amounts of money to be made from the huge public demand for new plays, which were produced and performed as soon as they'd been written. In the absence of copyright laws, rival companies eagerly spied on each other's latest productions, made notes during the performances and instantly produced their own versions.

In 1596, the City of London imposed a total ban on theatrical productions due to the "great disorder rampant in the city by the inordinate haunting of great multitudes of people, especially youth, to plays…" and this ensured the South Bank of the Thames became the social hot-spot for entertainment.

The public thronged to the playhouses to see full-length theatrical drama that fell into three basic categories: comedy, tragedy and history. Advertising was simple but effective. A flag was flown above the theatre and its colour proclaimed the type of drama being performed that day: white for comedy, black for tragedy, red for a history play.

Interestingly, it was the red flag that drew the biggest crowds. History plays were enormously popular with Elizabethan audiences and there is reason to suppose that Shakespeare's *Henry IV Part One* was the most popular of all. Its text was reprinted more than any other.

The story is filled with intrigue, rivalry for power and the constant threat of war as King Henry IV, having stolen the English throne from Richard II, struggles to secure his newly-acquired kingdom. What gives the play a touch of genius is the way Shakespeare alternates the main storyline with comic lowlife scenes from medieval England's underbelly, as the wayward Hal, Prince of Wales, joins forces with the fat and merry Falstaff to create drunken havoc.

The climax, when it comes, is worthy of any Hollywood Western. Hal rises above his dubious reputation and joins his father, the king, on the battlefield at Shrewsbury to face their enemies. Sergio Leone would feel right at home when, in the midst of the fray, Hal comes face to face with one of the chief rebels, young Henry Percy nicknamed 'Hotspur' because of his impetuous nature.

Yes, it's time for the showdown, not a gunfight at high noon, because the Colt .45 revolver has yet to be invented, but swords are lethal enough and we know that only one man will leave the field alive.

As Hal himself declares:

Two stars keep not their motion in one sphere,
Nor can one England brook a double reign
Of Harry Percy and the Prince of Wales.

They fight and, predictably, it is Hotspur who is killed and the reformed Prince Hal who is triumphant:

Hotspur (clutching his mortal wound):
O Harry, thou hast robbed me of my youth!
I better brook the loss of brittle life
Than those proud titles thou hast won of me....

Like a dying gunfighter in a spaghetti western, Hotspur has just enough time to utter a few final words:

O, I could prophesy
But that the earthy and cold hand of death
Lies on my tongue. No, Percy, thou art dust,
And food for... (dies)

Prince Hal: *For worms, brave Percy. Fare thee well, great heart....*

One must forgive William Shakespeare for trampling on historical accuracy in favour of high drama, because Hotspur and Prince Hal never met in personal combat at the Battle of Shrewsbury, in 1403. Hotspur was killed by troops loyal to King Henry, most probably by an arrow rather than a sword, and his dead body was displayed before Prince Hal and King Henry after the fighting had ended.

I must have watched the *Hal vs Hotspur* showdown in 1964, performed by the Royal Shakespeare Company at Stratford, when, as an eighteen-year-old aspiring intellectual, I camped by the River Avon and went to the theatre every day to see the entire 'history cycle' of eight plays, with the Bard escorting us through the Wars of the Roses from Richard II thru Henry IV (Parts 1&2), Henry V and Henry VI (parts 1,2&3) to Richard III.

But, afterwards, it all became one long blur of battles, executions and crowns. I'd imagined I was immersing myself in culture, but really I was drowning in a theatrical overload. I just recall how important it was to have an aisle seat, so that I could race to the bar in the break in order to down an ice-cold lager before the bells called us back for the next power struggle.

Nevertheless, *Henry IV, Part One* is an enjoyable play and it's easy to understand how Elizabethan Theatre shared the same basic *raison d'etre* as our contemporary Hollywood productions on the silver screen: to entertain the public. This hasn't changed one bit in more than 400 years.

It's important to remember this, because we tend to forget that even William Shakespeare, for all his fine poetry and profound social commentary, was in the entertainment business. If no one had come to his plays, the Bard's career would have ended there and then. He would, indeed, have been the 'upstart crow' that one of his jealous rivals, Robert Greene, judged him to be, and would have faded quickly into obscurity.

With this in mind, let us shuffle along with the crowd, pay one penny as an entrance fee and join the common folk in The Globe's cheapest viewing area, the so-called 'pit'. While munching on pork pies and sipping mugs of ale, we shall watch the beginning of *Hamlet*. Needless to say, the flag flying above the theatre on this day is black.

The play is gloomy from the outset. Even before learning of his father's murder, Hamlet is in distress, shocked by the speed with which his mother remarried, barely two months after burying her husband.

With his very first appearance in the play, it's clear Hamlet takes a dim view of life:

> *How weary, stale, flat and unprofitable,*
> *Seem to me all the uses of this world!*
> *Fie on't! Ah fie! 'tis an unweeded garden,*
> *That grows to seed; things rank and gross in nature*
> *Possess it merely...*

Thus, from the play's second scene until the final words of the fifth act, we are invited to accompany Hamlet and the other characters on a long procession of suffering and anguish.

What is remarkable, though, when seen from our perspective in the theatre pit, is the eagerness of the Elizabethan public to watch it. The apprentices, we assume, lapped it up and not just because it provided an excuse to skip work.

Clearly, to them, tragedy was highly entertaining. The sight of a young man helplessly railing against the blind and bitter forces of destiny was not depressing. On the contrary, it was enjoyable. It was exactly what they'd come to The Globe to see.

Such plays may have had tragic themes, but they were not taken seriously. After all, it was only the sons of royalty who could afford to laze around, idly speculating about the meaning of life. Everyone else had to earn a groat or two to buy their daily bread.

Like our modern-day movies, Elizabethan drama had the capacity to lift people out of their ordinary lives and carry them off into fantasy. In what manner they did it, with comedy, tragedy or history, wasn't really the issue. The fact that Hamlet ended sadly, compared, for example, with a modern-day, happy ending like the one in *Star Wars VII*, may not have been the least bit important from an apprentice's point of view.

Perhaps the real connection here is between Shakespeare's poetic skills and the *Star Wars* producers and cinematographers who used a combination of real locations, scale models and computer-generated imagery to create the space saga. The poetry and the producers perform the same function: offering a vehicle for the public to ride into dreamland. And it is a nice coincidence that *Star Wars VI*, the predecessor to the latest epic, was given the name 'The Undiscovered Country' after a line in Hamlet's famous soliloquy:

But that the dread of something after death,
The undiscover'd country from whose bourn
No traveller returns, puzzles the will...

The Bard's poetry, rather like modern pop songs, may seem significant while it is being delivered onstage, but does it stand up under scrutiny? As I see it, it's easy to pick holes in Hamlet's argumentation. Take, for example, these immortal lines:

To sleep: perchance to dream: ay, there's the rub;
For in that sleep of death what dreams may come
When we have shuffled off this mortal coil...

This is nonsense. People don't hold back from suicide because they are afraid of after-death dreaming. Death, in fact, brings an abrupt end to all dreaming. They may be afraid of heaven and hell, but, from the Christian theological perspective, these are not dreams. They are realities. So this is beautiful poetry, but with no real basis.

It is for this reason that I cannot take Hamlet's 'to be or not to be' too seriously. Granted, it is the world's best-known quotation, embedded in the world's most frequently performed play. But still, it is poetry, and therefore to be embraced as entertainment rather than reality, otherwise there is bound to be confusion and trouble.

I am reminded of the well-known American singer, Bob Dylan, who rose to fame in the early sixties with acid-tongued folk ballads that soon evolved into protest songs about social injustice, the evil of war, civil rights and the exploitation of labour.

To a young generation of Americans that was blossoming into the hippie era, complete with LSD-inspired visions, sexual liberation and anti-Vietnam war demonstrations, Dylan was hailed as a prophet of great social change that many people felt was about to sweep through the land, transforming mainstream America.

Though Dylan denied this role, his songs seemed to confirm it. For example, in one of his best-known songs from that era, *The Times They Are A-Changin*, he clearly predicts that parents in America will lose all control over their sons and daughters in a new dawn of radically changed moral values.

When Dylan, as a song-writer and performer, moved on, picking up an electric guitar and ignoring all kinds of worthy social causes in favour of rock songs and country music, many people felt betrayed. Joan Baez and David Bowie both wrote songs pleading with Dylan to return and lead the revolution.

He declined. Why? Because he wasn't emotionally involved in the protest movement. His passion wasn't engaged in it. At heart, he was not a revolutionary. He was a poet, a singer and a songwriter.

I suspect the same goes for Shakespeare. He wasn't so much concerned with creating a meaningful world view. Indeed, his views changed with each play he wrote. He was, essentially, a poet who enjoyed entertaining people with his love of language and its endlessly flowing imagery.

Nevertheless, the impact of what the Bard wrote stays with us, because, centuries later, his musings have been absorbed as part of our cultural atmosphere. Whatever the Bard originally intended is no longer relevant. It is the effect that his plays have on us that has to be considered and that is why Mrs Shakespeare needs to turn the plot of *Hamlet* upside down.

The apprentices in the pit were of a different era. They had the privilege of hearing the Bard's living words, raw and fresh, as something new, exciting and barely respectable. Now, four hundred years later, we must deal with the opposite effect. Why? Because Shakespeare has become too respectable, too much part of the cultural establishment. His plays have been embraced by the 'First Order' if I may borrow a *Star Wars*' term for the social elite and are being used to control our minds and enslave our energy.

It is time to break loose.

How do we do that? For one moment, stop reading, close your eyes and listen closely to your own heartbeat.

Can you feel it? Can you hear it?

Yes, the Force is awakening...

CHAPTER 16

Falstaff's Raw Deal

Falstaff got a raw deal. He didn't deserve his fate. So, if you will excuse me, I will extend this detour from my play's storyline in order to air a long-standing grievance on behalf of Sir John. There are lessons to be learned from the Bard's most popular comic character and his demise.

It's worth remembering that, in the years immediately following Shakespeare's death, when his plays at the Globe proved less attractive to the theatre-going public – presumably, because most people had already seen them – the three Falstaff plays always drew big crowds.

The adventures of this swaggering, vain, affable rogue with a poetic tongue and philosophical mind have proved immensely appealing, both then and now.

We first meet Falstaff in *Henry IV Part One*, bantering and boozing with Prince Hal and soon running into trouble, when the Prince and Ned Poins, another lowlife character, trick Falstaff and his fellow thieves into robbing a band of pilgrims and then, in disguise, they ambush the robbers themselves.

Panic stricken, the thieves run off, leaving their ill-gotten gains behind. Afterwards, when Prince Hal exposes Falstaff's cowardice, his quick-witted friend immediately has an answer, saying that he knew it was the Prince who attacked them:

"By the Lord, I knew ye as well as he that made ye. Why, hear you, my masters. Was it for me to kill the heir apparent? Should I turn upon the true Prince?"

But this rowdy relationship is not all it seems. There is a coldness to Prince Henry in his mockery of Falstaff and calculation in his friendship that bodes ill for the fat knight, who, one feels, is the more genuinely affectionate of the two men.

Sure enough, at the end of *Henry IV Part Two,* in one of the most poignant scenes ever written by the Bard, the newly-crowned King Henry V disowns his former companion:

I know thee not, old man: fall to thy prayers;
How ill white hairs become a fool and jester!
I have long dream'd of such a kind of man,
So surfeit-swell'd, so old and so profane;
But, being awaked, I do despise my dream....

The transformation of the wayward Prince is complete. In rejecting Falstaff, he publicly renounces those qualities that are deemed unacceptable in a monarch and reveals his 'true nature' as a noble English king.

As a piece of theatre, it works wonderfully and audiences down the ages seem to have readily accepted the necessity of Henry's action. But, personally, I would have been more impressed with the new king if he'd taken responsibility for his enjoyment of those bygone days of drinking, joking, whoring and making mischief.

If you ask me, Henry should have thanked Falstaff for supporting him in sowing his wild oats, while at the same time making it clear that those days were over, and then pensioned him off with a small annual income and a nice little house in Chelsea. Falstaff could have been the very first Chelsea Pensioner.

Instead, the king made an elaborate show of renouncing his past by vilifying Falstaff and sending his former companion to the notorious Fleet Prison. To me, this is cowardly. It shows Henry's fear of public opinion, his desperate need to be taken seriously as a king and his cold-heartedness in using his former friend as a sacrificial pawn. It is sheer hypocrisy.

Just why Prince Hal enjoyed Falstaff's company in the first place is a puzzle and one that has been the subject of many long, boring student essays across the United Kingdom, so I don't need to go there.

Suffice it to say that either Prince Hal wished to distance himself from his father, King Henry IV, or he wanted to indulge in fast living while he was free to do so, before taking on serious matters of state. Either way, he owed a debt of gratitude to his portly companion.

There is no evidence to show that the historical Prince Hal was anything like Shakespeare's character. Really, it was just a clever dramatic device by the playwright, taking Henry down into the depths of depravity before raising him up and exalting him as a great king. As the lowly caterpillar becomes the high-flying butterfly, so the delinquent youth transforms into the magnificent monarch.

Historically, however, Henry wasn't that great a king. True, he managed to unite the quarrelsome nobles of England by taking on France – adopting the classic political strategy of creating a common enemy abroad to ensure peace at home – but his conduct was often questionable.

At Agincourt, he killed most of his prisoners after they had surrendered. At the siege of Rouen, when the starving citizens pushed their women and children out of the gate in the hope that Henry would allow them to pass through his troops to safety, he refused to let them do so. The women and their babies died of hunger, thirst and cold in the ditches outside the city walls.

Militarily, his campaigns achieved little. Henry's victory at Agincourt was followed almost immediately by a defeat for his army at the Battle of Baugé, and his short military career came to a sudden and ignominious end when he died of dysentery in a French chateau at the age of thirty-six.

Discharging one's bowels of blood, mucus and liquid faeces at the rate of one litre an hour and dying of dehydration, as victims of dysentery generally tend to do, hardly makes for a dignified ending for an allegedly illustrious king. Even Shakespeare would have had a problem spin-doctoring that one, which is why the Bard gives no explanation as to the manner of Henry V's death at the beginning of his next play in the history cycle, *Henry VI Part One*.

Instead, his characters lament the late king's passing with purple prose, uttered by a mourning English nobility:

Duke of Bedford:
King Henry the Fifth, too famous to live long!
England ne'er lost a king of so much worth.
Duke of Gloucester:
What should I say? his deeds exceed all speech:
He ne'er lift up his hand but conquered.

Within a few decades of Henry's death, English claims to the French throne lay in ruins, so nothing came of his efforts to unite the two kingdoms. Nobody at the time – least of all Henry V – seemed bothered by the sheer impracticality of ruling two countries divided by a wide, rough, unpredictable stretch of water called the English Channel.

So, one may legitimately ask, what was the point of this fake glorification of a mediocre monarch? Well, the repudiation of Falstaff by King Henry sends a clear message to the public, not least to the youthful apprentices who flocked to the Globe Theatre to see these hugely popular history plays:

There comes a time when the wildness of youth must be replaced by dignified, sensible social behaviour. This is called 'maturity' or 'growing up'.

What is not addressed is the questionable value of the uses to which this so-called 'maturity' is then put. After all, is there any greater merit in conducting long, futile military campaigns, causing great suffering and loss of life, than in enjoying oneself in pubs and brothels?

Here we come to the crux of the matter. What Shakespeare created out of his cocktail of historical fact and dramatic fiction was a myth of English glory and power that is still being used today in shaping the minds of young people being educated in the United Kingdom.

They are encouraged to look back on a glorious past in order to be persuaded to accept their role as obedient citizens within a certain social structure. That's why the British public still loves the monarchy, because it's a link back to a time of mythological greatness.

People say the Queen is above politics, but it's hard to see how. Her function, as the embodiment of historical sovereignty, gives her a central role in the political process. If British politics is a circus, then it is she who acts as the ringmaster, inviting clowns like Tony Blair and David Cameron to make brief appearances and to do back-flips to entertain the audience. When the public gets bored with their antics, they have to leave, and the ringmaster invites somebody new.

To conclude: the past is a kind of national glue, a collective adhesive that sticks people together and gives them an identity. This identity may be fanciful, but it is powerful. The Brexit lobby, which in the June 2016 referendum successfully urged UK voters to leave the European Union, drew on historical mythology to promote its case for an 'independent' Britain. By the way, I'm not suggesting that we discard British glue in favour of some other brand…German, Russian,

American or Chinese. As long as glue is being used, the sticky British stuff is probably as good as any. But perhaps we shall discover, as this book progresses, that there are benefits to getting oneself unglued.

Theatrical flashback: I had the honour of briefly rubbing shoulders with Falstaff during a school play, back in the early sixties, when our history teacher, who fancied himself as a theatre director, staged *Henry IV Part Two*. As Justice Silence, a very minor character, my main task was to fall off a stool in a drunken stupor while Falstaff was busy recruiting soldiers.

To me, at that time, Shakespeare was a kind of pantomime. The characters weren't real. But the following year I was given a role that changed my view of both history and acting.

I was asked to play Thomas Cromwell in Robert Bolt's play *A Man for All Seasons* which focuses on the sixteenth century conflict between King Henry VIII and his philosopher-chancellor, Thomas More.

In Bolt's play, King Henry is desperate for a son and is determined to divorce his wife, Catherine of Aragon, so that he can marry Anne Boleyn. But the high-principled More refuses to help the king's campaign against Pope Clement VII, who is blocking the divorce.

Thomas Cromwell enters the fray as an upwardly mobile civil servant, working for the king, and what I liked about the man was his ordinariness. He wasn't trying to live up to some noble ideal like More. He was a pragmatic, politically-minded, fallible, human being.

Somehow those qualities resonated in me and I found myself becoming genuinely irritated by the sanctimonious Thomas More. I loved the moment when Cromwell lost his temper with the king's chancellor for stubbornly clinging to his principles against the practical necessity of helping the king produce an heir for his throne.

As More loftily paraded his 'conscience' onstage, Cromwell shouted:

"A miserable thing whatever you call it that lives like a bat in a belfry tower! A shrill incessant pedagogue about your own salvation!"

Cromwell had a point. In Bolt's play, More comes across as a near-saint, justifying his loyalty to Clement VII as reverence for the Pope's sacred role as the only link to Jesus Christ. But in refusing a divorce to Henry VIII, the Pope was acting purely politically, pressured by the Holy Roman Emperor, King Charles V, who was Catherine's nephew. It was a power struggle that had nothing to do with religion.

Taking on the role of Cromwell was an eye-opener for me and the fact that More was played by a pompous head boy whom I thoroughly disliked helped a lot. I really lost my temper and the history teacher, directing the play, was delighted.

"That was good acting, Peter," he complimented me, after the scene had ended. He didn't know it wasn't. But it did show me how acting provides a wonderful excuse for releasing socially-inappropriate emotions and being applauded for it at the same time.

In my final year at school, I was given the best possible gift by the same director: the opportunity to play Azdak, the maverick judge, in Bertolt Brecht's *The*

Caucasian Chalk Circle.

I won't go into the whole story, but what I adored about Azdak was that he lived outside the box of conventional thinking. Of course, he had to survive amid the rapidly shifting power politics that surrounded him, but he didn't care for any of it.

He was mercurial, unpredictable, willing to act spontaneously in whatever way his own intelligence dictated. The fact that justice prevailed at the end of the play because of his ingenious device of the chalk circle revealing the true mother of a disputed child was a double bonus.

In a way, these three roles Justice Silence, Thomas Cromwell and Azdak gave me a taste of my own future, mirroring my personal transition from blindly obedient citizen to politically astute observer to renegade individualist.

And, as we shall see, there is an Azdak-like figure in my own play who will emerge before very long. And now it really is time to get back to the action.

CHAPTER 17

The Story of the West

We are approaching that moment in the play where my wife, Mrs Shakespeare, single-handedly demolishes Western materialism. Or, rather, she puts it firmly in its place. Since I am the one who wrote the words she is about to utter, I must take responsibility, while at the same time pointing out that I'm not against materialism. I like my laptop, mobile and refrigerator as much as the next guy.

But it's time for a reality check; time to see how smug and satisfied we are with living on the surface of human consciousness, surrounded by pleasant consumeristic distractions, not even considering the possibility of diving deeper.

As a loyal husband, I am required to support my wife, so I'm using the phrase 'single-handedly' rather loosely. The truth is, as the Bard, I'm not as convinced as Mrs Shakespeare about the shallowness of Western values, but once in a while a husband has to stand by his woman – or face the consequences.

As she comes on stage, I rise from my seat and together we address the audience. Mrs Shakespeare begins, "You seem like an intelligent group of people, so let me ask you a question. Don't you think it's odd that in the whole history of Western culture nobody knew anything about meditation?

Will: "All those European geniuses..."

Mrs: "French Impressionist painters..."

Will: "Russian novelists..."

Mrs: "Italian sculptors...."

Will: "German composers..."

There is a brief pause as I wait for my wife to realize there's an important omission in her list of Europe's most talented artists.

Mrs: "Oh yes, and not forgetting the English playwrights."

Will is relieved and gratified. "Thank you, dear," he murmurs, acknowledging his rightful place among the cultural elite.

Mrs: "And not one of them ever sat down, closed his eyes and meditated."

Will: "They knew everything about the human ego."

Mrs: "But they didn't know anything about dropping the ego."

Will: "They knew how to be *Somebody*."

Mrs: "But they had no idea how to be *Nobody*."

At this point, we move into a kind of poetic dialogue:

Mrs: "Don't you think it's kind of odd? Don't you think it's kind of strange?"

Will: "Such a funny situation, no one's heard of meditation."

Mrs: "If you say the world is Maya..."

Will: "You will just be called a liar."

Mrs: "If you point towards nirvana..."

Will: "They will say you've gone bananas."

Mrs: "If you tell them not to think..."

Will: "They will send you to a shrink."

Mrs: "If you ask them to be still..."

Will: "They will offer you a pill."

Mrs: "If you talk of inner vision..."

Will: "They will think of television."

Mrs: "If you sit silently alone..."

Will: "Don't switch off your mobile phone."

Mrs: "If you want to clear your head..."

Will: "You can Google it instead."

Mrs: "If you want true happiness..."

Will: "Just send an SMS."

Mrs: "If you want to raise your spirit..."

Will: "Any shopping mall will do it."

Mrs: "You can find out who you are..."

Will: "At Manchester United Café Bar...."

I have to interrupt our repartee at this point to explain that in Pune, one of the most chic places to be seen having coffee or drinking beer is located in the city's most fashionable shopping mall, Amanora, which is packed with brand clothing, jewellery and every symbol of foreign fashion you can imagine. There, amid the Louis Vuitton handbags, Calvin Klein jeans, Victoria's Secret lingerie and Marks & Spencer socks, you find the Manchester United Cafe Bar, where you can buy expensive drinks and be seen watching big-screen reruns of England's most successful football club in action on the field. It's supposed to be the height of cool, especially for men.

That's why I chose to include it in our diatribe against Western values. It also happens to be the only trendy cafe in Pune whose name rhymes neatly with "find out who you are." In Europe, I'd simply say "You can find out who you are, in your local pub or bar."

Now we can continue:

Mrs: "That's the story of the West."

Will: "There's no time to stop and rest."

Mrs: "Just to be..."

Will: "And let the rest..."

Mrs: "Disappear..."

Together: "In emptiness."

For a moment, we stand silently together with eyes closed, illustrating the inner state about which we speak. Then we turn to face each other, give a namaste greeting, and Mrs Shakespeare quietly leaves the stage.

I watch her go and then feel free to distance myself from what has just occurred. Turning to the audience, I comment "My wife's in love with Eastern philosophy. Oh, it's interesting, I grant you, but what can you do with it? It's not going to pay the rent is it? It's not going to get me out of trouble with the Queen. So, it's back to work for me."

I have to say this, or the play would end right here. We would simply declare, *"Hey Ram! All is God! All is One! Duality is but a fleeting illusion created by an even more illusory Self!"* Thereafter, we would sit cross-legged on the stage, contemplating our navels, until the audience became bored and left. End of story, end of play, end of just about everything you can imagine.

But we're not done. The play must continue.

By the way, in case, you're thinking that my wife's speech is relevant only for the newly-enriched Indian middle class, may I remind you that almost everything in the UK is now branded. The corporate consumer culture has swallowed us all and we happily wear their logos on our t-shirts, jeans, jackets, handbags…

Brands are advertised on the caps of racing drivers, the racquets of tennis champions, the shirts of football players and on the stadiums in which they perform. It gets worse every year. Soon they will be calling Westminster the Coca-Cola Commons and repackaging the Windsor franchise as the Ladbrokes Monarchy.

I can tell you one thing: if my grandfather had been told he had to wear the name of his tailor on the outside of his jacket, he would have shot himself. I kid you not. That's an indication of how far we've come in the last sixty years.

Okay, that concludes my rant about materialism. Now we can proceed with the story…oh, I almost forgot…after these messages from my sponsors:

"This book is being written on a Lenovo laptop *(I went for a cheap deal on Amazon and have regretted it ever since)*…while I drink my morning Nescafe Gold *(I ran out of coffee beans and was desperate)*…after sending a quick SMS to my publisher on my Samsung Galaxy S5 Mini *(couldn't afford an iPhone)* and eating a bowl of Kellogg's Frosties *(sugar is really, really bad for you and your children)*…at my summer home in sunny Jutland *(ha!)* an ideal summer vacation spot for British holidaymakers *(you've got to be kidding...it's thirteen degrees Celsius and pouring with rain outside my window right now, in the middle of June!!!).*"

CHAPTER 18

Young Women, Old Men

Ophelia is not a happy thespian. She feels frustrated. She wants a bigger slice of dramatic action, and I can't say I blame her. After her Lady Raga dance routine, she doesn't have many lines to speak, even though she's onstage for a big chunk of the time.

So I need to come up with a new idea. She's a young, good-looking blonde and I've just finished reading a book about the trials and tribulations of Marilyn Monroe as she attempted to forge an acting career for herself.

Typecast as a bimbo blonde, Marilyn struggled through many 'casting couch' situations, sometimes refusing the advances of producers and studio directors, but more often furthering her career by giving them what they wanted: the chance to make love with a fantasy symbol of sex and glamour which they themselves had created out of a very ordinary young woman.

Thus inspired, I created a casting couch scene between William Shakespeare and Ophelia. Will is sitting in his chair at the side of the stage, as per usual, writing his tragic masterpiece, when Ophelia hesitantly approaches him. Having tasted freedom as Lady Raga, she now envisions a different role for herself.

"Excuse me, Master Shakespeare," she says, timidly.

Will doesn't want to be disturbed and feels irritated by this intrusion.

"Yes, what is it now?" he snaps.

"I... I want to change my character," ventures Ophelia, not really believing she's got the guts to say this to the great playwright.

"You... what?" Will can't believe he's hearing this defiant whisper of rebellion from such an insignificant member of his acting troupe.

Remember, in those days, age was respected and youth counted for nothing. It's changed now, of course, but I really don't see why. Young people look pretty, seem open to new ideas and can text at lightning speed on their mobiles, but it turns out that the only thing on their minds is which selfie to post, what video clip to upload and which app to download. Frankly, I haven't seen a flicker of intelligent rebelliousness in any of the younger generations since the sixties.

"I want to change my character," repeats Ophelia, more determinedly, gathering courage.

The Bard waves his quill pen in a dismissive gesture. "No, no. That's not going to happen. The play is almost finished."

Pleadingly, the young woman sinks down close to Will's chair, catching hold of his arm, begging him with her big innocent eyes.

"Please, sir! It's not much to ask, is it? I just want to live my own life. And you are such a clever genius, you can make anything possible."

Flattery will get you everywhere. Will stops writing, focuses attention on the beautiful girl in front of him and, in the time-honoured manner of every horny guy who ever found himself in a position of power over a helpless female, changes his tune. Suddenly, he's more accommodating, friendlier, more willing to listen.

Stroking Ophelia gently on the face and trying not to gaze too long at her heaving, emotion-filled bosom, he murmurs, "Hmm... You're a pretty little thing, aren't you? Listen, tomorrow my wife goes out of town to take care of her sick mother. Why don't you come to my house and we'll... talk about it... together... hmm?"

If it had been Monroe, she might have said yes. But Ophelia, innocent girl that she happens to be, isn't ready to accommodate the Bard's unbridled lust. She backs off to centre stage and addresses the audience thus:

"My God, this horny old goat is trying to seduce me! I've heard of the Hollywood casting couch, I've heard of the Bollywood casting couch, but I've never heard of an Elizabethan casting couch! Oh well, I guess it's always been the same. Right then...."

She adjusts her hair, as if looking in a mirror, makes her dress a little more tidy, puts on a winning smile and turns towards the Bard. Approaching him seductively, she brushes her hand lightly over his bald head, and, whispering in his ear, offers him this little poem:

Oh Master Shakespeare, you're such a handsome man

And if you agree to help me, I'll give you what I can.

She's all over the guy, caressing his face, bringing her lips close to his, giving green lights to his desires, reducing his keen intellect to a mush ball....

Would you like to taste my cherry? It's so tender, it's so sweet!

Would you like to squeeze my plums, while I'm lying at your feet?

Here, she thrusts her cleavage into his face, half-burying the Bard in almost-undressed breast...

Shall I feed you some papaya, while we're lying on your bed?

She stretches back over his lap in a delicious gesture of surrender....

Or would my lover rather have... a twisted nose instead!

Suddenly, she grabs hold of his nose and twists it violently, making the startled Bard cry out in pain.

"Ow! You hurt me, you little bitch!"

Ophelia jumps up, shrinking back from his anger but is unrepentant, replying defiantly, "Well, you asked for it! You dirty old man!"

Will is enraged and points a condemning literary finger at the poor girl.

"You will regret this young lady. You will die before this play is done. Your fate is sealed!"

Ophelia gasps in shock, then sobs and sinks to the floor. Will sits back in his chair, nurses his aching nose for a few moments, then goes back to writing his play.

Here, I must pay my dues to Monroe, who inspired this scene with her account of how she once turned down the advances of a studio head in Hollywood. Monroe was asked to strip naked for the movie mogul in his office, which she obligingly did. At his direction, she bent over, but as he approached her, penis in hand, she declined his advances. Said Monroe, "I had never seen a man so angry". He banned her from his studio.

Monroe's career survived the experience and so, as it happens, does that of Ophelia. As she weeps in despair, Mrs Shakespeare comes to the rescue once more, gliding onstage from the wings, kneeling down next to Ophelia and tenderly stroking her arm.

Slipping cosily into the role of an older, sympathetic girlfriend, Mrs Shakespeare begins to sing. It is a song that contains her philosophy of life and is inspired by a ballad titled *I've Never Been to Me* that, way back in 1982, became a one-hit wonder for a little known American R&B singer called Charlene.

Charlene's message, sung by an experienced 'woman of the world' to a younger woman, intrigued me because it comes close to conveying the message I had in mind, while at the same time completely missing the point.

In her folksy ballad, Charlene, as the older woman, addresses a desperate young wife and mother who would like to exchange her mundane existence for a glamorous jet-set lifestyle.

The older woman describes how she has travelled the world, allowing herself to be seduced by wealthy, powerful men, but never found fulfilment in any of her adventures. After each verse, she announces:

I've been to paradise, but I've never been to me.

She describes many sexual encounters, such as being 'undressed by kings' and then, somewhat coyly, confesses that while being seduced by such people she's seen some 'things' that a woman 'ain't supposed to see'.

Just as an aside: it's hard to let Charlene get away with this attitude. If she had been singing about Victorian times, it would've been okay with me, but by the seventies, in the USA and in Europe, most women were, I suspect, liberated enough to keep the lights on in the bedroom and get acquainted with the sight of a man's naked body.

I'm also irritated by Charlene's assertion, later in the song, that having a couple of babies would have made her feel more complete and less lonely. That's not necessarily the case. A new mother can feel isolated at home, especially if her girlfriends are out partying and her husband is drinking with his pals at the pub. Moreover, as everyone knows, babies soon become kids, kids become teenagers and then one day teenagers walk out the door to lead their own lives, a traumatic moment for any mom that can leave her feeling lonelier than ever.

Really, there's so much wrong with Charlene's song. For example, if the young woman's relationship with her husband is unhappy, as seems to be the case, it's really not going to help to know that a globe-trotting whore isn't any happier. Is she supposed to smile, say "Gee, thanks!" and feel better about the fact that her husband is an insensitive asshole?

But this is beside the point. What caught my attention was the hook line. After each romantic adventure in some distant part of the world, Charlene returns to the same theme:

I've been to paradise, but I've never been to me.

To a meditator like me, this line is fascinating, because it describes the condition of ninety-nine point nine percent of the human race. Not that we are all jet setters, but if we take 'paradise' as a metaphor for all those activities that promise to deliver fulfilment, that keep us preoccupied with external reality, then the line works perfectly.

Most of us have never looked 'in' and have therefore no real acquaintance with ourselves. In other words, we have 'never been to me'. We are too busy looking for paradise in the outside world: a new house, a happier marriage, a better job, a new career, a family, children…whatever we desire is part of that outer reality. Our inner world, where our authentic sense of self is to be found, remains unexplored.

However, as you can imagine, Charlene was no meditator and her words did not mean anything faintly resembling my interpretation. In her view of life, as expressed in her song, a young mother and wife is more in touch with the real 'me' than a jet-setting, sexy, gold digger. She is advising the young woman to be grateful, because in the end it is more fulfilling to have a family than chasing illusions of glamour and wealth.

Charlene herself had an extraordinary career in which she got to see both sides of the coin: the glamour and the anonymity. When she first tried to break into the music industry in the late seventies, signing on with Motown Records, her songs – including *I've Never Been to Me* – never reached higher than number ninety-seven in the charts.

Eventually, she gave up her showbiz dreams, married an Englishman, left the United States and descended into total obscurity, working in a sweet shop in a tiny English town called Ilford.

Then, in 1982, at the urging of his girlfriend, a Florida DJ started playing *I've Never Been to Me*. This time, the track caught fire and it rose from the ashes to become a classic sleeper hit, reaching number three in the *Billboard Hot 100*, occupying the number one spot in the UK charts and becoming a global sensation. For a moment, it seemed like a new career was being launched for Charlene and she returned to the recording studios.

But, alas, she had no further success and was never able to convert that one-hit into a string of successful albums. Both she and the song became known as the all-time, number one, one-hit-wonder.

Returning to the theme of the song itself: to me, Charlene's predictable, wholesome message of placing family values above the jet-set lifestyle is off-track, because when you become interested in meditation, you don't necessarily change your way of living.

Wife, mother, businesswoman, movie star, singer, secretary, international escort...the external role you play in life is irrelevant to the inner journey. A jet-setter can be as good a meditator as a housewife, and vice versa.

Which is not to say that changes don't happen. They do. For example, Meera, India's most famous enlightened female mystic, was a beautiful Rajput princess, belonging to a royal family in Rajasthan, living around 1500 AD. She became a devotee of Krishna and then – to the horror of her family – wandered the streets, singing and dancing in public, completely uninterested in her status as a princess.

But Charlene isn't singing about the kinds of changes that arise from spiritual transformation. She's simply moralizing in favour of staying home and being a good wife and mother rather than seeking adventure in the big wide world.

Inspired by Charlene's song, I changed the hook line from *I've Never Been to Me* to a more profound assertion pointing in the same direction: *I'd Rather Be with Me*. I created a new tune and changed all the lyrics. This is how our song emerged reborn from this musical mutation:

Oh lady, sweet lady, weeping for your life,
You want to be a princess and you want to be a wife.
I can see you long to be
His sweet beloved one
And I hope for you that your dreams come true,
Now your life has just begun.
I've searched and roamed many miles from home

Looking for that special man,
Enjoyed a fling with a foreign king
And we danced until the dawn.
I met Will and I love him still
And yet I want to be free
I've been around the world
But I'd rather be with me.

Oh lady, sweet lady, you will have your day
From my heart I want to tell you
That everything's okay.
I can see your destiny
Reflected in your eyes
You won't be apart and your open heart
Can see through all the lies.

It's strange but true, and I'm telling you
That nothing ever lasts.
The future will be present
And the present will be past.
Now the hardest thing is to look within
And find the real me
I've been around the world
But I'd rather be with me.

Mrs Shakespeare did well, lifting Ophelia out of her misery with this reassuring ballad, reviving her spirits after her shocking encounter with the sleazy Bard. Taking the younger woman by the hand, Mrs Shakespeare offers her the favourite English solution to any personal difficulty:

"Come on, dear, let's have a nice cup of tea."

And, yes, we will ignore the fact that tea, in Elizabethan times, was still confined to China and those precious plants had not yet been stolen by English 'entrepreneurs', polite term for pirates and thieves, and then cultivated in Northern India on a massive scale, so that their leaves could be harvested and exported to the UK. The accurate Elizabethan equivalent, "Come on dear, let's have a mug of ale", just doesn't convey the same comforting feeling.

The women exit, arm in arm, two sisters brought together by their mutual determination to survive Shakespeare's message of gloom and doom.

CHAPTER 19

Nobody Likes to Dance

I must now present the mysterious character called Nobody. He has been waiting too long, standing in the wings for over half the play, ready to spring into action and twist the plot around his enigmatic finger.

Perhaps the best way to introduce him is by way of a quotation from Lewis Carroll's story *Through the Looking Glass*, written in 1871 as a sequel to *Alice's Adventures in Wonderland*.

In a fantasy world, beyond the mirror, Alice is listening to a conversation between the King and the Messenger:

> *"Who did you pass on the road?"* the King asked.
> *"Nobody,"* said the Messenger.
> *"Quite right,"* said the King, *"this young lady saw him too. So of course Nobody walks slower than you."*
> *"I do my best,"* the Messenger said in a sullen tone. *"I'm sure Nobody walks much faster than I do!"*
> *"He can't do that,"* said the King, *"or else he'd have been here first."*

And so it continues. This is a play on words, created by the Reverend Charles Dodgson – Lewis Carroll's real name – to amuse a pretty young girl of his acquaintance, Alice Liddell, with whom he was infatuated. However, the Rev. Dodgson managed to curb his paedophile passion and instead channelled his lust into a literary masterpiece.

In her looking-glass world, Alice never gets to meet Nobody, but if she happened to find herself in my play she most certainly would. Because my Nobody isn't just nobody. My Nobody is a real character.

Nobody is a time-warp wizard who gives the play its mystical dimension: a bit like Doctor Who, a bit like Merlin the Magician, and a whole lot like the little man behind the curtain, pulling levers to create illusions, in *The Wizard of Oz*.

I notice I've been referring to Nobody as 'he' but the part is androgynous. It can be played by a man or a woman and, indeed, for this quirky role, I invited a young Indian woman of my acquaintance who was a dynamo of energy, both onstage and off.

For years, Nobody had worked in the resort canteen – for so long, in fact, that when I close my eyes I can still see her scraping vegetarian lasagne off the serving trays. She had a thick mop of black hair, a pretty face and a wide mouth that could either give you a brilliant smile or utter inconvenient truths. Tact wasn't her strong suit.

I recall one moment, in the mid-nineties, when writing and directing a musical show, I carefully created a part for her that would, coincidentally, prevent her from being part of the show's glamorous all-female chorus line. I thought I'd handled the situation with diplomatic aplomb, when all of a sudden Nobody announced loudly to the rest of the cast: "Subhuti doesn't want me in the chorus line because my legs are too fat."

OMG, how embarrassing *pour moi*! Because, of course, it was true. Nobody possessed a body that was 'comfortably round' and shrank only with a great deal of dieting. She had been skinny, a couple of years earlier, during our first show together, but it was hard work for her to keep the kilos off, requiring rigid calorie control. In the end, she decided that if a little roundness was needed to regain her natural mood of easy-going happiness, then it was cheap at the price.

This year, she'd come to Pune to study Craniosacral Healing, but she had a soft spot for theatre and, after checking her busy schedule, agreed to squeeze our rehearsals into her daily programme.

Now, back to the play: we take up the tale where Hamlet is recovering from the traumatic experience of being temporarily dead. He limps across the stage, nursing the wounded leg where Will Shakespeare unkindly stabbed him with a poisoned sword. He sees the skull, lying beside my chair, and picks it up, as if to deliver the famous soliloquy which, as I mentioned earlier, begins:

"Alas, poor Yorick, I knew him Horatio,
A fellow of infinite jest..."

My interpretation is a little different. Instead, Hamlet uses this opportunity to reaffirm his decision to have nothing to do with Ophelia:

"Alas, poor Yorick! You lost your head over a woman, didn't you? Well, that's not going to happen to me!"

Carelessly, Hamlet tosses the skull over his shoulder. Its sails through the air and lands perilously close to the chair where I'm sitting. Fortunately, even if it hit me, it wouldn't do any damage. It's made of rubber.

At this moment, Nobody walks on stage. Far from being dressed in a classical Elizabethan costume like the other players, she is wearing blue jeans and a white t-shirt with the word "NOBODY" printed in capital letters across her chest. She has a denim cap, with its peak turned cheekily to one side. Her mood is upbeat and playful, like a fairy or imp who enjoys the foolishness of mere mortals and once in a while decides to mess with their minds.

Nobody glances quizzically at Hamlet. "Hi, how's it going?" she inquires.

Hamlet: "Well, to be honest, I could use a few laughs. Who are you? What's your name?"

Nobody: "Nobody."

Hamlet: "Nobody? C'mon, you must be *somebody*."

Nobody: "Everybody tells me that: 'You *must* be *somebody*.' But *anybody* can be somebody. And everybody *wants* to be somebody. Nobody wants to be *nobody*. Except me."

Hamlet: "Can you say that again, slowly please?"

Nobody: "Everybody says that, as well. *Nobody* understands."

Hamlet: "But you *are* Nobody, so *you* must understand."

Nobody: "Anybody *could* understand, and I keep thinking one day somebody *will* understand. But believe me, nobody has any idea what Nobody is talking about."

Hamlet: "Well, nobody's perfect."

Nobody: "Thank you, I agree!"

Hamlet: "No, that's not what I meant!"

Nobody: "No worries. Nobody cares."

What Nobody is saying here, is not just a play on words. She's touching on a subject close to our hearts: the desire in all of us to be special, to make our mark, to be *somebody*. We cannot all carve our name in golden letters on mythical Mount Sumeru, where, according to Hindu legend, the great world conquerors write their signatures. But still, we might, somehow, be able to squeeze ourselves into a footnote of the history books.

When you think about it, however, the urge we all share to be special actually makes this kind of desire very common; in fact, very un-special, because everybody has it.

As an Indian mystic once told me, "The desire to be extraordinary is a very ordinary desire. Everybody has it. To be ordinary is really extraordinary."

To which, you may sensibly respond: "Okay, but what's the pay-off in being ordinary? What's in it for me?"

Patience. All will be revealed at the appropriate time.

Hamlet: "Okay, Mister Nobody, where are you from?"

Nobody: "I'm from the Land of Not To Be."

Hamlet (sarcastically): "I should have guessed."

Nobody: "Not to be, you see, is the only way to be."

Though you may disagree, just listen carefully:

The more you think you've got, the more you have to drop.

But, the more you find you're not, the more you've really got."

Hamlet: "That's nonsense, don't you see? Or would nobody agree?"

Nobody: "Nonsense it may be, but would you agree, to check it out with me?"

Hamlet: "Well, okay...maybe."

Nobody: "Watch closely...you will see."

At this point, Queen Elizabeth and her two attendants arrive on stage. In their company, we are transported to her Royal Court, where the daily business of the realm is being conducted. One of the attendants unrolls a scroll containing supplications to the Crown. My aim here is to reinforce the Queen's image as a cold-hearted bitch, in urgent need of transformation.

By the way, I must emphasize that the Queen's gold dress looked wonderful, a triumph for Ritu's tailoring skills. As for the lace ruff around her neck...well, my dear friend carried it off as best she could, but, alas, it flopped down on her shoulders. How the original queen's dress-makers managed to make her ruff stand up like a perfect fan, I have no idea. Either it was, as I have already speculated, supported by a frame of whalebone, or they used enough starch to stiffen the River Thames.

The day's Royal business continues:

First Attendant: "Your Majesty, the people of London have no bread to eat."

Elizabeth: "Let them eat cake."

A line borrowed, of course, from Marie Antoinette, who, by the way, never said it, but got her head chopped off anyway.

First Attendant: "Your Majesty, the people of York say your taxes are too high."

Elizabeth: "Let them work harder."

First Attendant, with a big toady grin on his face: "Your Majesty, the people of Lancaster wish you a happy birthday."

Elizabeth allows a small, contemptuous smile to lighten up her grim features: "Indeed? How touching. Let them make a statue of me, in gratitude."

Today's business is concluded and the Royal trio freezes, standing motionless on the stage.

Nobody: "Tell me, who is she?"

Hamlet: "Of course, 'tis Her Majesty."

To Hamlet's amazement, Nobody walks over to the Queen and reaches up, as if to take away Elizabeth's crown.

Nobody: "And if I remove her attire?"

Hamlet is alarmed at the prospect of such a foolhardy act: "Oh, I wouldn't do that, sire!"

Not in the least worried, Nobody gently lifts the crown from Queen Elizabeth's head. The Queen, otherwise motionless, gasps as she feels the crown being taken away. Nobody gives the crown to one of the Queen's attendants and turns once more to address Hamlet.

Nobody: "Who is this woman now, before whom you love to bow?"

Hamlet: "Well, no matter what it seems, she will still say she's the Queen."

Nobody: "Without a crown with golden teeth?"

Hamlet: "Why certainly, 'tis her belief."

Nobody: "This belief, she wears it like a mask. So this gives me another task."

Again, she approaches Queen Elizabeth and gently removes the golden mask from her eyes, leaving her looking vulnerable and astonished. Again, the Queen gasps as if being robbed of her status and power.

Hamlet can't quite believe what he's seeing and in an aside to the audience, whispers: "This Nobody is quite insane, she'll cut his head and eat his brains!"

Nobody: "Your queen is stripped of power and glory
Who is she now in your Tudor story?"

Hamlet: "Why, looking simple, sad and sorry
This woman is just...ordinary."

Exactly. That's the very point Nobody wishes to emphasize. The denuded Queen looks out across the audience, dazed and confused.

"Who am I?" she asks, like a lost, innocence child.

Nobody seizes this opportunity to coach Hamlet on how transformation works.

Nobody: Hamlet, you have hit upon the truth
And now the Queen will give you living proof
Now anything can happen, you will see
How 'not to be' makes everybody free....

This is where things get surreal. Modern pop music with a hip-hop flavour starts to play and Nobody pulls Hamlet to one side as Mrs Shakespeare and Ophelia come onstage in tight, black, sexy leotards and perform a passable imitation of Beyoncé's *Single Ladies* dance routine. It's cool, it's slick, and it's unmistakeably twenty-first century, and therefore has absolutely nothing to do with Elizabethan England. Only Nobody could pull off a time-warp stunt like this.

The Queen remains under some kind of hypnotic spell, cast upon her by Nobody, and she is enchanted by these two women, watching their dance moves closely. She has forgotten all about her royal dignity and prudery. When the music suddenly stops, Elizabeth has only one thing in mind.

Elizabeth: What is this dancing that you do?

Can I learn to dance with you?

Mrs Shakespeare: Dear Madam, come and dance with us.

Ophelia: We'll show you how to shake your ass.

The music starts again and the Queen makes a hilarious sight, trying to dance like Beyoncé in her long royal robes. Here, the medium is the message. I'm not sure if Canadian philosopher Marshall McLuhan meant it this way, when he coined the famous expression back in the sixties, but what we're seeing is a visual illustration of what happens when we drop our attachment to a certain public image and let our energy freely express itself.

Just think for a moment: how many times have you felt an impulse to spontaneously express yourself by dancing, laughing, singing, jumping, being silly, maybe even hugging someone, but stopped yourself because of your reputation, your social image, your concern over what others may think?

For Elizabeth, the good times don't last long. After a few minutes, the music starts to fade and simultaneously the spell begins to wear off. The Queen is emerging from her trance and returning to her old self. Mrs Shakespeare and Ophelia look apprehensive.

Ophelia: Uh-oh, I think we're in trouble.

Mrs Shakespeare: Get ready to run.

Predictably, the Queen is outraged by the sight of these two skimpily clad female forms. Her next move is equally predictable:

"What is happening in my court? These women are naked! Off with their heads! Off with their heads!"

Mrs Shakespeare and Ophelia run off, pursued by the Queen and her attendants. Nobody, disappointed by this turn of events, watches her go, then shrugs his shoulders.

Nobody: "Of course, it doesn't always work.

That Elizabeth is such a stupid jerk!"

He turns to Hamlet:

"Now, Hamlet, think what I have said,

Take off *your* mask and lose *your* head!"

Hamlet is genuinely confused: "I have no mask! It's not on me."

Nobody laughs: "Oh yes, you have. You just can't see!"

Hamlet gets irritated: "You've gone quite mad; I'll say good day!

And this Nobody can go his way."

He starts to walk away, but Nobody catches him gently by the arm to prevent him. This is the moment of truth. If Hamlet can understand that he's wearing a false mask of personality, just like the Queen, he can achieve a breakthrough. But, since I don't want this play to become preachy, it needs to happen playfully.

Nobody: "Wait, spare a moment, let me ask,

This noble fellow *with no mask*,

This gloomy guy so filled with sadness

Who thinks that I am touched by madness.

Can you smile and sing and dance

If I give you half a chance?"

Hamlet: "Of course I can, if I so choose.

I've really nothing left to lose."

Nobody: "Then why be miserable and glum

When you can dance under the sun?"

Hamlet: "It isn't me who feels this way..."

He points at Will Shakespeare, sitting in his chair, scribbling away.

"...it's this bloody Bard who writes this play!"

Nobody seizes the opportunity presented by Hamlet's remark.

Nobody: "Come then, let's show this anti-fun guy

How they move it down in Mumbai!"

Cue for a Bollywood song and dance routine. The part of Nobody, as I've said before, is played by a young

189

Indian woman. She is a therapist by profession, but in her heart she's a dancer and a showgirl – she's been in all my musicals. So it's completely natural for her to boogie onstage, doing those cute-and-corny Bollywood moves that we've all seen in Hindi movies.

Hamlet watches her and does his best to follow, but can't get the hang of it. Eventually, he gives up.

Hamlet: "Stop! Stop! Enough! It's plain to see,

This Bollywood is not for me."

Nobody is disappointed. She folds her arms and looks at Hamlet in disgust.

"You're giving up because you're foreign?

Oh Hamlet, this is really boring!"

But she's in for a surprise.

Hamlet: "But I *can* dance, please have no fear,

He takes out a pair of sunglasses, puts then on and gives the audience a wide smile.

"Hi! My name's Psy... I'm from Korea!

Dressing classy, dancing cheesy

Gangnam Style is really easy!"

If there's one moment in the play which is really surprising and has the audience gasping in delight, it's this sudden transition from Hamlet to Psy. Born to Korean parents, all this actor has to do is put on a pair of sunglasses and start making those famous moves we've all seen on YouTube's record-breaking *Gangnam Style* video. Two billion people can't be wrong. The whole audience cracks up.

Hamlet leaps across the stage and drags me into the act, as well as Mrs Shakespeare and Ophelia, so when the music takes off, we move, all together, into Psy's cowboy dance routine. Pretty soon, I'm standing at the front of the stage with my legs apart, doing hip thrusts, while Hamlet is lying on the floor, poking his head through – another classic scene from the video. The song ends with enthusiastic applause from the audience.

Will Shakespeare staggers to the front of the stage, shakes his head, and exclaims, "My God, what in the name of Her Majesty is happening to my play? I will be thrown into the Tower of London and left to rot forever!"

An aside from the author: At this point in the play, I seriously considered having the Bard stand on his head, in the classic yoga position of sirsasana. *It would be a perfect metaphor for what is happening to him. But I gave up the idea for two reasons: first, it would take too long and second, at the age of sixty-seven, I can't guarantee I'd manage it.*

Instead, Will returns to his seat and continues writing. Meanwhile, Hamlet is beginning to realise that Nobody's peculiar but intriguing way of looking at life might be just the thing he needs to escape his gloomy destiny. He wants to know more.

Hamlet: "Okay Mr Nobody, I'm beginning to see things differently. But there's one thing I don't understand. What would I gain from becoming a *Not To Be*?"

Nobody: "Well, let's see...you wouldn't be the Prince of Denmark any more...so you wouldn't be obsessed with trying to avenge your father's death...so you wouldn't spend all your time thinking "to be or not to be" … *and* you wouldn't tell your beautiful girlfriend to get lost."

Hamlet: "Really?"

Nobody: "Really."

Hamlet: "How do I do it?"

Nobody: "Ah, that can be a *little* challenging. Come with me."

Here, we are approaching the crucial moment in the play when I try to show how people can escape from their own psychological limitations through meditation. Not an easy task, let me tell you, especially with the twin threats of sermonising and proselytising hanging over my head.

But Hamlet is ready to make the change and so, it turns out, is Ophelia. As Hamlet leaves with Nobody, she comes on stage with Mrs Shakespeare.

Ophelia: "Oh Mrs Shakespeare, it was wonderful being Lady Raga. But I don't want to imitate anybody else. I want to be me."

Mrs Shakespeare: "Really?"

Ophelia: "Really."

Mrs Shakespeare: "Really...*really*?"

Ophelia: "Yes really. I just want to be myself."

Mrs Shakespeare: "Well, that can be a *little* challenging. Come with me."

The stage is set for a visual presentation of spiritual transformation. Let's hope we don't fall flat on our faces.

CHAPTER 20

Prophecy, Politics and Power

First Witch
When shall we three meet again, in thunder,
lightning, or in rain?

Second Witch
When the hurlyburly's done, when the battle's lost
and won.

Third Witch
That will be ere the set of sun.

My version of *Macbeth* is short. So short, in fact, that I can guarantee it will be never performed onstage. Not surprising, really, because there is zero suspense and therefore nothing to grip the audience.

You will recall that Macbeth, who in the opening scene fought so valiantly for King Duncan on the battlefield, is walking home with Banquo when he encounters three witches on the heath, who greet him thus:

First Witch: "All hail, Macbeth! Hail to thee, Thane of Glamis!"

Second Witch: "All hail, Macbeth! Hail to thee, Thane of Cawdor!"

Third Witch: "All hail, Macbeth! Thou shalt be king hereafter!"

The prophecy has been made. Macbeth goes home and tells his wife, the notorious Lady Macbeth, and she eagerly feeds his ambitious dreams, helping him plot the murder of the king that very night as he sleeps in their castle.

But in my version of the play, in the middle of their plotting and scheming, Macbeth suddenly laughs, scoops up his wife in his arms, whirls her around and declares:

> *Such fools are we, to hatch a plot like this*
> *When we can be transported into bliss.*
> *For if the witches' prophecy be true*
> *There's really nothing left for us to do.*
> *It will happen by itself, you see,*
> *A murderer, I just don't need to be!*

Macbeth has a point. Either the prophecy is true, or it is not. If true, why should he do anything? Why should he try to make it happen? He can just relax, sip his favourite Scotch whiskey, eat a plate of haggis, listen to the mournful wailing of bagpipes on his castle wall and wait for events to overtake him.

No illusory daggers for Macbeth to clutch at, in his guilt and shame. No "Out damned spot!" for Lady Macbeth to scream at, in her madness and remorse. On the contrary, they can sit back and let it all unfold: King Duncan accidentally expires after choking on a bowl of Scott's Porridge Oats, Banquo suffers a fatal heart attack when Rangers beat Celtic, and the Macbeths are graciously invited to share Scotland's throne. End of story and curtain down.

But Will Shakespeare wasn't an idiot and he understood human nature. He knew that a certain human weakness called 'lust for power' lies as a dormant seed within each and every one of us. All it lacks is opportunity. If such an opportunity presents itself, the hunger for power awakens and consumes us – and anyone else who stands in its path. This is the human frailty he portrays in *Macbeth*.

A few hundred years after Shakespeare died, Lord Acton declared:

Power corrupts. Absolute power corrupts absolutely.

Osho disagreed with the noble aristocrat. Power does not corrupt, he explained to us on many occasions. The corruption already exists within us but, most of the time, lacks the opportunity to manifest. Possession of power simply allows whatever is unmanifest to show itself.

Historically speaking, Queen Elizabeth knew all about power, both as a victim and as a tyrant. For years, she lived as a helpless royal relative, in constant fear of execution by her elder sister, Mary Tudor. Then, after her sister's death, she clung to a shaky English throne by executing others.

The most serious threat to Elizabeth came from her Roman Catholic subjects. Her excommunication by the Pope in 1570 was a virtual invitation to all English

Catholics to try to overthrow her, so from that time onwards, after eleven years of religious tolerance at the beginning of her reign, the number of executions skyrocketed.

However, I do need to mention, just as an historical titbit, that the daughter's track record of beheading her English subjects came nowhere near her father's astonishing achievement. According to one contemporary chronicler, Henry VIII authorized no less than 72,000 executions during his thirty-eight-year reign. Other historians challenge this figure as excessive, but they generally agree Henry kept up a steady demand for sharp axe blades and necks on which to use them.

So now, as Elizabeth sweeps imperiously onto the stage and confronts William Shakespeare, it is perfectly in tune with her naturally suspicious and slightly paranoid nature that she feels something is amiss. Instinctively, she senses the rebellious atmosphere brewing among the players and intends to stomp on it without further ado.

"Master Shakespeare, we are not pleased with the way this play is progressing," she informs him.

Will sinks to one knee and bows his head. He's in an impossible situation, stretched to breaking point between Her Majesty's demand for tragedy and his wife's determination to do everything in her power to sabotage it.

"A thousand apologies, Your Majesty," he stutters.

"We have not yet seen enough suffering and death to call it a tragedy."

Will's cunning mind searches for an escape route. Smiling in a show of pathetic submissiveness to the Royal Presence, he stalls for time.

"Fear not, Your Majesty..."

Fear not? He's the one filled with fear, quaking in his boots under the Queen's fierce stare. Like a drowning man clutching at straws, he offers a feeble explanation:

"I'm... er... I'm planning a surprise. The play will seem to be heading in the direction of happiness, but, at the very end, I shall kill them all, I swear it!"

Her Majesty is mollified, up to a point, but there's a sting in her tail.

"Very well. See that it is done..." her tone becomes more menacing... "or I promise you, thine head shall be impaled on a stake before the Tower of London!"

Just what a desperate playwright needs to hear.

"Oh no! I mean... oh *yes*, Your Majesty." He bows low with grovelling humility as the Queen strides away, then returns to his chair to write the ending she commands. The time for hesitation is past. From now on, no more Mister Nice Guy. The Bard is about to become the executioner of his own characters.

CHAPTER 21

Good Thoughts, Bad Thoughts

Meanwhile, the rebellion continues. Two chairs are brought to the middle of the stage and placed facing the audience. Nobody brings Hamlet and indicates he should sit on one chair. Mrs Shakespeare brings Ophelia and asks her to sit in the other. Then Nobody and Mrs Shakespeare explain the basic guidelines for this exercise, in which they will help Hamlet and Ophelia free themselves from their identities.

"*Not To Be* requires an empty mind," says Nobody.

"A clear and quiet head," confirms Mrs Shakespeare.

Pointing to herself and to the Bard's wife, Nobody continues, "We will represent your thoughts."

"When a thought enters your head, we will speak it for you," adds Mrs Shakespeare.

"In this way, you will become aware of your own thoughts," continues Nobody.

"And most important, you will become aware of the silence *behind* your thoughts," instructs Will's wife.

Nobody concludes, "In that silence you will discover the *Land of Not to Be*."

Okay, so let me review the build-up so far, just to prevent any misunderstanding. Onstage it's pretty clear, but in print it might seem a little confusing.

Ophelia is desperate to break out of her role as the fated, rejected lover of Hamlet. She tasted liberation as Lady Raga and now wants more. Hamlet is less certain what he wants, but after a wild dance routine as Psy in *Gangnam Style*, he realizes he's missing out on life.

From a meditator's perspective, they're both in the situation of a spiritual seeker who realizes he is trapped in his personality and wants out. Perhaps I should add, here, that relatively few people ever come to this point. Most people are more or less satisfied with who they are – or at least pretend to be.

Many mystics have insisted that you cannot experience yourself as pure consciousness while you're identified with your personality. Why? Because your personality is your outermost layer, while consciousness is your innermost centre. If you're glued to the outside edge of a circle, you can't go in to the middle.

Let's take a look, for a moment, at the common British expression "Who the hell do you think you are?" We use it to address someone who is being arrogant. But, in reality, this saying applies to all of us. Thinking creates who we are. It's our ideas about ourselves that create personality and, of course, we've been collecting these ideas ever since we were born, so there's going to be lots of them.

So, how do we free ourselves from all this? According to Bodhidharma, the first patriarch of Zen, we do it by "beholding the mind". According to Gautama

Buddha, we do it by "self-remembering". According to Osho, we do it by "witnessing" learning to watch our own thoughts. In fact, all three mystics are saying the same thing, using different expressions to describe the same process.

As soon as we become aware of a thought, it loses its grip on us. For example, Ophelia feels hurt that Hamlet has dumped her. But if she becomes *aware* she is hurt, a distance opens up between herself and her emotion. Through this distance, she may come to realise that she is not the emotion. She will still feel the pain, but it won't totally consume her.

I'm not saying this is easy. Not at all. Most probably, when you've just been dumped by your boyfriend, you want to kill him, or jump off a cliff, or post nasty remarks on *Facebook* about his new girlfriend. The last thing you want to do is sit down, close your eyes, meditate and realise that you're not your emotions.

This is hard work. It's not like instant coffee. Most people don't have the time for it, nor the dedication needed to patiently explore their inner world. But, like it or not, that's the name of the meditation game and that's what I'm trying to convey in this scene.

One more thing: over time, when you meditate, a kind of flexibility is gained. You're not so controlled by your personality. You become more authentic, more real, because your way of thinking arises from a deeper source within you. That's the payoff.

"Close your eyes. Let us begin," says Mrs Shakespeare. She and Nobody then crouch down behind the chairs on which Hamlet and Ophelia are sitting. Mrs

Shakespeare hides behind Ophelia, Nobody is behind Hamlet. When a thought enters Hamlet's head, Nobody will jump up and speak it aloud. The same goes for Mrs Shakespeare and Ophelia.

Nobody goes first. She stands up, cups her ear to listen to what's going on inside Hamlet's head and declares: "This is easy... oh no, that's a thought!" His thought vanishes and she ducks down.

Mrs Shakespeare stands up, listens to the chatter inside Ophelia's head and announces: "I just want to be myself." Puzzled, Mrs Shakespeare remains standing, turns to look at Nobody and asks: "Is this a thought?"

Nobody stands up, surprised at the question: "Of course it is!"

"But it's such a nice thought," objects Mrs Shakespeare, not ready to let it go.

Nobody shakes her head impatiently: "Nice thoughts... nasty thoughts... they all have to go!"

Mrs Shakespeare shrugs. "Oh well... bye-bye nice thought!" she says and they both duck down behind the chairs.

Now here's a thought: many people who meditate make a distinction between good thoughts and bad thoughts. Indeed, the whole American philosophy of 'positive thinking' is based on the idea that spirituality can be cultivated by disposing of negative thoughts and emphasising positive ones.

Naturally, being America, this pop philosophy found its way into a song and in 1944 Bing Crosby and the Andrews Sisters topped the charts with their call to 'Ac-Cent-Tchu-Ate the Positive' and thereby eliminate negative thinking.

To an experienced meditator, this approach is childish, because meditation has nothing to do with good and bad. It's a method of dis-identifying with the mind *in its totality*, regardless of content. So meditators are neither moral nor immoral people. They go beyond the duality.

Nobody rises from behind Hamlet's chair, picking up a thought: "I'm hungry!" she declares, rubbing her stomach, then ducks down.

Mrs Shakespeare rises, speaks for Ophelia and announces: "I'm thirsty!"

Thoughts follow in rapid succession:

Nobody: "I'm restless."

Mrs Shakespeare: "I'm sad."

Nobody: "To be or not to be? Oh, not again!"

Then Ophelia sinks a little deeper, into her heart, and Mrs Shakespeare echoes a poignant thought arising from this sweet young woman's breast: "I wonder if Hamlet still loves me?"

Hamlet's mind, on the other hand, is straying in a slightly different direction, which Nobody picks up.

Nobody: "I wonder what Ophelia looks like in the shower?" She interrupts the action by looking at Mrs Shakespeare and exclaiming, "Now there's an interesting thought!"

Mrs Shakespeare is uncomfortable with this unexpected turn of events. Standing up, she looks indignantly at Nobody and protests, "Hey, keep your mind on your job, *Mister Not to Be!*"

Nobody doesn't mind the rebuke. She's more interested in what's going on inside Hamlet's head.

"Well, it's the first time he's actually expressed interest in her," she explains.

Mrs Shakespeare leaves her post and comes to stand behind Hamlet. Giving the audience her very best, deeply ironic smile, she places her two hands gently on Hamlet's head and declares "Isn't the male mind wonderful? If it's not drowning women in lakes, it's gazing at them under the shower."

This produces a big laugh from the audience, especially from the women. But then Nobody raises a hand to interrupt her.

"Wait... Listen! Listen!"

"What do you hear?" asks Mrs Shakespeare.

With a big smile, as if announcing the winner of the National Lottery, Nobody gestures towards the sitting couple and says, "Nothing!"

Mrs Shakespeare was so caught up in her feminist view of male psychology that she forgot, temporarily, the purpose of the exercise. Now she realises just how successful it's been. Joining Nobody in her delight, she looks at Hamlet and Ophelia, who are both still sitting with eyes closed, and exclaims in triumph to the audience, "Oh my God, they've done it. They've stopped thinking!"

Nobody and Mrs Shakespeare turn towards each other, each raising a finger to her lips and softly hissing: "Sssshhhhh!" Then, joining the lovers in this unexpected moment of deep meditation, they both close their eyes and stand in silence behind Hamlet and Ophelia.

There is the long dramatic pause. Meditation has dawned and all four minds are quiet. The gateway to the Beyond has opened.

I'm not sure if this has ever been done onstage before, although variations have manifested in several movies, most notably in the 1954 Japanese epic, *The Seven Samurai*, and more recently in *The Last Samurai*, where Tom Cruise, as US Army Captain Nathan Algren, is seen training as a samurai in a remote mountain village. Tom keeps getting beaten in mock fights until a friendly warrior tells him he has 'too many minds' and needs a quick dose of 'no mind' if he is to be victorious.

Stretching his modest acting abilities to the maximum, Tom closes his eyes for a second and then, presumably with a blank space between his ears, charges at his foe. Presto! His combat skills acquire an extra edge and he earns an honourable draw in the contest.

Oh, Tom, if only it was that easy....

As any experienced meditator knows, it's difficult to remain in the space of no-mind for more than a few seconds. Sooner or later, a thought is going to arise that will grab your attention and carry you off.

In my play, it's Mrs Shakespeare who cracks first. Opening her eyes and looking slightly vacant, as if trying to remember something important, she gently bites on one of her fingers and ponders, "I wonder if I left my cooking pot on the stove?"

Mind is like that. It keeps throwing thoughts at you until eventually one catches your interest and you start chewing on it.

Nobody rolls her eyes in frustration. "Oy vey! Now *you're* thinking!" she protests.

But Mrs Shakespeare refuses to be embarrassed so easily and quickly retorts, "Well, now *you're* thinking about me thinking."

This kind of spiritual one-upmanship can continue indefinitely, with characters accusing each other of thinking about them thinking about them thinking....

But Nobody has noticed Ophelia is slowly opening her eyes. He raises a hand to stop their little tiff.

"Wait! She's going to say something," she informs Mr Shakespeare, pointing towards Ophelia.

What words of wisdom will be uttered by this young vision of loveliness, now that she been to no-mind and back? Will she reject Hamlet? Will she still be hooked? What does the future hold for these sweet young people?

We will know soon enough. But first, a few words about the state of meditation from which she is emerging. Quantum physics would probably consider it to be similar to the Zero Point Field Theory, which asserts that even when there are no particles present in a given field, some kind of wave-like energy still persists.

In other words, even when there is nothing, there is something. Likewise with consciousness: even when there are no thoughts, there is something we might describe as...*the great nothing*.

CHAPTER 22
The Great Nothing

Here's the skinny, the bottom line, on how we experience our inner world:

Nothing happens.

On the outside, everything is continuously changing. Even mountains are changing, eroding slowly over time; even suns and galaxies are born, grow old and die. But on the inside, nothing ever happens.

To better understand this phenomenon, we must take a short break from the dramatic action and examine our relationship with nothingness. Or, as writer Ernest Hemingway would have said, after introducing the Spanish term into the American language, *Nada.*

Hemingway took it negatively and felt that the universe is indifferent to us. He used the idea of *nada* to illustrate man's struggle in a life where God is absent and existence is at best neutral and at worst downright hostile towards human beings.

In protest, he spoofed the Lord's Prayer thus: *'Our nada who art in nada, nada be thy name, thy kingdom nada....'* It was a tribute to the author's nihilistic and accidental view of the universe.

John-Paul Sartre and the Existentialists of the 1950s struggled with the idea of nothingness. On the one hand, it was attractive because it freed man's consciousness from the grip of divine will and pre-determination. But, at the same time, it made everything meaningless. Unlike Hemingway, however, Sartre declined to blow his brains out as an existential solution to this philosophical problem.

Hemmingway and Sartre are not exceptions. Generally speaking, nothingness has been given a bad rap in Western culture. Why? Because people are afraid of it. It implies an absence of meaning, morality and value in our lives...scary stuff.

Here, one might be tempted to make an exception of the Nihilists, a movement born in the nineteenth century and popularized by Russian novelist Ivan Turgenev, which rejected all authority, especially that of the Tsar and the Eastern Orthodox Church. But Nihilism wanted to demolish Russia's revered social icons only to replace them with new ideals, such as the liberation and education of the masses.

This, by the way, made the assassination of Tsar Alexander II by a group of Nihilists in 1881 both unfair and unfortunate. Unfair, because he was the man who, in 1861, had emancipated the serfs, ending feudalism in Russia; unfortunate because his death triggered a repressive backlash in which his plans for a modern, democratically-elected parliamentary assembly came to...umm...nothing.

Postmodernism, arising in the late twentieth century, also embraced Nihilism, deconstructing fixed attitudes or beliefs in recognition of a world seen to be in a state of perpetual flux and incompleteness. But, again, it ended up with *something*, rather than *nothing*, a new *something* that was ever-changing, but *something* nevertheless.

The greatest children's story ever written – ignoring Harry Potter and leaving aside my personal favourites, Rupert Bear and Winnie the Pooh – is the epic German fantasy novel by Michael Ende called *The Neverending Story*.

The tale takes place in a fabulous world called Fantastica, which is being destroyed by a mysterious force. This terrible, unstoppable force eats up all the beautiful, strange and wonderful characters of Fantastica, who can only be rescued by a human child participating in the story.

And what, one may ask, is the name Michael Ende gives to this dark force? *The Nothing*. This provides us with an intriguing insight into the writer's mind. It seems that nothingness is regarded by Ende as the ultimate threat, the destructive opposite of creative fantasy and imagination.

In the tale itself, *The Nothing* is explained as the effect of all the lies humans tell in their greed for power, but I happen to know Ende really was afraid of nothingness. Late in life, he told a friend of mine – just back from India – that he felt Europeans should stick to Western methods of meditation and not experiment with Eastern techniques.

Carl Gustav Jung, one of the founders of modern psychology, said more or less the same thing after his own trip to India in 1937, where he studied Hinduism and became greatly interested in Ramana Maharshi, an enlightened mystic who, at the time, was living on Mount Arunachala in South India.

Jung described Ramana as 'something quite phenomenal' and a 'true son of the Indian earth' who had 'struggled earnestly all his life to extinguish his ego'. But Jung shied away from meeting the man, fearing his own understanding of the human psyche would be shaken if he encountered Ramana personally. He also advised Westerners against dabbling in yoga and other Eastern methods of meditation.

What was the fear? The basic difference between East and West is that the Western approach to spirituality is a form of contemplation, or prayer, and thus remains within the realm of intellectual thought. Western philosophy does the same. Renee Descartes, the seventeenth century Frenchman who is regarded as 'the father of modern philosophy', summed it up in his famous declaration: "I think therefore I am."

About 300 years later, my philosophy professors at Bristol arrogantly informed me they had improved on Descartes. All that can really be said, they argued, is: "There is a thought." You cannot rationally infer "I am" from the thinking process.

However, if Gautama Buddha had been passing through Bristol at the time, he might have asked them "How do you know? How do you know there is a thought? There must be a deeper sense of 'amness' that is aware of the thought, otherwise you wouldn't be able to say even this much."

Siddhartha is right. Consciousness precedes cognition.

Western philosophy stops here, because it depends on thought for its existence. No thought, no philosophy. Of course, some academic who enjoys playing mind games can write a book titled *The Philosophy of No Thinking* (I can even be accused of doing this myself), but make no mistake, the author of such a book is only thinking about not thinking. He isn't *not thinking*. If he's not thinking, he's not a philosopher. He's a meditator.

Eastern meditation embraces no thought, or nothingness, and that's what Descartes didn't get, and both Jung and Ende didn't want to know. None of them understood that, in reality, all things – from children's stories to the human mind to the universe itself – arise from the creative womb of no-thing, or nothingness. They couldn't fathom the paradox that you can't have *something* without *nothing*. They didn't realize the two go together.

Shakespeare seemed to be heading in the right direction when he gave one of his comedies the title *Much Ado About Nothing*. But the 'merry war' between Beatrice and Benedict – the play's central theme – derives its humour from romantic mischief and misunderstanding, not mysticism.

The Bard does, however, enrich his comedy with a neat word-play that embraces handwritten notes, musical notes and nothingness all in one breath:

Balthasar: "Note this before my notes: There's not a note of mine that's worth the noting."

Don Pedro: "Why, these are very crotchets that he speaks – Note notes, forsooth, and nothing!"

Returning to our twenty-first century, Eckhart Tolle, spiritual teacher and best-selling author of *The Power of Now*, encourages people to explore the gaps between their thoughts. That's how you can plug into what Tolle calls 'space consciousness' – a fancy name for nothingness.

To most of us, such practices seem unappealing because all you find is...well...*nothing*. Faced with this inner void, many people prefer the conventional approach to spirituality offered by mainstream religions, which all agree on one thing: It is better to offer people any kind of divine *something*: salvation, redemption, transubstantiation, reincarnation, rather than tell them to face their inner emptiness.

Anything rather than nothing seems to be the underlying attitude. The fact that all of these religious *somethings* are worth absolutely nothing doesn't seem to worry most people.

For those brave souls who do have the courage to explore their inner nothingness, there is good news: if you go deep enough, you will experience another awesome paradox:

"This nothingness is not negative," explained Osho, while discussing the Big Zero that lies within us all. "Just a little more acquaintance with it and you will be surprised, you start feeling an immense fulfilment and overflowing energy.

"Nothingness is your very nature," he added. "Out of this nothingness arises everything, and into this nothingness dissolves everything. If you can return to nothingness consciously you have found the source. That's what I call meditation."

For scientists, confronted with nothing, there is a disturbing new hypothesis with which they need to wrestle: If *nothingness* is the absolute substratum of all things, then the formation of star systems and, indeed, the so-called creation itself, are just small, temporary manifestations of *somethingness,* twirling, pirouetting and boogying in an endless dance of birth, life, death and rebirth within the context of an infinite and eternal *nothingness*.

In this context, the 'Big Bang' turns out to be a little bang that was preceded by many other bangs as the unmanifest became manifest, hung around for a while, then disappeared back into the womb of nothingness once more.

For theologians, it's pretty much the end of the trail. How can you make a religion out of nothing? Unless, of course, you publish a completely empty tome called *The Holy Book of Nothing*, create a divine trinity of *Nothingness*, *Emptiness* and *Space Consciousness*, then add a messiah-like figure called *Zero the Nonbeing*, who, out of compassion, came out of *nothing* and briefly took form as *something* in order to redeem us…

Hmm, maybe it could work, after all!

And what about the rest of us humans? Shall I tell you the truth? *Tat Tvam Asi…that art thou.* The ancient seers of the Vedas knew their stuff when they declared that *you are it*. When everything you think you are has disappeared, only space consciousness remains…and hey, guess what? That's you.

So, to Ernest Hemingway, Jean Paul Sartre, Michael Ende and Carl Jung, I need to say: bite the bullet, guys, and face it. Like it or not, you are *The Nothing*.

Nothing and non-doing go hand in hand. It's only when you're doing nothing, *not even thinking about doing nothing*, that space consciousness manifests itself and the sound of one hand clapping deafens your inner eardrums.

Even when you sit down to 'do' meditation, you're off-base, which poses a tricky problem for mystics who want to encourage others to experience the inner world. Every meditation technique, however subtle, is a kind of effort, a kind of doing, so, how to give people a taste of no-mind?

Osho hit on the idea of using opposite extremes. He encouraged people to be vigorously active in the first half of a meditation, then relax and let go all effort in the second half. The principle was simple: intense activity creates the opportunity for its polar opposite, non-doing, to arise naturally.

"Doing cannot lead to being…."

I remember some New Age guru uttering this apparently wise statement. But it's not the whole truth, because if you exhaust yourself through doing, you have a better chance of relaxing into being. However, I do need to point out that 'doing' is a modern disease and that's why active meditations are necessary. We are so busy, so mentally stressed, so physically tense, that we need to 'overdo' and release all this pent-up pressure before we can relax.

It wasn't always so, especially in India. This place got its reputation for being a country full of bone-lazy people because, for centuries and centuries, non-doing and meditation were embraced and respected as a way of life.

This reminds me of a story concerning the first railroad track ever to be laid in India, sometime towards the end of the nineteenth century. A gang of local labourers was working hard, laying track, under the supervision of a British engineer.

Every day, a young Indian man, dressed only in a simple *lunghi* or sarong, would come and sit under a nearby tree and watch the work as it progressed.

The engineer noticed the young man's regular appearance at his viewing spot and eventually became curious. One day, he walked over to the tree and asked the young man, "What are you doing here?"

"Nothing," he replied.

The engineer snorted his disapproval. "You should come and work for me," he advised.

"How would that benefit me?" the young man enquired.

"Well, if you work hard, you will soon be able to earn a considerable sum of money," the engineer explained.

"And what would I do with this money?" asked the young man.

"When you have saved enough money, you will be able to relax and enjoy life," said the engineer.

The young man laughed and shook his head, saying "But I'm relaxed and enjoying now!"

I don't know if this incident really happened, but it nicely enshrines the old India and its lifestyle, contrasted with modern Western values. Of course, it's all changing now. You walk along a street in Bengaluru (Bangalore) today and you think you're in New York City – the hustle is infectious and you can sense the urgent, hungry feeling that money is just waiting to be made in India's software capital. And remember, time is money!

That's not how it used to be. The lingering atmosphere of a subcontinent awash with idleness was still present when I landed at Mumbai airport in 1976. Everything was slower, less important. Time stretched forever, forwards and backwards both....

You wish to be rich? Hey Ram! If God so wills, one day it may happen. If not in this life, maybe in the next....

The taxi that conveyed me from the airport to the train station was old and rusty. Its AC wasn't working. When we turned off the highway, traffic consisted mostly of bullock carts, bicycles and lots and lots of people walking on foot. Nobody seemed to be in a hurry.

When I got to the station, families were sitting on the ground in the entrance hall, eating from their lunch boxes, their packages spread out around them, as if their trains were days away from departure. When I got to the counter, the ticket seller had gone for chai, but anyway it wasn't a problem because my train was an hour late. And, more important than any of these separate incidents: *none of it seemed to matter*.

Getting something done could be terribly frustrating, but only until you realized it didn't need doing in the first place. For example, trying to find an electrician to fix a wall socket in my rented Pune apartment drove me nuts, until I gave up trying to fix it. Later, when it was finally fixed, it looked worse than before.

Indians hate to be reminded of those days, when any kind of service was simply lousy. That's why Prince Philip, England's favourite racist, caused such a stink in 1999 when he looked at a scrambled mass of wires in a fuse box, while touring some factory, and commented, "It looks as though it was put in by an Indian."

Hey Ram! I never thought I'd agree with old Phil about anything, but we are both nostalgic for a bygone era of sub-continental ineptitude and indolence. It's far from politically correct, I agree, but it contains a great secret, now in danger of being lost forever.

Oh, the peace that comes with non-doing! I remember one warm and sunny morning, sitting for hours on a tree stump in a run-down park in Pune called 'Empress Gardens' named after the late, great Queen Victoria.

At first I was restless, waiting for a friend who hadn't showed up, but slowly, slowly, the atmosphere of non-doing got to me. Little by little, I understood the real reason why I'd come to Empress Gardens. Not to meet anyone. Not to do anything. Not to think about anything. No, I'd come to be seduced by an ancient, invisible, underlying atmosphere of nothingness that was permeating the very air I was breathing.

I stopped looking at my watch. I stopped fidgeting and somehow, for a while, I even stopped thinking.

Pretty soon, I was listening in awe to the silence, feeling the stillness in my bones, gratefully sensing the relief and relaxation in my heart. Nothing was happening, inside or out. No motors running, no car horns blaring, no radios playing, no ring-tones chiming, no machine tools hammering...nothing. Even the occasional birdsong only served to deepen the silence in which each sweet note arose and disappeared.

Here, I understood, was the doorway to a different world in which nobody needed to do anything. Here, time stopped. Here, the most to which one might aspire, after several hours of inactivity, would be to rise slowly to one's feet and stroll to a local street stall in search of a delicious, sugar-saturated cup of chai.

Here, and only here, in this precious space, might one bow down in awe to those compassionate mystics who, not content to remain in their blissful silence, tried to make the deaf hear, the blind see, the sleeping humanity awaken...no task for the faint-hearted.

In any case, on that April morning in Empress Gardens, it was way too hot to do anything. When you pass through the hot season in India, you understand how a culture of non-doing is born.

Perhaps it's just as well that meditation didn't become popular in the United States back in the fifties, when the Un-American Activities Committee of Congress was busy rooting out communists and other social deviants. Meditation is neither communist nor anti-communist, but it is, essentially, un-American.

Why? Because Americans are great doers. All their cultural icons, from Superman to Batman, from Dirty Harry to John McClane, are action heroes. The whole nation is hooked on hyperactivity...doing something, getting somewhere, *making it happen.*

Let us reflect on John F. Kennedy's famous utterance: "My fellow Americans, ask not what your country can do for you. Ask what you can do for your country." Either way, it's the 'doing' that's important, right, Jack?

JFK certainly practiced what he preached. He was a hyperactive president, always on the go. When he wasn't busy 'doing' government business, he was busy 'doing' nineteen-year-old White House intern Mimi Alford and many other women who willingly lined up and lay down for 'Jack the Zipper'.

Now, for a moment, stop and think of all the labour-saving devices that have been invented in the United States since the 1950s. You'd expect, by now, that everyone would be on permanent holiday – nobody would need to do anything. But no. Paradoxically, introducing faster and more efficient technology has made us faster, too, as if we must run to keep up with our own innovations, becoming ever more busy and stressed.

And none of it has helped us become richer. If you believe the statistics, a middle-income couple who are both working today generate no greater wealth, in real terms, than in those unliberated days when the wife kept house and the guy earned the bread. *Hey Ram!* That's progress.

Meditation is the exact opposite of this all-American attitude. It is the art of enjoying inactivity, of relaxing into *that which is* – unhooked from the idealism of *becoming*. It is feeling so at ease with life that you naturally and effortlessly sink deeper and deeper into yourself, coming closer and closer to the core...and there, and there alone, you find the fulfilment you have been seeking in a thousand different ways elsewhere.

In short, it is a revolution, a 180-degree turn. And it is a revolution whose time has come.

Chai, anyone?

CHAPTER 23

Happy Ever After

This is the moment. Now is the hour. Hamlet and Ophelia are free. They have experienced the silence behind their thoughts. They have entered the land of *Not To Be*. They have dived into the inner ocean and returned.

Practically speaking, this is a bit of a stretch. To have such deep experiences, spiritual seekers sometimes need to meditate for as long as thirty years, maybe even several lifetimes. Theatrically speaking, however, we need to do the job in a few minutes. After all, you can't stop the show and tell the audience: "Come back in a couple of decades and we'll show you what happens next."

Nobody and Mrs Shakespeare stand waiting behind the lovers. What will happen now? What will be their response, now that they understand they are no longer confined within the limitations of their former attitudes?

Slowly, Ophelia opens her eyes and turns her lovely head towards the man she loves.

"Hamlet," she says softly, "you still love me, don't you?"

Hamlet slowly opens his eyes, now fresh with innocence, and turns to look at Ophelia.

He smiles. "Yes, I do," he replies gently.

Ophelia's heart bursts with joy and her face becomes radiant as the secret hope she has been nursing for so long comes true at last. As a theatrical aside, I must add that this scene is greatly assisted by the fact that Ophelia and Hamlet are lovers in real life, so Ophelia has no trouble at all showing her love for this man. It overflows like a fountain from her heart.

"I knew it!" she cries, in relief and happiness.

The first notes of a beautiful song begin to play and Hamlet rises from his seat, turns towards Ophelia, bows slightly and enquires, "Shall we dance?"

"I'd love to," she replies.

The song to which they dance is original. I wrote the lyrics and a friend added the music. It's titled *A Country Far Away* and the opening lines go like this:

> *There is a country far away,*
> *There is a land, far away and lost.*
> *There is a healing, there is a feeling,*
> *There is a country, a country of the heart...*

Who says I'm not an incurable romantic? I recorded the song last year with a woman from Taiwan who has a fabulous voice and many other showbiz talents. She's the only person I've ever seen tap-dancing in the Pune ashram and she puts Fred Astaire to shame.

However, the way Hamlet and Ophelia dance is formal, Elizabethan-style. There's lots of ritualistic parting and coming together, with little body contact. Nevertheless, it's an opportunity for them to show the deep affection flowing between them, now all obstacles have been removed. It's a metaphor for making love.

Touched by this romantic scene, Mrs Shakespeare skips lightly across the stage, grabs her husband by the hand and invites him to dance. He tries to refuse, not wishing to indulge in such feel-good trivia, but he's no match for her persuasiveness. Gently, she brings Will to his feet and soon they are dancing together, adding to the harmonious atmosphere.

By the way, I do need to add a word of caution here, lest those romantics among you start thinking that meditation is a sure-fire recipe for solving relationship problems and guaranteeing blissful reunions.

Not exactly. You see, it all depends on what kind of authentic feelings you discover inside yourself, beneath the superficial layers. For example, Ophelia may have opened her eyes, looked at Hamlet and said, "I understand now that you're not the man for me. Goodbye and thank you."

You never know. At this stage in the play, however, it looks like Hamlet and Ophelia are heading towards a happy ending. So let's hit the theatrical pause button for a moment and take a deeper look at the mystery called 'love'.

To be blessed by the love of a woman and to make her feel loved in return is one of the sweetest experiences available to the male species. It's a kind of magic that descends when two people open their hearts, allowing themselves to merge and complete each other.

Life acquires new meaning, new significance, thanks to this person holding your hand, gazing in your eyes, lying next to you at night. You can't get enough of each other and non-essentials like eating food, going to work, paying bills and staying in touch with the rest of humanity just fade into the background.

The experience of love is real – I want to make this clear. But, at the same time, biology and society are boosting the experience to dangerous heights, rather like a bull run on the stock market that gets out of control and everyone starts thinking they're going to get richer and richer forever and ever.

Opium-like chemicals, such as serotonin and dopamine, begin to flood the brain, stimulating the pleasure centre and suppressing our ability to think clearly. At the same time, Hollywood is pumping out a steady stream of fairy stories convincing us that...yes, true love can last a lifetime.

When the dream breaks, as one day it must, it's going to hurt – big time. That's why, when I walked into a shop in Mill Valley, California, with a new girlfriend in the first flush of a love affair, the thirty-something female sales assistant took one look at us, exclaimed "Oh my God, you're in love!" She put two fingers together in the sign of a cross in front of her, as if warding off evil spirits. She knew the pain that would follow...and she was right.

But, for me, that's no reason to avoid love. We just need to be strong enough to take the hit when it comes and to remember, as we roll around in agony on the floor, holding our stomachs to numb the aching void inside, that it's going to pass.

We just need courage enough, afterwards, to walk into those familiar places, a favourite coffee shop, perhaps, or an organic food store where we used to spend time together, and now, as we walk in through the door alone, we suddenly feel the vacuum caused by the absence of the lover, almost as if somebody has torn away one of our limbs, with no hope of reconstructive surgery.

It's because love affairs end mostly in suffering that we tend to think there's something wrong and blame the other partner, but, in fact, it's often the case that nobody's at fault.

"The very nature of relationship is that it turns sour at a certain point," commented Osho, in one of his many discourses on the subject. "Both partners feel frustrated and both try to throw the responsibility on the other, so that instead of love, fighting becomes their only relationship.

"The problem is that the man or the woman goes on clinging even though everything is going towards hell," he added. "It is better to be miserable, but with somebody, than to be lonely, because when you are lonely you have to face yourself."

Now, you may think a spiritual seeker devoted to meditation has no time to waste in love relationships. But you are wrong – at least as far as Osho's sannyasins are concerned. In fact, Osho himself encouraged it.

This makes him an exception to an ancient spiritual rule: keep the sexes apart. Historically speaking, mystics, monks and meditators have given sex, love and women a bum rap and run away from all three, hiding in monasteries, ashrams, or caves in the Himalayas. Not without reason. They found introspection impossible in a world filled with temptation.

Osho took the opposite view: get lost in temptation deeply enough, often enough, and you'll understand its impermanence – none of it lasts. Then you might look for something more timeless and eternal.

I love his critique of Gautama Buddha's instruction to his *bhikkhus* not to look at women: "If it had been me," said Osho, "I'd have given them a magnifying glass." In other words, don't look away, because that will only activate your imagination and sexual desire more strongly. Rather, look more closely. Then you'll see the imperfections, the pimples, make-up, hair dye, Botox lips, plucked eyebrows…in short, the transient nature of physical beauty and the fleeting nature of attraction.

Here, for a moment, Shakespeare and Osho see eye to eye. One of Will's most famous sonnets, dedicated to his mysterious 'Dark Lady' mistress, is a deliberate spoof of classical romantic poetry. In the romantic tradition, metaphors drawn from nature's splendour were used to praise the beauty of a certain woman, but instead the Bard drew on them to mark his mistress's ordinariness the Bard's point being that he loved her anyway:

> *My mistress' eyes are nothing like the sun;*
> *Coral is far more red than her lips' red;*

If snow be white, why then her breasts are dun;
If hairs be wires, black wires grow on her head.
I have seen roses damask'd, red and white,
But no such roses see I in her cheeks;
And in some perfumes is there more delight
Than in the breath that from my mistress reeks....

For centuries, the identity of the 'Dark Lady' has remained a source of intense literary speculation, but an historical detective recently identified her as Aline Florio, the faithless wife of an Italian translator, working in London. When the real woman is exposed, the 'Dark Lady' fantasy simply evaporates, which proves what I'm saying: the plain facts of love are less interesting than the air of mystery and romance that traditionally surrounds them.

However, it needs a lot of intelligence to give up the search for a soul mate, even in old age, when a man's testosterone levels are sinking faster than real estate prices in a subprime mortgage crisis.

One has only to see a movie like *Last Chance Harvey* to understand our longing for togetherness. As the storyline develops, we watch in hopeful suspense as a burned-out American advertising executive called Harvey Shine, played by seventy-two-year-old Dustin Hoffman, seeks a fresh start in the company of disillusioned British airport employee Kate Walker, played by fifty-year-old Emma Thompson.

Oozing talent, Hoffman and Thompson manage to pull off this otherwise corny romance, although judging by Harvey Shine's chronic heart condition, his new-found love will soon find herself in the role of nursemaid and caretaker, rather than a lover who enjoys walking around London with him.

We all know how difficult it is to be alone. Classic serial marriage addicts like movie actress Elizabeth Taylor have made the record books, but it's not just a girl thing. The personal lives of Tom Cruise, Paul McCartney and John Cleese all demonstrate – if proof were needed – how men, as well as women, can't really cope unless they have someone to 'be there' for them.

As I mentioned earlier, biochemistry doesn't help and it's not just the dopamine and serotonin that's to blame. There's evidence now that real merger occurs. Maybe this is the source from which we get the notion of a 'soul mate'. Researchers at the University of Virginia, studying MRI brain scans, recently announced that lovers become entwined at a neural level. "It's essentially a breakdown of self and other; our self comes to include the people we become close to," stated one brain researcher. No wonder it hurts when the times comes for two of these "neurally-entwined soul mates" to separate.

But it is churlish of me to dwell on such unfriendly realities. This is no time for bad news. This is a time for love. So, let us forget about such sobering and chilly truths as aloneness, meditation and the transient nature of human relationships. Let us rather melt with warm-hearted empathy as a young couple dance on stage to a romantic song:

There is a country far away,

There is a land far away and lost...

Ophelia is in love with Hamlet, and he with her. In this moment, time stops. The past has dropped away. The future does not exist. In this moment, they are one.

Can their love survive the stormy seas ahead? What about Queen Elizabeth's demand for a tragic ending? What about Will Shakespeare's determination to avoid having his head removed from his shoulders? How can all of this be reconciled?

In this moment of exquisite, romantic happiness... who cares?

CHAPTER 24

In the Name of the Father

Hamlet's Father's Ghost:
If thou didst ever thy dear father love,
Revenge his foul and most unnatural murder.
Hamlet:
Thy commandment all alone shall live,
Within the book and volume of my brain.

You must excuse me for returning to the subject of Elsinore's kingly ghost, but I cannot forgive Hamlet for being so spineless. He behaved as if he was nothing more than an extension of his father's ego. His father wanted revenge but, being somewhat handicapped as an insubstantial phantom, he ordered his son to do the job.

Still, the old man could have had a go at it himself. After all, if he could appear before his son and before the ordinary soldiers in the castle, why could he not appear in front of his brother, King Claudius? Why could he not torture the new king every night with his ghostly presence? Why couldn't he stand in front of his former wife, Queen Gertrude, and say "Boo!" every time she tried to enter the king's chamber? Why couldn't he sit on the bed while they were making love – after all, there's nothing more guaranteed to make a guy lose his erection than the sudden appearance of a ghost between the sheets.

But no, he asked his poor son to do the job for him, and Hamlet instantly agreed. If it had been me facing that miserable paternalistic apparition, I'd have told the ghost to do his own dirty work and invited Ophelia on an extended vacation.

Just as an historical aside, I was recently informed by a Shakespeare buff that Will himself liked to play the ghost in *Hamlet* at the Globe Theatre. The role, it seems, was close to his heart, which makes me wonder how the Bard's own son, Hamnet, would have turned out, reared by such a parent. But, alas, the young man died when he was eleven years old, so we shall never know if he was shaping up to be a wimp, like his near-namesake, Hamlet.

Even Ophelia had more guts than her boyfriend. She was ready to defy her father, Polonius, and her brother, Laertes, in order to marry Hamlet.

I tell you, this habit of obedience to our fathers is driving us all nuts. Make no mistake, our fathers have betrayed us. They deserve to be condemned, not obeyed. They should be ridiculed, not respected.

If this sounds unfair, just think for a moment: who has given us the framework of beliefs by which we live? Who has created a society that turns us into economic slaves? Who has made us so poor in spirit that we need to run madly after material wealth? Who has told us to believe in an angry father-figure in the sky who will punish us with eternal damnation if we dare to disobey him?

Who but our fathers?

Perhaps we should forgive our biological fathers. Poor guys. They really didn't have a clue how they were being manipulated. My own father worked in a bank for most of his life, relying on alcohol to get him through the mind-numbing activity of looking after other people's money.

But it's interesting to see how our early dependence on our fathers, as small children, has been used as a social tool to castrate us. Because, you see, we were never allowed to grow up. That would have been too much of a risk for those who benefit from our immaturity.

The Catholic religion offers one of the most obvious examples. The word 'pope', as most people know, is derived from the Greek word *pappas*, meaning 'father' and every Catholic priest is also to be addressed as 'father'. It's a simple and effective way of manipulating people by reducing them to children

Forgive me Father, for I have sinned....

You see the point? As long as we think we need fathers, we diminish ourselves to children, to lesser beings. That's why I say our fathers betrayed us. They did not teach us to be independent and strong; they taught us to obey authority. They did not teach us to be intelligent; they taught us to believe what we were told.

And if someone like Osho comes along to point out the absurdity of the situation, lampooning our respected authority figures, he automatically creates controversy.

Osho's irreverent description of Jesus Christ as a four-foot hunchback in need of electro-shock therapy, his dismissal of the Holy Trinity – Father, Son and Holy Ghost – as a 'gay trio' and his labelling of Pope John Paul II as 'the Polak Pope' all created headlines in the seventies and eighties, sparking indignant reaction.

One might argue that it's not very nice of Osho to say such things. But how else is a mystic supposed to help people grow up, other than poking fun at our sacred cows? He was just doing his job.

One paradox needs to be mentioned here. Anyone who observed the circus that surrounded Osho in the seventies and eighties would have seen hundreds of young people, all crowded into a meditation hall, singing songs of devotion to a white-bearded guru sitting silently on a podium in front of them.

So an objection must be raised: were we not creating our own father-figure? Were we not demolishing the authority figures imposed on us as children, only to transfer our dependency onto a new one?

The short answer is 'yes'. In accepting Osho's recipe of how to free ourselves, some hint of father-projection rubbed off on the man with the instruction manual. But, if you studied the manual, it was clear the journey didn't end there, which is why Osho was fond of quoting Gautama Buddha's advice to his *bhikkhus*:

If you meet the Buddha on the road, kill him immediately.

In other words, don't focus on the man; understand his teaching and take responsibility for liberating yourself.

"I am not a saviour," he once commented. "I have saved myself I think that's enough. Now you save yourself."

Which reminds me of another of Osho's comments that I liked very much:

Don't bite my finger, look where I am pointing.

A few hundred years earlier, when Shakespeare wrote his plays, there was no father-figure on the throne of England. Rather, it was a mother-figure in the shape of Queen Elizabeth.

Psychologically speaking, this kind of authority is trickier to handle.

When a father wields authority it's usually direct, obvious and backed by physical force: "Do as you're told, or else..." But when a mother has power, her authority is mixed with feelings of love and care as well as discipline, which, from a child's point of view, makes it confusing.

When Margaret Thatcher died in 2013, a former member of her Cabinet, reminiscing in a television interview, said something very significant about working with Britain's first woman Prime Minister. He explained that all of Thatcher's Cabinet ministers were male and most of them had been sent to private boarding schools as children, where the only female figure was Matron, who was supposed to look after the children's general health and welfare in a 'firm but fair' way.

"Margaret was Matron and we became her wards," confided the ex-minister.

Now let's hop across the English Channel for a moment and consider the political career of Angela

Merkel: Chancellor of Germany since 2005, de facto leader of the European Union and rated by Forbes magazine as the world's second-most powerful person – the highest ranking ever achieved by a woman.

At the time of writing this book, Merkel is enjoying her third term in office. What nickname has the public given her? 'Mutti,' which is a familiar German form of 'mother' – in other words 'mummy', or 'mom'.

In these times of economic and political uncertainty, the German people like the feeling that mom is holding their hand or, rather, they did until Merkel's open-door policy for hundreds of thousands of refugees finally shook the public's confidence in her.

Our need for parental permission manifests in many ways. Take, for example, a touchingly sensitive movie titled *The Sessions*, starring John Hawkes, Helen Hunt and William Macy. As a man crippled by polio, Hawke's character seeks spiritual guidance from his local priest, played by Macy, asking him if it would be a sin to lose his virginity without being married, using a surrogate sex worker played by Hunt.

For a moment, the priest silently communes with his divine employer, then reassures the crippled man, "In my heart, I feel he'll give you a free pass on this one." So the man in the iron lung gets a green light to enjoy sex out of wedlock.

The moment looks good onscreen and both Hawkes and Macy play their parts well, but the underlying implication disturbed me. It was saying, in effect, that we lack the maturity and intelligence to determine what's good for ourselves. We cannot act, even in our own best interests, without permission from a higher authority.

It's not my intention to single out Roman Catholicism as if it's the only culprit. The Vatican provides interesting examples, but the syndrome goes far wider.

My parents weren't particularly religious, but I got the message anyway, digesting it at a subliminal level along with my Kellogg's Cornflakes and Shredded Wheat: don't allow yourself to really live, don't step outside the sheep pen, don't think for yourself, don't explore your sexual energy....

Which leads us to an interesting question: why did we buy this toxic package? What was the payoff for Joe Citizen?

Well, in the old days, we bought it because we had no choice, unless you call being burned at the stake an option. It was certainly a convincing motive to conform. But there was, and still is, another motive: we happily embrace religious fairy stories to avoid the arduous task of exploring our own inner world.

Nothingness is a hard sell. Inviting people to meditate on a daily basis, over a period of many years, so that one day they might disappear into the void and thereafter exist only as some kind of indefinable 'amness' with no personal identity, isn't going to trigger a stampede of converts any time soon.

Promises of paradise seem a lot more appealing than emptiness. One notable exception to this general trend, however, was Chiyono, the world's first female Zen Master, who, in the thirteenth century, made the quantum leap from being a Japanese housewife to a spiritually awakened Zen Buddhist nun.

Her moment of enlightenment took place one full moon night, while she was carrying water in small bucket held by a frail bamboo frame. While she was watching the reflection of the moon in the water, the bucket suddenly broke and the water rushed out.

Chiyono's poem, describing the pivotal moment, goes thus:

This way and that way

I tried to keep the pail together

Hoping the weak bamboo

Would never break.

Suddenly the bottom fell out:

No more water:

No more moon in the water:

Emptiness in my hand!

Following her enlightenment, Chiyono was chosen by the great Japanese Zen Master, Rinzai, as his successor and, in spite of resistance from male chauvinist monks, she became the first abbess of the Keiaiji Temple in Northern Kyoto.

Chiyono's poem reminds me of a humorous cartoon, circulating around the social media. It shows the Dalai Lama being given a large box for his birthday by other

Buddhist monks. He opens it and, smiling with delight as his looks inside the empty box, declares, "Just what I always wanted for my birthday – Nothing!"

However, according to the purveyors of instant salvation, there is no need for the patient, persistent, lengthy introspection that Chiyono undertook and meditation demands. Why not take a short cut? Simply believe in an all-powerful father-figure in the sky, pay your dues to your local priest, receive a handy insurance policy against death and book your slot in the after-life.

In other words: "I don't need to take responsibility for my spiritual growth because daddy will take care of me".

Seen from this perspective, all one can say about the history of the human race, so far, is that it is the story of a retarded species that doesn't want to grow up, always wants to hold daddy's hand, and is willing to pay an enormous price for it.

As you can imagine, it took me a while to repair the damage from being spoon-fed this childish nonsense. That's why I condemn Hamlet for being such a wimp. Up to the time I became a sannyasin, it was the story of my own life, getting caught up in intellectual ideas about the meaning of life when the real thing – my own life energy – was suppressed, waiting impatiently to burst out from within my own body, heart and soul.

Hamlet, old chap, it's not about wondering whether 'to be or not to be'. It's about growing up and getting real.

How do you do that? Well, try this therapeutic exercise:

Imagine you are Hamlet. You have met your father's ghost on the castle ramparts. You listen carefully to his hard luck story and you understand that you don't need to take responsibility for his problems. When he has finished talking, you look into his ghostly eyes and slowly and deliberately say the following words: "Fuck off, asshole! Do your own dirty work. I'm taking the next flight to India with Ophelia."

You won't go mad. Trust me.

CHAPTER 25
All's Well That Ends Well

I almost forgot to tell you: the biggest drama on the opening night didn't happen onstage. It happened outside the theatre when the Pune police arrived uninvited and told us we couldn't put on the play.

It was a last-minute glitch of massive proportions. The audience was already seated. The actors had put on their make-up and were fully costumed. The radio mics had been tested and our technicians were in the control box, waiting to hit the lights and turn up the volume. Then Ragni, my co-producer, looking incredibly elegant and feminine in her evening sari, came to give me the bad news: the cops were shutting us down.

It was the third and biggest challenge to our production.

The first tsunami to wash over us came when Pune's local news media ran titillating excerpts from a tell-all book, written by one of Osho's former secretaries, describing the sexual antics in our ashram in the seventies.

Predictably, the media focused on the book's revelations about sexually transmitted diseases, crowded and unhygienic living conditions, and stomach trouble - amoebic dysentery being high on the list. Described in such a lurid way, the place sounded awful. There was little mention of the love we shared, the joy we felt in our singing and dancing, the peace we experienced in meditation.

The book was published just a few days before our two performances, and even though the events had occurred nearly forty years previously, they impacted our audience. About 500 local college students, whom we had invited free to the show, failed to turn up.

"I don't think my parents would want me to come," confided one nervous young woman. Strange, in my student days, if my parents didn't want me to do something, it guaranteed that I would. Clearly, the rebellious attitudes that once swept through the UK's citadels of learning has yet to penetrate the Indian educational system.

The second obstacle emerged when we discovered that our local agent, who'd promised to obtain permission for our production from the local authorities, hadn't done a thing.

Several types of authorization are required for putting on plays in Indian cities, including an okay from the Police Commissioner and another one from the Charities Commissioner. We knew this. We'd chosen an amiable, well-connected, local businessman to take care of this on our behalf, and had received daily assurances from him that it was happening... "Yes, yes, by tomorrow, don't worry."

It was only on the morning of our first show that Ragni realized nothing had been done. She shifted into high gear and, with a lot of running around and fast talking, managed to obtain both permits a few hours before curtain up. It was a close shave, but we made it. Situation sorted.

But neither of these difficulties prepared us for the final hitch. We'd put up the cash, rehearsed for weeks and rolled the production, only to be stopped seconds before curtain up.

I had to walk onto the stage, in my Shakespeare costume and announce, "There's been a slight bureaucratic hitch that's preventing us from starting the play. If you'll excuse me, I'll go out front and try to solve the problem. Meanwhile, just relax and enjoy the music."

We put on a CD of Indian sitar music, then I joined Ragni outside the theatre, where a Sikh police officer, looking smart in his colour-coordinated blue shirt, tie and turban, was speaking rapidly into a large walkie-talkie handset, conversing with the shopping mall's management.

Seeing me in my puffy pantaloons and Elizabethan jacket, he gave me a quick, embarrassed smile, but continued jabbering into his oversized mobile phone.

So, what was the problem? I couldn't figure it out.

Finally, when he got off his walkie-talkie, the police inspector told me apologetically: "Sorry to say, sir, government regulations state that special Home Ministry permission is an absolute necessity for foreigners to perform in this country... absolute necessity... *absolute necessity....*"

He was on a loop, but it was a key phrase and basically he was right. It was the law. It was something we didn't know and hadn't figured.

The owners of the shopping mall agreed with the cops. They were on the phone to Ragni, telling her they, too, wouldn't permit the show to go ahead without police clearance on all points – it was in the contract we'd signed with them.

Strange. I didn't recall signing any contract and neither did Ragni. She signed a cheque for the rent and that was all. But to tell you the truth, both of us had been so busy putting on the play we couldn't remember if we'd signed anything – not a very business-like attitude, I'm sure you'll agree.

We knew there was zero chance of obtaining Home Ministry permission to save the show, even if we flew to New Delhi with the speed of a Concorde jetliner. But the police and the managers were adamant we couldn't begin without it.

What to do? Silencing her mobile for a moment, Ragni looked at me, grimacing and smiling at the same time, indicating the challenge both frustrated and amused her. "There *must* be a way around this. In this country there's *always* a solution," she declared determinedly.

As it turned out, the police were easier to handle than the mall managers. The classic, time-honoured method of *baksheesh* took care of the inspector's requirements and I didn't really mind handing over ten thousand rupees – I'd lost so much money on this show, another couple of hundred bucks didn't make much difference.

But the mall owners were still blocking us, raising fears that they would be heavily fined by the government if the news got out that they'd allowed foreigners to perform without permission. And, no, they weren't interested in *baksheesh* – as I said, the owner was the wife of a gasoline king and she was loaded.

Ragni got back on her Galaxy, arguing fiercely with the management and after a long time her shoulders seemed to relax so I got the feeling something might be working. Eventually, she ended the negotiation and told me, "They're willing to let the show proceed, providing we sign a letter, drafted by them, guaranteeing we will pay any fines imposed by the Home Ministry," she informed me, then added, "Not just fines imposed on us, but also fines imposed on the mall."

No problem for this playwright. Theoretical fines for hypothetical offences imposed by invisible bureaucrats at some imaginary future date didn't worry me. I was ready to sign anything and go to debtor's prison later if necessary. All I wanted was to roll.

"Let's go for it," I said and she agreed.

For a moment, it seemed like we had a green light. But then Ragni's cell phone played its Bollywood tune and she raised a hand to stop me.

"Now what?" I asked.

"We can't start until we've signed the letter," she reported, grimacing in frustration once more.

"My God, how long is that going to take?" I wondered, but neither of us knew the answer.

Another ten minutes passed. No sign of any letter emerging from the mall's main office. Out of the corner of my eye, I saw a member of the audience coming out of the theatre and walking away. Later, I found out she was going to buy a bottle of water and was coming back, but at the moment I suddenly feared a mass walkout by an impatient audience.

I grabbed Ragni's mobile and screamed, "Look, people are leaving the theatre! We have to start the show now… NOW!" then handed the phone back to Ragni. Another fierce conversation in Hindi ensued.

"Okay, if I wait here to sign the letter, you can start the show," she told me. I think she spent the entire evening outside the theatre, waiting for the letter to come, and didn't see our performance until the second night.

As I went into the amphitheatre, my reappearance raised a cheer from the good-natured sannyasin audience, all of whom understood – some, no doubt, from personal experience – that in this country, bureaucratic intervention can abruptly derail any event at any moment.

Minutes later, the Prologue walked out onto the stage, unrolled his parchment and began:

The mark of greatness as we know
Is left for history to bestow….

After we had run the play successfully for two nights, Ragni and I sat down and drafted a letter to the Home Ministry in Delhi, seeking clarification.

We explained that, in our understanding, amateur actors from abroad who donate their services voluntarily, without being paid, need not apply to the Home Ministry for permission to perform in India – only professional performers need do that.

We asked the Home Ministry if our understanding was correct. So far, after three months of waiting, we have yet to receive a reply. There's an upside to the delay: as yet, no massive fines have been imposed on us, nor on the shopping mall, for what occurred.

Indian bureaucracy can drive you crazy if you want something. But if you don't want something – like a fine, or an embargo, for example – then, truly, it becomes a blessing. In this country, the hidden spirit of non-doing lives on, especially in government offices.

Long may it continue.

CHAPTER 26

A Thrilling Finale?

For one brief, shining moment, it looks as though true love is here to stay. Hamlet dances with Ophelia, Will Shakespeare dances with his wife, then they all join hands and dance together in harmony. What more could an incurable romantic wish for?

But then Will remembers the Queen's threat and, after a moment's hesitation, rudely breaks away from the other dancers, signalling for the music to cease.

"Stop! Stop!" he cries. "All this romantic nonsense... it just won't do!"

Of course, he feels bad about being a party pooper, but he's also a pragmatist. He knows what needs to be done to save his skin. He stalks back to his seat, picks up his quill pen and gets on with it.

Meanwhile, Hamlet is a changed man, open to an entirely different future. Wonderingly, he looks at Ophelia and Mrs Shakespeare and asks them, "What happens now?"

Mrs Shakespeare has the answer: "Well, if you take my advice you'll both get out of Denmark as quickly as possible. It's such a miserable country. Why don't you go to India for the winter?"

Ophelia likes this new turn of events. "India! That sounds like a wonderful idea!" she exclaims. She is a romantically inclined young woman and the promise of travelling to such an exotic country with her beloved sounds too good to be true.

Hamlet, however, has doubts. "My God, but from Elizabethan England it will us take six months just to get there!" he objects.

Mrs Shakespeare has all the answers. Pulling a couple of airline tickets from her copious bosom, she tells them, "No, no. I happen to know that Jet Airways is offering special flights from sixteenth century London nonstop to Mumbai. Look, here are the tickets. Now run along both of you."

Okay, let's back up a bit and take a look at this new development. First of all, as you may have noticed, Mrs Shakespeare is talking as if this young couple is living in Denmark, while giving them flight tickets from London. It's a question of parallel realities. In the play within the play, they are in Elsinore Castle. As Elizabethan actors they are in London. I'm comfortable with the confusion.

As for Denmark, I admit, I'm being too hard. It's not *such* a miserable country. For years, I've been going there every summer to live in a small sannyasin community, located in the countryside in Jutland – not far from where the legendary hero Amleth skewered his treacherous uncle with his sword.

When the sun shines and the temperature creeps above twenty degrees Celsius, Denmark is transformed into a paradise on Earth. But, unfortunately, that tends not to happen very often, which is why I'm happy to spend a few weeks on the beaches of Goa every winter before heading for Jutland. I fill up my personal sunshine quota, just in case.

News of Denmark's bad weather has spread across the internet, inspiring one cynical guy to spoof a web-search failure notice: *Error 404: Danish summer not found – try Thailand.*

Another humourist posted three photos on *Facebook*:

First photo: a man and a boy are sitting on a park bench, dressed in heavy coats, on a cold winter's day. The man asks the boy, "When does spring come?"

Second photo: the boy looks at the man with sad, tear-filled eyes and replies, "I live in Denmark."

Third photo: They embrace wordlessly, sharing a deep understanding of the hopelessness of the situation.

And then, of course, when summer ends and autumn begins, when the nights grow longer and darker and the temperature sinks toward zero...then it's definitely time to get out. I can't live in a country where daybreak comes at ten o'clock in the morning and nightfall arrives at four in the afternoon.

So Mrs Shakespeare has my sympathy in recommending a trip to India. By the way, when I first wrote this scene, the tickets mentioned in the dialogue were for Kingfisher Airlines, but, alas, the company went bust last year. Now it's Air India, Jet Airways, or British Airways.

The young couple are about to leave the stage to begin their journey, when Will, who's been pretending to write but was actually listening to all this, jumps to his feet.

"Wait! Hold everything!" he commands.

"Uh-oh," murmurs Mrs Shakespeare. She was hoping to get the couple safely away before her husband interfered. Fat chance, especially when the guy playing the part is also writing the script.

Will strolls with deliberate slowness towards his wife and with forced politeness enquires, "May I have a word with you... dear?"

Mrs Shakespeare tells Hamlet and Ophelia to wait a moment and comes close to her husband, smiling brightly with an expression of pure innocence on her face, as if nothing could possibly be the matter.

"Yes, dear?"

Will puts an affectionate hand on his wife's shoulder. He is, after all, human, and wants her to know it.

"Listen, beloved," he tells her. "I know you have good intentions and you want these young people to be happy, but if they don't die, I will. The Queen has threatened me with execution if this play does not end in tragedy."

This is news to Mrs Shakespeare. "Ooooh, that nasty woman!" she cries, but then inspiration strikes once more: "Wait... I know..." she pulls two more Jet Airways tickets from her bosom. "We'll all fly to India...right now, before she finds out."

Okay, never mind the implausibility of introducing airlines into an Elizabethan drama. We are approaching a significant moment, because there is only one thing preventing Will Shakespeare from agreeing with his wife and leaving this tortured situation. One tiny three-letter word called 'ego'.

Will folds his arms, looks at his wife indignantly and declares, "What? You want me to give up being the greatest playwright in England...just like that?" He snaps his fingers to emphasise the point.

Mrs Shakespeare looks at him with a mixture of pity and understanding.

"Oh, I forgot. You haven't learned how *not to be*, have you?"

Far from feeling hurt by her comment, Will agrees.

"No, indeed. Nor will I ever do so. My name is going to be remembered for centuries and centuries."

So, here we are, looking at the classic human condition in which a wonderful, juicy and exciting course of action is prohibited because of considerations of reputation, social image and personal prestige.

Just think for a moment: how many times have you felt an impulse to do something enjoyable, fun, life-enhancing, and prevented yourself because of your 'reputation' and what other people might think?

I'm reminded of one such moment in Marilyn Monroe's life. She was filming *The Prince and the Showgirl* in London and suffering immensely from the British stiff-upper-lip attitudes surrounding her. It wasn't only Laurence Olivier, the director, who was giving her a hard time (mainly because he wasn't able to seduce her). The stage crews at Pinewood Studios had perfected the art of inverted snobbery – pretending not to feel inferior to the film stars with whom they worked – so they ignored her and virtually cut her dead.

Of course, she should never have agreed to go there. Already deeply insecure about her acting abilities, Monroe, with her unerring sense of self-destruction, put herself in a situation that was guaranteed to make it ten times worse.

Anyway, one day, half-way through the filming, Marilyn figured she'd had enough and ran off with a young man called Colin Clark, who was personal assistant to Sir Laurence (and who subsequently wrote a book about his experiences). Clark and Monroe had a great time, touring Windsor Castle, walking in the fields and swimming in the River Thames, where Clark had the enviable distinction of being kissed on the mouth by the topless superstar.

Ecstatic at being freed from the stuffy atmosphere at Pinewood, Marilyn exclaimed, "This is reality!"

Clark instantly corrected her, reminding the celebrity sex symbol that the 'real world' lay in the film studios, in her movie career and in her difficult marriage with playwright Arthur Miller.

But here's my point: Clark was wrong. Both worlds were equally real and Marilyn was free to choose either one. She could have opted for the simple life, free from the pressures of being a popular actress. She could've run away with Clark, right then and there, and never looked back. What made her return to Pinewood was her investment in being a star – a totally understandable decision, but one that would ultimately destroy her.

I'm not saying Marilyn *should* have stayed with Clark. I'm saying the exhilaration she experienced with him happened because – for a few precious hours – she was leaving her image, her reputation, and therefore all her insecurity and anxiety behind.

That's a choice we all make. Will's dilemma is one that faces us all, almost every day of our lives. The paradox we need to fathom is that *not to be* offers us the freedom to be who we really are, moment to moment, while our lifelong obsession with *to be* keeps us restricted and imprisoned in our social image.

It looks like Will won't budge, but Mrs Shakespeare hasn't given up on the situation. Taking her husband by the arm, she leads him to where Hamlet and Ophelia are standing. She knows that, somewhere beneath his overweening ambition, her husband has a soft heart and she appeals to it now.

"Will, love, come here," she says gently. "Look at these beautiful young people. They've just discovered the joy of living. Do you want to take it away from them?"

Confronted by the dire consequences of his script, Will hesitates.

"Well, er...." For the first time, his resolve weakens and he just doesn't know what to do.

Ta-tata-taaaaaaa!

There is a loud fanfare of trumpets and Queen Elizabeth herself comes sweeping onto the stage, accompanied by two attendants carrying swords.

"Off with their heads!" she cries in a wonderful imitation of the foul-tempered Queen of Hearts in *Alice in Wonderland*.

Will is down on his knees in a second.

"Why are these young people not yet dying or dead?" she demands imperiously.

Immediately, the Bard suppresses whatever feelings he had for the lovers and succumbs to the necessity of *realpolitik* – in other words, the ignoble art of kissing ass.

"Soon, soon, Your Majesty. I'm just about to kill them," he assures her.

But the Queen will not brook any further delay. She is determined to see heads rolling on the floor this very instant.

"Do it now. I command it! Off with their heads!"

"Yes, Your Majesty," he says humbly, then turning to the young couple he apologises for what is about to happen: "I'm sorry, both of you. A thousand pardons, but it is your destiny to die in my play."

However, as I mentioned earlier, I like happy endings and so, at this critical moment, a strange and macabre figure with a skull-like head and black cape enters on the scene. Standing dramatically among the players, this ghastly apparition points an accusing finger at the Queen.

"Your time has come, Your Majesty," booms the figure in a hollow, ghostly voice.

The Queen is terrified. After all, it's all very well chopping the heads of other people, but it's a different matter when it's your turn to face the Grim Reaper.

"Eeeek! Oh God! Who are you, pray?" she cries, almost fainting in alarm.

"I am the Angel of Death. And it is your time to die!" booms the voice.

The Queen clutches at her heart and staggers to one side. "Ah, it is true!" she gasps. "My heart is giving out! It is my time! Farewell, cruel world! Farewell!"

Pushing melodrama to the max and going beyond even Bollywood-style histrionics, she falls back into the arms of her attendance and is half carried, half staggers across the stage, repeating loudly "I die! I die! I die....!"

Finally, when she's gone, the strange figure whips off its disguise to reveal the perpetrator of this eleventh-hour rescue operation: Nobody.

Nobody is immensely satisfied with her own performance and thinks Will Shakespeare should be, too. "That was pretty good acting, eh Will?" she asks.

Will is astonished. He's never seen this character before and doesn't know what she's doing in his play. "Well, obviously the Queen thought so; she's dying of fright," he replies. "Who are you?"

"I'll tell you later. But first, we must find a way to end this play properly," pronounces Nobody.

In one movement, Ophelia, Hamlet and Mrs Shakespeare turned towards Will and in a single voice demand, "A *happy* ending!"

But, even with the Queen off his back, Will isn't ready to agree.

"No. I refuse to write a happy ending," he tells them, stubbornly.

Nobody is genuinely puzzled. "But why?" she asks him.

"It's so ordinary, so predictable," he explains and gesturing towards the audience continues, "look at this sophisticated audience. You can't expect them to take me seriously as a playwright if I write a happy ending."

I love pulling in the audience, unexpectedly, like this, and it works well in a play in which I'm free to time-jump from Elizabethan England to the present day. It also reminds everyone – as I've said before – that comedy isn't respected as much as tragedy.

However, if Will can be stubborn, so can his wife. Folding her arms in a gesture of defiance, she tells her husband, "Well, we refuse to take part in a tragic ending."

Hamlet and Ophelia immediately take her side: "Right!" They've had quite enough gloom in their lives and here they draw the line. It looks like a stand-off, but then Nobody comes up with a possible solution.

"I know," she says. "How about a thriller?"

"A thrilling ending, yes!" agrees Mrs Shakespeare, immediately enjoying the idea.

Will is flummoxed. "But I've never, ever, written a thriller," he objects.

Historically speaking, this is perfectly true. All of Shakespeare's plays contain dramatic tension, that's obvious. You can't stage a drama without injecting some, well...*drama*. But he's never been one for nail-biting, fast-moving action like, for example, the kind of thing you find in *The Matrix*, or *The Terminator*. It's not his thing. There needs to be time for soliloquy, for lengthy poetic reflections on the deeper issues with which humanity wrestles.

Nobody has the solution. "It's easy. Listen, Will..." she whispers in his ear and slowly a smile creeps across Shakespeare's hitherto worried face.

"Okay. I'll try it," he agrees. "Take your places everyone!"

The lights dim, the atmosphere on stage becomes spooky, a familiar tune begins to play and Shakespeare starts to lip sync Michael Jackson's famous number *Thriller*:

It's after midnight... and something evil's lurking in the dark...

Behind him, the rest of the cast begin the classic zombie shuffle, staring vacantly towards the audience, twitching robotically back and forth. Then everyone suddenly breaks into a synchronised high-stepping chorus, with hands raised like claws, and the audience cracks up:

It's just a thriller... thriller night...

As you can see, we're throwing caution to the winds here, as far as paying royalties is concerned, because you just cannot find a substitute for *Thriller*. In this context, nothing else works. As with *Gangnam Style*, earlier in the tale, we will have to spend serious money if this show ever goes commercial.

As far as my own performance was concerned, it took me a while to learn the moves from Michael Jackson's video and I wouldn't say my sixty-seven-year-old body has the suppleness which the King of Pop's rubbery athletics demand. But we're all moving well, going great guns and are about two thirds of the way through the song when...

Ta-tata-taaaaaaa!

A royal fanfare interrupts our dance, announcing the return of the grim and malevolent Queen Elizabeth. She's not dead? *Oh shit.*

CHAPTER 27

Puritans Stop the Show

Puritans are not much fun. They seem to think that, in order to be pure, they have to make sure they spoil other people's enjoyment, especially by condemning those activities we commonly refer to as 'entertainment'. They believe that only by being serious and denying simple human pleasures can a puritan-minded person feel justified in calling himself spiritual.

So it was inevitable that, sooner or later, the swelling ranks of Puritans in England would come into conflict with the public's love of theatre. What is surprising is that it took so long to manifest: about one hundred years, in fact.

In the sixteenth century, Puritans in Europe developed as a kind of mutation from Protestantism, which in turn originated – as the name suggests – in a protest against the monopolistic excesses of the leaders of the Roman Catholic faith.

Led by Martin Luther, a German theologian and priest, the Protestants objected to the way the Vatican was exploiting Christians for financial gain. They were particularly critical of the commercialisation of *indulgences*, through which, via a generous donation, one could sin freely, safe in the knowledge that any divine punishment after death would be greatly reduced.

As one promoter of this lucrative business put it:

> *As soon as the coin in the coffer rings,*
> *The soul from purgatory springs.*

Luther began his crusade in 1517, and his teachings quickly spread across Europe. In England, the situation was complicated by King Henry VIII, who decided unilaterally to destroy the power of the Vatican, not for any theological reason, but simply because the Pope refused to give him a divorce.

King Henry created the Church of England, making himself its head, so the protest against mainstream Christianity and its shortcomings was rather muted, since the Vatican could no longer be the target.

By the time Queen Elizabeth came to power, there was a sizeable Puritan community in her country, but it was not nearly so great a threat to her throne as the Catholics. The Puritans were marginalised and sometimes forcibly suppressed, but generally survived without too many executions.

It was only after the Tudor monarchs gave way to the Stuarts that the Puritans began to strengthen their power, especially in Parliament, and even though King James I personally sponsored an excellent translation of the Bible from Latin to English, giving his people a new and elegantly-crafted holy book – the Authorized King James Version, which is still being used today, he became the target of Puritan hostility.

James' love of feasting and drinking, as well as his enjoyment of theatre, gained him a reputation as a foolish man and an indifferent monarch, an opinion shared by many historians until recently, when a reassessment took note of his skill at managing his financial affairs without the aid of Parliament, his attempts to reconcile the warring factions of Christianity, and his careful diplomacy which kept the country free from conflict with Spain.

Shakespeare's troupe, now proudly titled *The King's Men,* flourished under their Royal patron, as did The Globe, until 1613 when the theatre was burned to the ground. This was not an act of protest, but an accident, triggered, quite literally, by the discharging of a cannon during a battle scene in a history play, which set alight the thatched roof and sent the alarmed audience scrambling for the exits.

However, The Globe was rebuilt the following year and continued its successful run, outlasting Shakespeare, who died in 1616, and King James, who expired in 1625.

Here, perhaps I should mention an event, well known to us but totally ignored at the time: five years before the death of King James, a ship named *The Mayflower* carried a group of Separatists, fleeing from religious persecution in England, to North America, thereby exporting Puritanism to the New World and embedding its moralistic ideals in the collective psyche of the future United States.

Which reminds me of an Australian journalist who, in 1998, was covering the detailed interrogation of

Monica Lewinsky by the Starr Commission, which was probing her sexual encounters with President Bill Clinton. As the Commission pressured Lewinsky to confess every detail, the Australian wryly commented, "Thank God we got the criminals and they got the Puritans."

Meanwhile, back in the seventeenth century, King James was succeeded by his son, King Charles I, and the struggle between Monarch and Parliament escalated as the Puritan mood of the country increased.

An attempt in 1629 to introduce real women to play female roles in London theatres ran foul, not just of the Puritans, but of the public in general. When a French troupe of players, comprising both men and women, tried to perform in Blackfriars, the women were booed off the stage. A few years later, William Prynne, a prominent English lawyer and Puritan, described female actors as 'monsters', and condemned their performances as 'impudent', 'shameful' and 'unwomanish'.

Soon, it wasn't just female actors who were under attack. It was theatre itself. In 1642, at the outbreak of the English Civil War, the English Parliament, under pressure from the Puritans, issued an ordinance suppressing all stage plays in theatres. Two years later, the Globe was demolished and in 1648, all playhouses were ordered to be pulled down and all players were to be seized and whipped.

Meanwhile, on the battlefield, King Charles proved no match for the rising power of Parliament and its brutally efficient New Model Army, led by Oliver Cromwell, a fanatic Puritan and strong military commander. The king lost the war and soon afterwards his head. It was involuntarily removed from his shoulders in 1649.

For a moment, it seemed that Parliament had won, but Cromwell quickly became impatient with the institution, seized the Mace, dismissed its members and had himself pronounced Lord Protector, effectively making himself King of England for the remaining five years of his life, from 1553-58.

The austere atmosphere of the *Interregnum*, during which even holidays like Christmas and Easter were banned, did not last long after Cromwell's death. In 1660, the Restoration movement welcomed Charles II to the English throne and this was accompanied by an immediate renaissance of theatrical performances.

But the quality was low, compared to the Jacobean era. I have to say that if the Bard had been able to see what Restoration Theatre did with his plays – savagely editing, cutting and adapting them with scant regard for plot or poetry – he would have prayed for the return of Cromwell.

To its credit, however, Restoration Theatre finally allowed women to take to the stage. Nell Gwyn, long-time mistress of Charles II, was the most famous of these - "pretty, witty Nell" as Samuel Pepys called her, but it was actually Margaret Hughes, mistress of Civil War general Prince Rupert of the Rhine, who achieved the breakthrough.

The fact that both of these talented women were mistresses and not wives speaks volumes for society's attitude towards actresses. It would be a long time before it became as respectable for women to enter the theatrical profession as for men.

So, of Restoration theatre troupes, it can be said that, while they may have murdered Shakespeare, they at least opened the door to sexual equality.

It was not until the eighteenth century that Shakespeare came to be revered in his original form and style, influencing not only other playwrights but also poets, composers, philosophers and even social revolutionaries like Karl Marx.

Looking back, I have to admit that I have a soft spot for Puritans, which is a little eccentric of me, since in their rigid morality they exhibit no 'soft spots' of their own. But they had the right idea when they asserted there was no need for any professional, priestly intermediary to link an ordinary man with the divine.

But, alas, they were off target in believing that seriousness and strict moral behaviour were required for personal salvation. This particular delusion goes way beyond the Puritans. Even today, in the enlightened twenty-first century, codes of dress and prohibitive rules of conduct are still considered essential by many 'religious' people.

To a meditator, however, all outward behaviour is irrelevant. A self-realised soul can be an emperor or a beggar, a monk, a businessman or a naked *fakir*. The possibilities are endless. Among the many realized souls that India has produced, Janak was a king, Raidas was a leather worker, Kabir was a weaver, Chaitanya was a scholar, Saraha was a prince, Ramakrishna was a priest, Amrapali was a prostitute and Angulimala was a murderer…the outer role these people played in society had no bearing on their inner illumination.

But the human mind has a tendency to be impressed with people who give up the comforts of life and sacrifice themselves for others, which is why Mother Teresa is currently breaking the speed record for being declared a saint by the Vatican.

Clearly the people who support her canonisation do not understand that humbleness and service are as meaningless as pride or vanity – these are just different forms of human ego. Whatever the personality type, it needs to be set aside on the journey of self-discovery.

In other words, the inner state of consciousness, or nothingness, or *shunyata* as the Buddhists call it, is completely indifferent to our ideas about religiousness. Rather, it requires us to drop *all* ideas, bypass the chattering mind and move within.

As for William Shakespeare, he survived through many cycles of social fashion including the excitement of theatre in his own day, the righteous wrath of the Puritans, the indifference of the Restoration and the reverence of modern times.

This is, of course, because of his poetic and dramatic genius. But even he, for all his colourful portrayal of the various moods and qualities of human nature, did not come to the inner door where all distinctions cease and mysticism begins.

Hence the need for Nobody. Together with Mrs Shakespeare, he will need to bring this play to a conclusion that goes beyond the Bard. It's nice to know he can do so without fear of being whipped by Puritans.

Before we return to our own drama, a short anecdote about actors:

On several occasions, I heard Osho say that acting is a spiritual profession, because actors and actresses are required to slip in and out of so many different roles and characters. This can give them the experience that their own sense of identity is also a role, a mask. So it's easy for them to see beyond the personality to a deeper reality.

It's a nice idea, but I have to disagree. Why? Because, at least with the actors I've met, their egos get so inflated by public adulation that it's harder for them to become a 'nobody' in the land of 'not to be' than anyone else.

Singers, musicians, actors, TV personalities, newscasters…anyone who attracts the public's attention is going to find it difficult to free themselves from the addictive grip of fame. Applause is like mainlining heroin. People's admiration is like snorting a line of coke. You just keep wanting more.

Which means, of course, if this book becomes a best-seller and thrusts me into the public spotlight, my own spiritual growth is toast.

Ooops…

CHAPTER 28
The Land of Not To Be

Meditation is nobody's copyright. On the contrary, it is everybody's birthright. It's not something you need to obtain from somebody else in some kind of secret, esoteric transmission. It's already inside you, waiting to be discovered.

The bottom line of spiritual growth is that you need to find your own 'buddha nature'. It's helpful to hook up with mystics like Osho and other people who can teach you how to look within, but this doesn't absolve you from taking responsibility for your own personal growth.

So, as far as I'm concerned, anyone who has touched the inner core of consciousness can write his, or her, own ending to my play. However, there is one condition on which I must insist: all the characters need to end up in India.

Even though this country is doing its best to destroy itself as rapidly as possible, I still want Hamlet, Ophelia, Mrs Shakespeare, Will and even Queen Elizabeth to fly Jet Airways to Mumbai or Delhi and remain in the country for at least six months.

Why? Because the vibe of meditation still lingers here and that's a tremendous help for people setting out on the path of spiritual inquiry. I say 'spiritual' but it's a misleading term. Really, I'm referring to anybody who begins to understand that, even though we seem to be awake – walking, talking, acting normally – we are afflicted by a pernicious sleep that keeps the whole of humanity drugged.

You want to know the truth? Take a look at Michael Jackson's *Thriller* video, not at the star himself but the 'living dead' who dance with him. Yep, that's us. We are walking zombies, obeying a program of unthinking social conformity that has been hard-wired into our brains.

Never mind who did it. You can blame our fathers, our mothers. You can blame the Queen of England, the Vatican, the US Reserve Bank, the Illuminati, the Russian mafia, Exxon, Monsanto...it really doesn't matter who benefits from our 'waking sleep'. What matters is the understanding that we are, indeed, stacking *zzzzzzs* in slumberland. This realization alone begins the process of waking up.

Remember, though, we're all going to face the challenge of *not to be*. Like it or not, it's unavoidable. The rules of the game clearly state that we cannot simply add meditation to our nicely polished, sophisticated personalities and get on with life as before.

That's not going to work. As Jiddu Krishnamurti once observed, in his dry, elegant and ruthlessly uncompromising manner: "We are talking of something entirely different, not of self-improvement, but of the cessation of the self...."

JK is correct. We need to find a way of dropping the ego, dis-identifying with the personality, otherwise we may as well buy a lifetime subscription to the couch potato club and go on watching *Strictly Come Dancing* and *The X Factor* on Saturday evening television.

Now that I've given you the bigger picture, I can give you my own ending to the play.

You will recall that the Bard is onstage, doing a mean impersonation of Michael Jackson, dancing to the tune of *Thriller*. Then, to everyone's dismay, there is a fanfare of trumpets heralding the reappearance of Queen Elizabeth, who by now ought to have expired from heart failure.

The music stops and everyone falls to their knees as the Queen arrives with her attendants. Execution and tragedy are once again hanging in the air. But there's a difference in Good Queen Bess. She's changed. She's wearing neither her crown nor her mask. Her face looks calm and peaceful as she gazes lovingly upon her subjects and addresses them thus:

"One moment. Please don't be afraid
Of being hurt by this old maid.
If I may choose twixt life and death
I'd really rather keep my breath.
So let me join you in your gladness
And say goodbye to royal sadness."

A royal breakthrough has happened at last. The pressure is off. The young lovers are saved and Will gets to keep his head on his shoulders. All because the Queen, when taken to the verge of death, is able to understand that she really wants to live, and what is the use of being alive just to be miserable? Misery is a kind of death, a decision to turn away from life. Now the Queen is ready to enjoy herself.

Mrs Shakespeare is the first to congratulate her. Taking the Queen affectionately by the arm, she brings her to centre stage and confides:

"Your Majesty, I'm glad to see,
That, deep inside, you're just like me!"

Will goes over to Nobody, whom he hasn't really met until now. I'm not sure I had this intention when I started to write this play, but it's symbolic that the Bard connects with Nobody only at the end of the show. Up to now, Will has been clinging to his status as a famous playwright and, as his wife points out, he hasn't learned how *not to be*. Now the doors of understanding are beginning to open, even for him.

Will asks this mysterious stranger:

So tell me, Master Nobody
Where is this Land of Not To Be?
Nobody: Well, if you look beyond your mind
You'll find it's been there all the time.
But meditation is more fun
If to India you come!

Curiously enough, it is the Queen who is first off the starting blocks. She seizes enthusiastically on this notion, as if, having clung grimly to the polarity of misery for so long, she can hardly wait to swing to the opposite pole and have some adventures. She's like a terminally-ill patient who thought she was ready to die and then suddenly discovers she has a bucket list to check off first.

> Elizabeth: India! Oh yes, that's hip!
> If my old bones can make the trip.
> I think I'll go to Dharamshala
> And hang out with the Dalai Lama.

Well, of course, what do you expect of a monarch? She's not going to waste her time listening to any cheap *beedi wallah* guru. Her Royal Highness will settle for nothing less than an audience with His Holiness the Dalai Lama and we can confidently predict that the Indian press, addicted as it is to abbreviations, will emblazon its front pages with the headline "HRH Greets HH."

But there's a temporal-spatial issue: in the sixteenth century, during the reign of Good Queen Bess, the Dalai Lama was only in his third or fourth incarnation and residing in the Potala Palace in Lhasa, the capital of Tibet, which could conceivably render the Queen's trip to Dharamshala futile. However, as you will have noticed, time seems to be very elastic in this play, so let's assume that by the time Her Majesty reaches the

Dalai Lama's residence-in-exile in McLeod Ganj she'll find the fourteenth incarnation sitting there, ready to receive her.

But it seems she won't be alone. Her attendants, having lived for so long as extensions of her Royal will, naturally assume they'll be going with her:

Attendants: Oh yes, Your Majesty, it's true
Can we come along with you?
Elizabeth (*to her Attendants*): I think it's time for you to see
You really don't belong to me.
Nobody (*to Attendants*):
Find a path that suits *you* best,
And give this 'royal' thing a rest!

Sound advice to all sheep-like followers. Now it's Mrs Shakespeare's time to come forth and shine. Having been forced by Elizabethan convention to live in the shadow of her famous playwright husband, she's more than ready to break loose and pursue her own interests at last:

Mrs Shakespeare: Yoga is what I love best.
And so I'll go to Rishikesh.
Sitting by the Ganges stream
Enjoying yoga – that's my dream!
I'll practice my *asanas* daily
Standing on my head…well, maybe.

I can picture Mrs Shakespeare in Rishikesh. There are some lovely ashrams by the Ganges and lots of yoga courses. Every morning, the streets of Lakshman Jhula are full of slim, good-looking, young Western women walking purposefully to their daily classes, with a long, thin bag slung over one shoulder containing a rolled-up yoga mat. She'll be right at home.

One word of advice, though, as a concerned husband: don't spend more than a few seconds in the *sirsasana* headstand position, my dear. It may be called the 'King of Asanas', but too much blood flooding into the brain can damage those delicate little neural networks. Spirituality does not require one to be brain dead, unless of course you're following the mainstream religions, in which case it helps a lot.

The attendants, lost without a leader, turn to Mrs Shakespeare as a substitute authority figure:

Attendants (*to Mrs S*): Oh yes, we're good at yoga, too,
Perhaps we'll come along with you.

But Mrs Shakespeare, like the Queen, wants them to demonstrate some independence.

Mrs Shakespeare: Find a method of your own
Don't just follow… stand alone.

As you can see, the attendants, who have been more or less mute throughout the show, are getting more air time. That's because they add a touch of clowning to all these possibilities opening up for the other characters. I want to keep it light, otherwise it'll come across like a *Lonely Planet* guide to 'interesting places to meditate.'

Hamlet already knows where he wants to go.

Hamlet *(to Ophelia)*:
I'm sure we'll get enlightened sooner
If we meditate in Pune.
Ophelia *(alarmed)*:
But isn't that the 'free love' ashram?
Will I lose my love, my passion?

Ophelia is worried, and with good reason. The ashram's track record as a graveyard for long-term relationships is impressive. The basic problem is that two people in a partnership who come to Pune and start exploring personal growth rarely develop at the same speed.

For example, if the female partner starts doing emotional release work, she's going to open new energy channels inside her body, allowing all kinds of feelings to surface. She's going to feel more alive, more energized, which can be dangerous for a relationship that was moving along in a settled routine.

Maybe the male partner is more interested in Vipassana, a slower and more traditional method of discovering one's inner world. If the initial 'hot' phase of their relationship is over and the guy 'needs space' in order to meditate, the woman may start to feel – in the immortal words of Elizabeth Taylor – like a cat on a hot tin roof.

Moreover, lots of singles come to Pune, interested in new adventures, so, all in all, it's a pretty volatile place. Couples do come and some survive. Others, with the wisdom of experience, choose to come one at a time, while the other partner stays home and keeps his fingers crossed.

So, Ophelia's concern is well founded. Meanwhile, the attendants are seizing their chance to move in on this fair young maiden by offering their support. Placing their hands comfortingly on her shoulders, they reassure her thus:

1st Attendant: Don't worry, dear, we'll come with you
2nd Attendant: And sing and dance the whole night through!

Time for Hamlet to assert himself. Taking Ophelia's hand and pulling her gently away from the Attendants, he reclaims the relationship:

Hamlet: That won't be necessary, good fellows.
We can celebrate by ourselves.
We'll go to Pune as a pair
A challenge will await us there.
Ophelia (*no longer afraid, but courageous*):
Let's see if we can both be free
And true lovers still shall be.

My feeling is they'll be okay. They are too much in love to be distracted by other dating adventures. Now it's Will's turn. What's his decision? Where will he want to go?

> Will: All my life I've been a playwright
> Finding words to make you say right.
> So maybe I should shut up now
> And silently meditate somehow.
> I'll find a monastery in Ladakh
> And take the pressure off my back.
> 1st Attendant:
> Let's join the Bard in silence deep
> 2nd Attendant:
> If it doesn't put us both to sleep.

Not much chance of that, guys, I need to tell you. Apart from a few days in August, during an all-too-brief summer, Ladakh is an extremely cold place, with sub-zero temperatures guaranteed to keep you shivering and wide awake. You'll need lots of padded layers just to stay alive.

On top of that, meditation rituals offered by Tibetan Buddhist monks usually include plenty of crashing cymbals, banging drums and loud horns. Why? Because unlike our Sunday services and sermons, they know the idea is to wake up, not fall asleep.

I have a lot of respect for Tibetan Buddhism. It's not my cup of tea, but it's an alive spiritual tradition with some remarkable leaders. I've met enough radiantly-smiling abbots in monasteries on my trips through the Himalayas to know they have a real deal going on.

I recall one time, sitting in the Sakya Abode Hotel in Kaza, the capital of Spiti Valley, when a tall, elderly Tibetan monk walked gracefully through the lounge. Without thinking, my hands went into a namaste and he returned the greeting.

"Who's that?" I asked my companion, when the monk had gone.

"Him," he replied, pointing to an old black-and-white photo on the wall, showing a lama sitting grandly on a throne, somewhere in Tibet, back in the thirties. I think that's the first and only time I've seen someone in two incarnations at once.

Meanwhile, back on stage, Nobody admonishes the attendants for their attitude of slavishly following others:

Nobody (*to Attendants*):
Now stop this nonsense, both of you
Find something specially meant for you!
1st Attendant:
Okay, we'll walk the Himalayan hills
From end to end in search of thrills.
2nd Attendant:
We'll trek from Kathmandu to Kulu
And touch the feet of every guru.

That's it. All the characters have expressed their spiritual desires and are ready to depart. Only Nobody is left, but she is in a different category and will not be making the trip to India. Well, let me rephrase that: Nobody will be going to the non-geographical India that exists within us all, in a mystical sense – the place she calls the *Land of Not To Be*.

Nobody: Now I can say goodbye in style,
Let me vanish for a while.
Nobody was never here,
It's time for me to disappear.
If you wish, you can find me
In the Land of Not To Be.

The last lines go to Will. He's a changed man, ready to give up his reputation and embark on a journey of self-discovery, but he is, after all, a writer. He can't help it. So, naturally, he's thinking of turning this new situation into another play:

Will: Meet we all, here, in one year
There'll be so much for us to hear.
I'll write a new play, make amends,
Called 'Shakespeare the Meditator and His Friends'.

Cue for a closing song. I've chosen to repeat the opening number, using new lyrics:

Everyone:
Another drama for you to see,
Another story ends happily
In meditation, in ecstasy,
In the Land of Not to Be.
Another drama to make you smile,
Another story performed in style

We'll see you later, in a while,
In the Land of Not to Be.
Heroes, zeroes, kings and queens
Go to India it seems.
Cleopatra longs to be
In Rishikesh with Antony,
Juliet and Romeo
Left for Pune long ago.
Let your heart be open wide
Close your eyes and go inside.
There is more for you and me
In the Land of Not to Be.
Another drama for you to see,
Another story ends happily
In meditation, in ecstasy,
In the Land of Not to Be.
Another drama to make you smile,
Another story performed in style
We'll see you later, in a while,
In the Land of Not to Be...you gotta be there!
In the Land of Not to Be.

EPILOGUE

We performed several versions of the play: twice in Pune, in 2012 and 2013, and once at a festival in Denmark in the summer of 2013. It worked well, but I have to say, I don't know if I achieved my original aim in writing and staging this drama.

I wanted to see if I could present a piece of comedy theatre that would be able to communicate the basic Eastern philosophy of 'not to be' to the public. But since all five shows were attended mainly by sannyasins and people already familiar with meditation, I still don't know the answer. The jury is out and will probably stay out unless and until the show is staged again with a more mainstream audience.

In ending this book, I'd like to give the Bard the final word, but Will doesn't seem to possess the depth required for the occasion. You don't believe me? Listen to this lament by Macbeth:

"Life's but a walking shadow, a poor player,
That struts and frets his hour upon the stage,
And then is heard no more. It is a tale
Told by an idiot, full of sound and fury,

Signifying nothing."

Sheer nonsense. Every human being, in his or her essence, is pure consciousness – that's our significance, our dignity, our divinity. You just need to find it. You need to start the inner journey and go looking for it. Remember, though, it's expensive. The price you need to pay is everything you think you are.

So it's hard to see how Shakespeare can provide the 'PS' to round off this little saga of being and not being.

But wait...what's this? Among all the tragedies, comedies and tragi-comedies penned by the Bard, I have found one line that will suffice to end this book. How appropriate that it was uttered by my favourite character:

"The rest is silence."

Thank you, Hamlet.

COMPLETE SCRIPT

Enter Prologue with scroll.

Prologue

The mark of greatness, as we know,
Is left for history to bestow.
And who of us, now sitting here,
Will be remembered through the years?
Whose name to others will be shown
In golden letters, carved in stone?
William Shakespeare, there's a name,
Four hundred years of global fame.
His plays show man in good, in badness,
Our vanity, our pride, our madness.
The rise and fall of kings and queens,
Blind ambition, broken dreams.
Shakespeare's mighty pen described it,
What unkind critic will deny it?
But this I say, no hesitation,
Will never knew of meditation.
His busy mind was full of chatter,

He didn't think that silence mattered.
His characters did everything
But close their eyes and look within.
So come with me, let me invite you
With this small drama to excite you,
And meet Will Shakespeare and his wife
And give them both a different life.
And what we poor players lack in skill
Let your imagination now fulfil.

Queen Elizabeth walks swiftly onto the stage, followed by an attendant. Prologue becomes her second attendant. She is holding a manuscript in her hand and she is angry. William Shakespeare follows her.

Elizabeth: I will not have this play performed in my court, not while there is a single breath left in my body. No, no, no, Master Shakespeare!

Shakespeare (*protesting*): But your Majesty, it is a worthy play....

Elizabeth (*waving the papers at him*): I commanded a tragedy, Master Shakespeare.

Shakespeare: *Romeo and Juliet* is a tragedy, your Majesty.

Elizabeth (*shaking her head*): Ha! Do you take me for a fool?

Shakespeare: No indeed, your Majesty.

Elizabeth: It is a love story, Master Shakespeare, and what is more, it is an indecent love story! Will you have me sit on my throne, in front of the entire court, and watch while a young girl, barely thirteen-years-old, shares her bed with her lover?

Shakespeare: But they were married, Your Majesty.

Elizabeth: A hasty, secret wedding, performed against all wise counsel. It cannot excuse the scandal you will have us watch.

Shakespeare: But they both die in the end, your Majesty.

Elizabeth: Too late, Master Shakespeare, much too late! The romance has already happened. I will have none of it (*she rips up the manuscript and throws it on the floor*).

Shakespeare (*horrified*): My play!

He tries to gather the pieces, but the Queen stops him.

Elizabeth: Leave it there, I command you! And write me another play, to be performed in court within the week, or risk my deep displeasure. Do I make myself clear Master Shakespeare?

Shakespeare: Indeed, Your Majesty, very clear.

Elizabeth: So be it. One week, Master Shakespeare. Not a day longer.

Haughtily, she starts to walk away.

Shakespeare (*to the audience*): My God, what a bitch!

Elizabeth stops, turns slowly in a menacing way towards Shakespeare.

Elizabeth: What did you say, Master Shakespeare?

Shakespeare (*realizes the Queen was still within earshot, smiles and tries desperately to avoid having his head cut off*):

Er... I said... That I am rich...

Your patronage prevents me... from... er... falling in a ditch.

Queen Elizabeth gives a scornful snort of contempt and leaves the stage, with her attendants. Shakespeare waits until she has gone, then starts to pick up the pieces of his torn manuscript. As she leaves, two players belonging to the same theatre company as Shakespeare come running onstage, the girl being chased by the boy, and laughing.

First Player (*approaching Shakespeare and mocking him*): How now, what grave misfortune have we here?

Second Player: Her Majesty was not too pleased, I fear!

First player: Why Will, what ails you man? Why this distress?

Second Player: Have you been fighting with our Royal Mistress?

Shakespeare: Leave me alone, good fellows, I entreat you.

I lack the time and humour now to meet you.

First player picks up two of pieces of paper and hands one to her companion. They tease Will by exaggerating and over-playing the roles of Romeo and Juliet.

First Player (*playing Juliet*):

Oh Romeo, Romeo! Wherefore art thou Romeo?

Second Player (*playing Romeo*):

But soft, what light through yonder window breaks?

It is the East and Juliet is the sun!

First Player (*surrendering*):

Take me, Romeo, for I am yours!

Second Player (*running towards her*): My love! My angel!

They collapse together on the floor with giggles of laughter.

Shakespeare (*irritated*): Stop it, both of you! Leave me in peace. For I must write a tragedy, within a week.

First Player: What story will you tell? Hast thou begun?

Shakespeare: Alas, I know not. Inspiration have I none.

The two players look at each other and nod agreement.

Second Player: Will, we can help you...

First Player: ...if you so desire.

Shakespeare: How now? What mischief do you two conspire?

First Player: Last month, in Denmark, we played before the king...

Second Player: In his great castle did we dance and sing...

First Player: A mighty feast was held, with many plays...

Second Player: Heroic tales and legends from the grave...

First Player: One story was admired above them all...

Second Player: The greatest tragedy, wherein a king did fall...

First Player: The king's own brother did most treacherously take his life...

Second Player: And then he forced the Queen to be his wife!

Shakespeare: So far so good... and then?

First Player: Then her poor son, Hamlet, tortured by this stealth...

Second Player: Knows not whether to kill the new king, or himself...

First Player: And so he struggles on, quite desperately

Second Player: Not knowing whether to be, or not to be....

Shakespeare (*intrigued by the story*): It is a worthy tale. What happens next?

The two players look at each other and scratch their heads and look puzzled.

First Player: Er... we forget! It matters not, Will, draw upon thy skill...

Second Player: And let your clever mind write what you will.

First Player: Just make it up, you shall invent the rest,

Second Player: After all, it is what you do best!

First Player: As long as they all die when the play ends...

Second Player: The Queen will love you...

First Player (*rubbing fingers to indicate money*): ...and make sweet amends!

Shakespeare: It shall be done. I'll write this '*Hamlet*' now.

For I must save my precious neck somehow!

Henceforth, Will Shakespeare's plays shall ever be,

Remembered for their gloom and tragedy!

All gather together for the opening song. Queen Elizabeth comes onstage with her attendants and stands separately, looking proud and aloof, and she does not sing.

Another drama for you to see,
Another ending in misery,
It's oh-so tragic, it has to be
It's for her Royal Majesty.
Another drama to make you sad,
Another story that's going bad
If you enjoy it
You must be mad!
It's for her Royal Majesty.
Heroes, zeroes, kings and villains
Kill each other with precision.
Cleopatra's destiny
Dying with Mark Antony,
Juliet as we all know
Killed herself for Romeo,
Star-crossed lovers, heartbreak endings
Tragedy and gloom descending
Is there more that we can't see?
Is this all that's meant to be?
Another drama for you to see,

Another ending in misery,
It's oh-so tragic, it has to be
It's for her Royal Majesty.
Another drama to make you sad,
Another story that's going bad
If you enjoy it
You must be mad!
It's for her Royal Majesty...we're going crazy!
It's for her Royal Majesty.

Actors depart, leaving Will Shakespeare (WS) sitting alone, writing with a quill pen (Attendants remain standing at the back).

WS: "To be or not to be, that is the question" ... Yes... that is *the* question... (*writing*)...

Enter Shakespeare's wife (SW). She has a crochet circle in her hand. She looks at her husband, recognizing that he is completely preoccupied.

WS: "...Whether 'tis nobler in the mind..."

SW: Will dear.... Will.... WILL!!! Fetch another basket of firewood, there's a good fellow.

WS: Er... what?

SW: Wood, dear, the fire's going out and there's a winter chill in the air today.

WS: "To suffer... the slings and arrows of outrageous fortune..." (*writing*) yes, I like that!

SW (*wearily*): Writing again, I see.

WS (*not looking up*): Hmm...

SW: Not another tragedy I hope.

WS (*frostily*): Her Majesty, Queen Elizabeth, happens to be very fond of tragedies.

SW: That's because she's old and sick and dying.

WS (*shocked, indignant and scared*): Hush, woman, hold your tongue! Such things may not be said without immediate arrest and punishment.

SW (*shrugs*): Everyone's saying it except you. The gossip is all over London that the Queen will die before the year is out.

WS: Alas, I fear it. And what will happen to our poor company of players then?

SW comes over to him, smiling and seductive.

SW: Will, sweetheart, write me a nice comedy... something to make me smile and laugh... like you used to in the old days... to please me?

WS: Dearest, I will... but not now. (*stands up*) This new play, *Hamlet*, is going to be my greatest triumph. The great tragedy of the young Prince of Denmark, torn between action and inaction, decision and indecision, life and death... (*dramatically with a flourish*) ... "To be, or not to be, that is the question!"

SW remains unimpressed. She picks up the bucket and hands it to him.

SW: Firewood, or no firewood? *That* is the question. Now get along with you or we'll both die of cold tonight.

WS (*taking the bucket*): Oh very well... But wait! I see how it must continue... (*sits down and writes furiously*) "To sleep, perchance to dream – aye, there's the rub: For in that sleep of death what dreams may come..."

SW: I give up. Give me the bucket (*picks it up*). (*addressing the audience*). Equal rights for women is going to come a little too late for me. (*smiling deviously at WS*) But I have my ways. Buy me a new dress, Will, and I'll forgive you everything."

WS (*not looking up*): Yes dear.

SW (*pleased at herself for persuading him*): Ha! (*to the audience*) You see? It's better to *be*. How can you wear a new dress if you choose *not to be*!

SW exits with her basket. An actor come onstage carrying a human skull and approaches WS. He has come to audition for the role of Hamlet. He was one of the two players who teased Will earlier, giving him the idea to write this play.

H (*coming close to WS, he accidentally almost thrusts the skull in his face*): Excuse me, Will.

WS (*looks up, sees the skull and is frightened*): Aaaargh! For God's sake, man, what do you think you're doing?

H (*hides the skull clumsily behind his back*): Sorry, Will. I've come for the audition.

WS: What?

H: The part. I've come to play Hamlet.

WS: But why the skull?

H: Well, you said it's a tragedy, so I brought along my grandfather to add a little atmosphere.

WS: Oh, very well (*takes skull to inspect*). After all, if I fail to please the Queen, this is what I will look like in a week! (*gives him a script to read*): Let's put him down... stand here, face the audience and read this.

Hamlet strikes a very theatrical pose.

H: To be, or not to be, that is... such a stupid question! (*laughs*)

WS: What do you mean, man?

H: Nobody asks questions like this, Will.

WS: I don't believe this! You and your colleague gave me that line yourselves, from the play in Denmark!

H (*shrugs*): I guess it sounds better in Danish.

WS (*annoyed*): Just read the script.

H: ...Whether 'tis nobler in the mind to suffer

The slings and arrows of outrageous fortune,

Or to take arms against a sea of troubles,

And by opposing end them.

WS: That's better.

Enter Shakespeare's Wife, looking sceptically at Hamlet.

SW: So, let me get this straight. This handsome-looking young man is called Hamlet.

WS: Right.

SW: Hamlet's father was the King of Denmark, but he was killed by a rival. The rival becomes the new King of Denmark and marries Hamlet's mother.

WS: Right.

SW: Hamlet wants to kill the new king, to revenge his father, but instead spends a long time wondering whether to be or not to be, which makes everything very complicated. And how does it all end...?

WS: In tragedy, of course.

SW: Hamlet dies...?

WS: Yes.

SW: Hamlet's mother dies?

WS: Yes.

SW: The new king dies?

WS: Yes.

SW: The king's prime minister dies?

WS: Yes.

SW: The king's prime minister's son dies?

WS: Yes.

Enter Ophelia, looking dreamy and sad. She was the other player who was teasing Shakespeare in an earlier scene.

SW: And who might this young lady be?

WS: This is Ophelia, the Prime Minister's daughter. She's in love with Hamlet.

SW: Ah, something to be happy about, at last!

WS: Not exactly. You see, the murder of his father has driven Hamlet almost mad, so he rejects Ophelia. Watch and see!

H (*to Ophelia*): I did love you once.

O (*sad yet still hopeful*): Indeed, my lord, you made me believe so.

H: You should not have believed me. I loved you not.

O (*hurt and crushed*): Alas, I was the more deceived.

H: Get thee to a nunnery: why wouldst thou be a breeder of sinners?

O: O, help him, you sweet heavens! I fear that my true love is going mad!

H: Get thee to a nunnery, go: farewell. Or, if thou wilt needs marry, marry a fool; for wise men know well enough what monsters you make of them. To a nunnery, go, and quickly too. Farewell.

O: O heavenly powers, restore his troubled mind to peace and sanity!

Ophelia sinks down in despair. SW looks at the scene and moves slowly towards the couple.

SW: So Hamlet told her he loved her, and now he doesn't... and now what will she do?

WS: Er... she will throw herself in a lake.

SW: And drown herself and die?

WS: Yes, in her grief and her despair.

SW (*slowly*): Will...

WS: Hmmm...?

SW: Don't you think you're overdoing it, just a little bit? All this doom and gloom...?

WS: The Queen will love it.

SW: Yes, well, the Queen is sixty-seven years old and still a virgin. (*goes to Ophelia*) But what about all the young women who will watch your play? "Breeder of sinners"? "Get thee to a nunnery"? What kind of example are you giving them?

WS (*wearily*): You don't understand, woman.

SW: Oh but I rather think I do... (*to Ophelia*) Come here, sweetheart.

Ophelia looks surprised.

O: Who me?

SW: Yes, dear (*takes her by the hand and leads her to one side*). Now listen, you're much too young to go drowning yourself in a lake.

O (*looking at Hamlet*): But... but I love him!

SW: There are plenty more idiots where that one came from, I assure you. What you need is a role model...

O: What is a role model?

SW: Oh, I forgot, that phrase doesn't come into fashion for another 300 years. Well, someone to look up to... someone to give you hope... someone to show you a new vision of life...

O: Like who?

SW: Well, how about Lady Raga?

Note: As we shall see, Lady Raga is a copy of Lady Gaga in her dress and mannerisms. Attendants bring forward Lady Raga props.

O: Who's Lady Raga?

SW: I can't explain. You need to experience it. Bring on the curtain! Let's have a little music.

WS (*alarmed*): Hey, what's going on? This isn't in my script!

Music plays. Attendants bring on a curtain to screen off Ophelia. She changes into her Lady Raga outfit while the music-intro is playing. Ophelia bursts out from behind the curtain in a skimpy, white top, very tight shorts and a blonde wig and sings the blues song "Raga and her Baba":

Raga and her Baba, we don't get along,

Raga and her Baba, this man he done me wrong.

Broke my heart in pieces and threw it on the floor,

Still I come back crying, begging him for more....

It's a crying shame.... oooh yes it is... it's a crying shame...

Raga and her Baba, the man I love to hate,

Raga and her Baba, a passion that can't wait.

Broke my heart in pieces and threw it on the fire,

Still I come back crying, burning with desire...

It's a crying shame... oooh yes it is... it's a crying shame....

Song runs for approx. 1:45 min, then SW stops the music with a wave of her hand.

SW (*to Ophelia*): Stop! You've got the right idea, sweetheart, but you're still focusing on Hamlet. Take all the energy back and give it to yourself. You are free to be you.

Ophelia: Free to be me?

Music begins with a solo violin as background to words that are half spoken, half sung.

It's not the first time that you've said goodbye,

It's not the first time that you've made me cry,

But this time I have found a golden key,

Without you, I have freedom to be me….

The music changes to a fast, driving beat. There's a wild dance routine by Ophelia, with Shakespeare's wife and the two Attendants doing a very hip backing routine to support her.

I'm free to be me, yeah, free to be me,
Free to be me, yeah, free to be me…
Free to say "No!" and free to say "Yes!"
Free turn on, say goodbye to the rest
Free to get high and dance all night long
Grab any guy and this is my song.
Free to say "Hi, I'm single and free,"
Free to say "You! You're coming with me!"
Free to say "Guy, are you looking at me?"
Free to say "Yeah, now, you're coming with me!"
I'm free to be me, yeah, free to be me,
Free to be me, yeah, free to be me…

At the end, Ophelia and SW dance offstage, leaving Hamlet alone with WS.

WS (*Hamlet*): What are you smiling at?

H (*looking after Ophelia*): She's kinda cute, isn't she?

WS (*slowly and deliberately*): Young man, I am a genius in the use of English language and the word 'cute' does not appear in any of my plays. Ophelia is a tragic figure who is doomed to drown in a lake. Now, the big question is: how should YOU die?

H (*nervously*): Do I have to, Will?

WS: Of course, man. How can *Hamlet* be a tragedy if you don't die? (*calling out*) Where are the instruments of death?

An attendant brings a tray with a wine cup, a bottle of poison, an old flintlock pistol and two swords.

WS (*picking up the wine cup and bottle of poison*): Now, suppose the new king pours a glass of wine, sprinkles poison in it, then offers it to you to drink?

Hamlet reluctantly accepts the glass, then deliberately drops it.

H: Ooops! Sorry, I dropped it.

WS (*handing him the pistol*): Or, perhaps, in your despair, you put a pistol to your head and pull the trigger...

Hamlet does so and pulls the trigger, but there is just a 'click' and nothing happens.

H: Will, you forgot to load it!

WS: I have it! Hamlet must die in a sword fight. Come on man, take one of these and defend yourself.

H: (*to audience*): My God, do I really have to fight? Maybe I can scare him with my Clint Eastwood impersonation. (*to WS*) "Will, you've got to ask yourself one question: 'Do I feel lucky?' Well, do ya, punk?"

WS: You can't threaten me. I'm a Master Swordsman.

H: (*still imitating Clint Eastwood*): "Go ahead, make my day!"

WS: Where are you getting these cheap Hollywood lines from? Fight, man, fight!

H: (*to audience*) When all else fails... Arnold Schwarzenegger. (*to WS*) "Hasta la vista baby!"

Hamlet charges at WS, taking him by surprise. They fight. Shakespeare is losing and falls on the floor.

WS: Wait! Wait! I forgot. There must be treachery involved. (*to the attendant with the tray*) Give me that bottle of poison! (*drips it on his blade*) Your enemy has put poison on the tip of his sword. One small cut and all is lost. *(to Hamlet)* Look over there! *(he points behind him)*.

Hamlet looks behind, Shakespeare makes a quick jab and cuts Hamlet's leg. Hamlet gasps and performs a long, overly-dramatic death, collapsing in a heap on the stage.

WS: That's much better!

Enter Queen Elizabeth.

E: Where is our playwright, Master Shakespeare?

WS *(kneeling immediately)*: Here, your Majesty... your humble servant awaits your bidding.

E: We are interested in the progress of your new play.

WS *(still kneeling)*: Yes, Your Majesty, it's coming along nicely.

E: What is this drama to be called?

WS: *Hamlet, Prince of Denmark*, Your Majesty.

E: Indeed? We are curious as to how you intend this play to end... in *tragedy*, we trust?

WS: Oh yes, indeed, madam. *(Pointing to Hamlet's dead body)* All the main characters die.

E: Excellent. Our people must be continuously reminded that life is filled with melancholy, suffering and death.

Elizabeth exits. WS nudges Hamlet's body with his foot.

WS: Arise, O Corpse!

H (*looking up, surprised*): But I'm dead!

WS: No, no. That was just a temporary death to keep Her Majesty the Queen off my back (*helps him up*). Don't worry, you will die permanently later in the play.

H *(sarcastically)*: Gee, thanks Will!

Hamlet limps offstage. Will goes back to his chair and starts writing. Enter Mrs Shakespeare. She walks to the front of the stage and addresses the audience directly.

SW (*to audience*): You seem like an intelligent group of people, so let me ask you a question. Don't you think it's odd that in the whole history of Western culture nobody knew anything about meditation?

WS (*standing up and joining his wife*): All those European geniuses...

SW: French Impressionist painters...

WS: Russian novelists...

SW: Italian sculptors....

WS: German composers...

Brief silence, as Will coughs and waits to be acknowledged.

SW: Oh yes, and not forgetting the English playwrights...

WS: Thank you, dear.

SW: And not one of them ever sat down, closed his eyes and meditated.

WS: They knew everything about the human ego...

SW: But they didn't know anything about dropping the ego.

WS: They knew how to be Somebody.

SW: But they had no idea how to be Nobody.

SW: Don't you think it's kind of odd?

Don't you think it's kind of strange?

WS: Such a funny situation

No one's heard of meditation.

SW: If you say the world is Maya

WS: You will just be called a liar.

SW: If you point towards Nirvana

WS: They will say you've gone bananas.

SW If you tell them not to think

WS: They will send you to a shrink.

SW: If you ask them to be still

WS: They will offer you a pill.

SW: If you talk of inner vision

WS: They will think of television.

SW: If you sit silently alone

WS: Don't switch off your mobile phone.

SW: If you want to clear your head

WS: You can Google it instead.

SW: If you want true happiness
WS: Just send an SMS.
SW: If you want to raise your spirit
WS: Any shopping mall will do it.
SW: You can find out who you are
WS: At your local pub or bar.
SW: That's the story of the West,
WS: There's no time to stop and rest,
SW: Just to be...
WS: And let the rest...
SW: Disappear...
SW & WS: In emptiness...

WS and SW close their eyes for a moment, in silent meditation. Then they turn to face each other and give a Namaste. Mrs Shakespeare leaves the stage.

WS *(watching her go):* My wife's in love with Eastern philosophy. Oh, it's interesting, I grant you, but what can you do with it? It's not going to pay the rent, is it? It's not going to get me out of trouble with the Queen. So, it's back to work for me...

He sits down and starts writing. Ophelia enters. Her 'Lady Raga' mood has disappeared and she is again hesitant and insecure.

O: Excuse me, Master Shakespeare.

WS *(irritated at being disturbed):* Yes, what is it now?

O *(hesitantly):* I... I want to change my character.

WS *(astonished):* You... what?

O (*gathering courage*): I want to change my character.

WS (*dismissively*): No, no. That's not going to happen. The play is almost finished.

O (*kneels down by his chair and comes close with an appealing look*): Please, sir! It's not much to ask, is it? I just want to live my own life. And you are such a clever genius, you can make anything possible.

WS (*noticing for the first time that she's beautiful and playing with her hair and cheeks*): Hmm. You are a pretty little thing, aren't you? Listen, tomorrow my wife goes out of town to take care of her sick mother. Why don't you come to my house and we'll... talk about it... together... hmm?

O (*getting up and addressing the audience*): My God... this horny old goat is trying to seduce me! I've heard of the Hollywood casting couch... I've heard of the Bollywood casting couch... but I've never heard of an Elizabethan casting couch! Oh well, I guess it's always been the same. (*making herself look nice, as if she's giving in to his desire*) Right then...

O goes over to him seductively.

O: Oh Master Shakespeare

You're such a handsome man

And if you agree to help me

I'll give you what I can

(*She is all over him, caressing his face, etc.*)

Would you like to taste my cherry?

It's so tender, it's so sweet!

Would you like to squeeze my plums

While I'm lying at your feet?

Shall I feed you some papaya

While we're lying on your bed?

Or would my lover rather have

A twisted nose instead?

(*Ophelia gives a hard yank to Will's nose*)

WS: Ow! You hurt me, you little bitch!

O: Well, you asked for it! You dirty old man!

WS: You will regret this young lady. You will die before this play is done. Your fate is sealed!

WS sits down with his play. Ophelia collapses weeping. Enter Mrs Shakespeare, who sits down beside her, gently takes her hand and comforts her with this song:

-Oh lady, sweet lady, weeping -for your life,
You want to be a princess and you want to be a wife.
I can see you long to be

His sweet beloved one
And I hope for you that your dreams come true,

Now your life has just begun.
I've searched and roamed many miles from home
Looking for that special man,
Enjoyed a fling with a foreign king
And we danced until the dawn.
I met Will and I love him still
And yet I want to be free
I've been around the world
But I'd rather be with me
Oh lady, sweet lady, you will have your day
From my heart I want to tell you
That everything's okay.
I can see your destiny
Reflected in your eyes
You won't be apart and your open heart
Can see through all the lies.
It's strange but true, and I'm telling you
That nothing ever lasts.
The future will be present
And the present will be past.
Now the hardest thing is to look within
And find the real me
I've been around the world
But I'd rather be with me.
Mrs Shakespeare holds Ophelia's hand.

Mrs S: Come along dear, we'll have a nice cup of
tea.

They exit. Hamlet wanders on, sees the skull next to
Will's chair, picks it up and looks at it.

H (*limping onstage*): Ow, that fake swordfight wasn't quite as 'fake' as I hoped. (*sees skull and picks it up*). But, on the other hand, it could have been worse! (*strikes a pose, holding up skull*) Alas, poor Yorick. You lost your head over a woman, didn't you? Well, that's not going to happen to me!

Hamlet tosses the rubber skull carelessly over his shoulder.

The character 'Nobody' comes onstage. He is dressed rather like an Indian sadhu, or holy man, but a little more jolly and friendly.

Nobody: Hi, how's it going?

Hamlet: Well, to be honest, I could use a few laughs. Who are you? What's your name?

N: Nobody.

H: Nobody? C'mon, you must be *somebody*.

N: Everybody tells me that: you *must* be *somebody*. But *anybody* can be somebody. And everybody *wants* to be somebody. Nobody wants to be *nobody*. Except me.

H: Can you say that again, slowly please?

N: Everybody says that, as well. *Nobody* understands.

H: But you *are* Nobody, so *you* must understand.

N: Anybody *could* understand, and I keep thinking one day somebody *will* understand. But believe me, nobody has any idea what Nobody is talking about.

H: Well, nobody's perfect.

N: Thank you, I agree!

H: No, that's not what I mean!

N: No worries. Nobody cares.

H: Okay, Mister Nobody, where are you from?

N: I'm from the Land of Not To Be.

H: I should have guessed.

N: Not to be, you see,

Is the only way to be.

Though you may disagree

Just listen carefully:

The more you think you've got,

The more you have to drop.

But, the more you find you're not

The more you've really got.

H: That's nonsense, don't you see?

Or would nobody agree?

N: Nonsense it may be,

But would you agree

To check it out with me?

H: Well, okay... maybe.

N: Watch closely... you will see.

Enter Queen Elizabeth with attendants. It is time for the daily business in her court. First Attendant unrolls a scroll with a list of supplications from her people.

First Attendant: Your Majesty, the people of London have no bread to eat.

E: Let them eat cake.

First Attendant: Your Majesty, the people of York say your taxes are too high.

E: Let them work harder.

First Attendant: Your Majesty, the people of Lancaster wish you a happy birthday.

E (*slight smile*): Indeed? How touching. Let them make a statue of me, in gratitude.

The Royal group freezes, standing motionless.

N: Tell me, who is she?

H: Of course, 'tis Her Majesty

N (*reaching up towards her crown*): And if I remove her attire?

H (*alarmed*): Oh, I wouldn't do that, sire!

Nobody, not in the least worried, takes off her crown. The Queen reacts with a little gasp, as the crown is removed, but is still in trance. Nobody gives the crown to one of her Attendants.

E: Ah!

N: Who is this woman now, before whom you love to bow?

H: Well, no matter what it seems, she will still say she's the Queen

N: Without a crown with golden teeth?

H: Why certainly, 'tis her belief.

N: This belief, she wears it like a mask.

So this gives me another task (*takes the mask off her face, gives it to Attendant*).

H *(to the audience)*: This Nobody is quite insane,
She'll cut his head and eat his brains!

E (*bigger reaction but still in trance*): Oh! Who am I?

N: Your queen is stripped of power and glory
Who is she now in your Tudor story?

H: Why, looking simple, sad and sorry

This woman is just... ordinary.

Nobody (*very pleased*): Hamlet you have hit upon the truth

And now the Queen will give you living proof

Now anything can happen, you will see

How 'not to be' makes everybody free....

Nobody pulls Hamlet to one side. Hip-hop dance music starts to play. Mrs Shakespeare and Ophelia come onstage in tight black leotards and start dancing like Beyoncé, or similar style.

The Queen, under some kind of spell cast by Nobody, is enchanted and watches closely. At a certain point in the dance, the music stops.

E: What is this dancing that you do?

Can I learn to dance with you?

SW: Dear Madam, come and dance with us

Ophelia: We'll show you how to shake your ass.

Music starts again (from the beginning). The Queen joins in. The music continues for a while, then suddenly stops. The Queen looks shocked as she returns to her old self. Mrs Shakespeare and Ophelia look apprehensive.

SW: Uh-oh, I think we're in trouble.

Ophelia: Get ready to run.

Queen: What is happening in my court? These women are naked! Off with their heads! Off with their heads!

Mrs Shakespeare and Ophelia run off quickly, pursued by the Queen and Attendants.

Nobody (*to audience*): Of course, it doesn't always work.
That Elizabeth is such a stupid jerk!
(*turns to Hamlet*)
Now, Hamlet, think what I have said,
Take off *your* mask and lose *your* head.
H (*confused*): I have no mask! It's not on me.
N (*laughs*): Oh yes, you have. You just can't see!
H: You've gone quite mad, I'll say good day!
And this Nobody can go his way.
N: Wait, spare a moment, let me ask,
This noble fellow with no mask,
This gloomy guy so filled with sadness
Who thinks that I am touched by madness.
Can you smile and sing and dance
If I give you half a chance?
H: Of course I can, if I so choose.
I've really nothing left to lose.
N: Then why be miserable and glum
When you can dance under the sun?
H: It isn't me who feels this way.
It's this bloody Bard who writes this play!
N: Come then, let's show this anti-fun guy
How they move it down in Mumbai!

Music begins and Nobody leads Hamlet into a popular Bollywood dance routine. Nobody does it easily. Hamlet does his best to follow but soon gives up.

H: Stop! Stop! Enough! It's plain to see,
This Bollywood is not for me.
N: You're giving up because you're foreign?
Oh Hamlet, this is really boring!
H: But I *can* dance, please have no fear... (*he puts on a pair of dark glasses*)
Hi! My name's Psy... I'm from Korea!
Dressing classy, dancing cheesy
Gangnam Style is really easy!

Music for Psy's Gangnam Style is played. Mrs Shakespeare and Ophelia come onstage and join in. Hamlet drags Will off his seat to dance. Everyone joins in and dances like crazy. As the music ends, Mrs Shakespeare and Ophelia exit. Will comes centre stage.

WS: My God, what in the name of Her Majesty is happening to my play? I will be thrown into the Tower of London and left to rot forever!

WS returns to his seat. Nobody and Hamlet are left on stage.

H: Okay Mr Nobody, I'm beginning to see things differently. But there's one thing I don't understand. What would I gain from becoming a Not To Be?
N: Well, let's see... you wouldn't be the Prince of Denmark any more... so you wouldn't be obsessed with trying to avenge your father's death... so you wouldn't

spend all your time thinking "to be or not to be" ... *and* you wouldn't tell your beautiful girlfriend to get lost.

H: Really?

N: Really.

H: How do I do it?

N: Ah, that can be a *little* challenging. Come with me.

They exit. Ophelia enters with SW.

O: Oh Mrs Shakespeare, it was wonderful being Lady Raga. But I don't want to imitate anybody else. I want to be me.

SW: Really?

O: Really.

SW: Really... really?

O: Yes really. I just want to be myself.

SW: Well, that can be a *little* challenging. Come with me.

Enter Queen Elizabeth, with crown and mask.

E (*to WS*): Master Shakespeare, we are not pleased with the way this play is progressing.

WS: A thousand apologies, Your Majesty.

E: We have not seen enough suffering and death to call it a tragedy.

WS (*thinking fast*): Fear not, Your Majesty. I am... er... I am planning a surprise. The play will seem to be heading in the direction of happiness, but, at the very end, I shall kill them all!

E: Very well. See that it is done, (*menacing*) or I promise you, thine head shall be impaled on a stake before the Tower of London.

WS: Oh no! I mean... oh yes, Your Majesty.

The Queen exits. Shakespeare goes to his chair. Attendants bring two chairs to the front centre of the stage. Nobody brings Hamlet to sit in one. SW brings Ophelia to sit in the other. Nobody stands behind Hamlet's chair. SW stands behind Ophelia's chair.

N: Not To Be requires an empty mind.

SW: A clear and quiet head.

N: We will represent your thoughts.

SW: When a thought enters your head, we will speak it for you.

N: In this way, you will become aware of your own thoughts

SW: And most important, you will become aware of the silence *behind* your thoughts.

N: In that silence you will discover the Land of Not To Be.

SW: Close your eyes. Let us begin.

N and SW crouch down behind Hamlet and Ophelia. Each time a thought comes, they will stand erect and speak it.

N (*standing up*): This is easy... oh no, that's a thought! (*ducks down*)

SW (*standing up*): I just want to be myself... is this a thought?

N (*standing up and looking at SW*): Of course it is! (*ducks down*)

SW: But it's such a nice thought!

N: (*standing up again*): Nice thoughts... nasty thoughts... they all have to go! (*ducks down*).

SW (*shrugs*) Oh well... bye-bye nice thought (*ducks down*).

N (*standing up*): I'm hungry! (*ducks down*).

SW (*standing up*): I'm thirsty (*ducks down*).

N (*standing up*): I'm restless (*ducks down*).

SW (*standing up*): I'm sad (*ducks down*).

N (*standing up*): To be or not to be? Oh, not again! (*ducks down*).

SW (*standing up*): I wonder if Hamlet still loves me? (*ducks down*).

N (*standing up*): I wonder what Ophelia looks like in the shower? (*as himself*) Now that's an interesting thought...

SW (*standing up, amused but firm*): Hey, keep your mind on the job, Mr Not To Be!

N (*laughing*): Well, it's the first time he's actually expressed interest in her.

SW (*comes behind Hamlet and holds his head gently with her hands*): Isn't the male mind wonderful? If it's not drowning women in lakes, it's gazing at them under the shower...

N: Wait... listen! Listen!

SW (*puzzled*): What do you hear?

N (*in wonder*): Nothing!

SW (*looking down at Hamlet and Ophelia*): Oh my god, they've done it. They've stopped thinking!

At the same moment, N and SW put a finger to their lips, then turn towards each other.

N & SW (*simultaneously*): Sssshhhhh!

They both stand with eyes closed, their hands in a mudra – Buddha-like. But SW isn't very good at it and occasionally takes a quick peek at Nobody to see if he still has his eyes closed. Then she goes back to trying to meditate.

SW (*opening her eyes*): I wonder if I left my cooking pot on my stove.
N (*opening his eyes and rolling them upwards, while making an Italian gesture with his hands*): Oy vey! Now *you're* thinking!
SW (*rebuffing him*): Well, now *you're* thinking about me thinking. (*glances at Ophelia*)
N: Wait! She's going to say something.

Ophelia opens her eyes and looks lovingly at Hamlet and takes his hand. He opens his eyes and looks at her.

O: Hamlet, beloved, you still love me, don't you?
H: Yes, I do.
O: I knew it!
H: Shall we dance?
O: I'd love to!

They smile lovingly at each other.
Nobody and Mrs Shakespeare take away the chairs. Hamlet and Ophelia dance to "There is a Country Far Away."

There is a country

Far away,

There is a land

Far away and lost.

There is a feeling

There is a healing

There is a country

A country of the heart.

Can this beauty that's there

Something so rare

Touch your heart, touch your heart, touch your heart?

Can this love in the air

Something so rare

Ever let us part?

Mrs Shakespeare runs over and drags Will onto the dance floor. He is reluctant, but gives in and dances with his wife. Then all four dance together.

There is a secret in my soul

There is a deep mystery of love

There is a first time

There is a last time

There is a deep mystery of love

Can this beauty that's there

Something so rare

Touch your heart, touch your heart, touch your heart?

Can this love in the air...

WS breaks away from the other dancers and signals for the music to stop.

WS: Stop! Stop! All this romantic nonsense... it just won't do!

He shakes his head in frustration and goes back to his seat.

Hamlet (*to SW*): What happens now?

SW: Well, if you take my advice you'll both get out of Denmark as quickly as possible. It's such a miserable country. Why don't you go to India for the winter?

Ophelia: India! That sounds like a wonderful idea!

Hamlet: My God, but from Elizabethan England it will us take six months just to get there!

SW: No, no. I happen to know that Jet Airways is offering special flights from sixteenth century London. Look, (*removes tickets from her dress*) here are the tickets. Now run along both of you.

Will: Wait! Hold everything!

SW: Uh-oh.

Will (*walks forward a short way, then stops*): May I have a word with you... dear?

SW (*to Hamlet and Ophelia*): Just a minute. (*goes over to WS*). Yes, dear?

WS: Listen, beloved. I know you have good intentions and you want these young people to be happy, but if they don't die, I will. The Queen has threatened me with execution if this play does not end in tragedy.

SW: Ooooh, that nasty woman! But wait... I know... (*pulls more tickets out of her dress*) We'll all fly to India... right now, before she finds out.

WS: What? You want me to give up being the greatest playwright in England... just like that?

SW: Oh, I forgot. You haven't learned how Not To Be, have you?

WS (*indignant*): No, indeed. Nor will I ever do so. My name is going to be remembered for centuries and centuries.

SW (*takes him by the hand*): Will, love, come here (*takes him over to Hamlet and Ophelia*) Look at these beautiful young people. They've just discovered the joy of living. Do you want to take it away from them?

WS (*hesitating*): Well... er...

Queen Elizabeth enters with crown and mask. Two Attendants follow her, carrying swords.

E: Off with their heads

WS (*bowing*): Your Majesty.

E: Why are these young people not yet dying or dead?

WS: Soon, soon, Your Majesty. I'm just about to kill them.

E: Do it now. I command it! Off with their heads!

WS: Yes, Your Majesty. I'm sorry, both of you. A thousand pardons, but it is your destiny to die in my play.

Enter Nobody, disguised as Death, with black hood and skull face.

N (*hollow voice*): Your time has come, Your Majesty.

E (*shrieks in fright*): Eeeek! Oh God! Who are you, pray?

N: I am the Angel of Death. And it is your time to die!

E (*clutches her heart*): Ah, it is true! (*staggers forward a little*). My heart is giving out! (*theatrically brushes her forehead with her hand*) It is my time! (*sinks to her knees*) Farewell, cruel world! Farewell! I die! I die! I die!

Elizabeth staggers off, supported by her Attendants. Nobody takes off his death mask.

N: That was pretty good acting, eh Will?

WS: Well, obviously the Queen thought so. She died of fright. Who are you?

N: I'll tell you later. But first, we must find a way to end this play properly.

SW, Ophelia, Hamlet (*together*): A *happy* ending!

WS (*stubbornly*): No. I refuse to write a happy ending.

N: But why?

WS: It's so ordinary, so predictable. Look at this sophisticated audience. You can't expect them to take me seriously as a playwright if I write a happy ending.

SW (*folding her arms*): Well, we refuse to take part in a tragic ending

H and O (*also folding their arms*): Right!

N: I know. How about a thriller?

SW: A thrilling ending, yes!

WS: But I've never ever written a thriller.

N: It's easy. Listen, Will... (*he whispers in WS's ear*).

WS (*smiling*): Okay. I'll try it. Take your places everyone!

Lights down. Music starts from Michael Jackson's "Thriller." WS dances like Michael Jackson and lip-synchs the words, while the rest are dancing as zombies.

WS (lip-synching): "It's close to midnight and something evil's lurking in the dark..."

The song continues for a couple of minutes, including two choruses of "It's Just a Thriller, Thriller Night..." Then, suddenly, the music is interrupted by a Royal fanfare of trumpets. Queen Elizabeth comes on to the stage, followed by Attendants. Everyone kneels down and is worried.

E: One moment. Please don't be afraid
Of being hurt by this old maid.

If I may choose twixt life and death
I'd really rather keep my breath.
So let me join you in your gladness
And say goodbye to royal sadness.
SW (*taking Elizabeth warmly by the arm*):
Your Majesty, I'm glad to see
That, deep inside, you're just like me!
WS (*to N*):
So tell me, Master Nobody
Where is this Land of Not To Be?
N: Well, if you look beyond your mind
You'll find it's been there all the time.
But meditation is more fun
If to India you come!
E: India! Oh yes, that's hip!
If my old bones can make the trip.
I think I'll go to Dharamshala
And hang out with the Dalai Lama.
Attendants (*still wanting to please her*):
Oh yes, Your Majesty, it's true
Can we come along with you?
E (*to her Attendants*):
I think it's time for you to see
You really don't belong to m.
Nobody (*to Attendants*):
Find a path that suits *you* best,
And give this 'royal' thing a rest!
Mrs Shakespeare:
Yoga is what I love best.
And so I'll go to Rishikesh.
Sitting by the Ganges stream

Enjoying yoga – that's my dream!
I'll practice my asanas daily
Standing on my head... well, maybe.
Attendants: Oh yes we're good at yoga, too,
Perhaps we'll come along with you.
Mrs Shakespeare:
Find a method of your own
Don't just follow... stand alone.
Hamlet *(to Ophelia)*:
I'm sure we'll get enlightened sooner
If we meditate in Pune.
Ophelia (*worried*):
But isn't that the 'free love' ashram?
Will I lose my love, my passion?
Attendants:
Don't worry, dear, we'll come with you
And sing and dance the whole night through!
Hamlet (*taking Ophelia's hand and taking her away from the Attendants*):
That won't be necessary, good fellows.
We can celebrate by ourselves.
We'll go to Pune as a pair
A challenge will await us there.
Ophelia (*no longer afraid, but courageous*):
Let's see if we can both be free
And true lovers still shall be.
Will: All my life I've been a playwright
Finding words to make you say right.
So maybe I should shut up now
And silently meditate somehow.
I'll find a monastery in Ladakh

And take the pressure off my back.

1st Attendant: Let's join the Bard in silence deep

2nd Attendant: If it doesn't make us go to sleep.

Nobody (*to Attendants*):

Now stop this nonsense, both of you

Find something specially meant for you!

1st Attendant:

Okay, we'll walk the Himalayan hills

From end to end in search of thrills.

2nd Attendant:

We'll trek from Kathmandu to Kulu

And touch the feet of every guru.

Nobody: Now I can say goodbye in style,

Let me vanish for a while.

Nobody was never here,

It's time for me to disappear.

If you wish, you can find me

In the Land of Not To Be.

Will: Meet we all, here, in one year

There'll be so much for us to hear.

I'll write a new play, make amends,

Called Shakespeare the Meditator and His Friends.

Everyone: Another drama for you to see,

Another story ends happily

In meditation, in ecstasy,

In the Land of Not to Be.

Another drama to make you smile,

Another story performed in style

We'll see you later, in a while,

In the Land of Not to Be.

Heroes, zeroes, kings and queens

Come to India it seems.
Cleopatra longs to be
In Rishikesh with Anthony,
Juliet and Romeo
Left for Pune long ago.
Let your heart be open wide
Close your eyes and go inside.
There is more for you and me
In the Land of Not to Be.
Another drama for you to see,
Another story ends happily…

The End